THE LORD AND THE LADY ASTRONOMER

The Grantham Girls
Book Three

By Alissa Baxter

ARE YOU SIGNED UP FOR DRAGONBLADE'S BLOG?

You'll get the latest news and information on exclusive giveaways, exclusive excerpts, coming releases, sales, free books, cover reveals and more.

Check out our complete list of authors, too!

No spam, no junk. That's a promise!

Sign Up Here

www.dragonbladepublishing.com

Dearest Reader;

Thank you for your support of a small press. At Dragonblade Publishing, we strive to bring you the highest quality Historical Romance from some of the best authors in the business. Without your support, there is no 'us', so we sincerely hope you adore these stories and find some new favorite authors along the way.

Happy Reading!

CEO, Dragonblade Publishing

Dedication

For John, with love

CHAPTER ONE

ABIGAIL GRANTHAM PEERED through the carriage window into the darkness. After a series of travel mishaps that had become almost comical in their varied nature and number, they had finally driven through the gates of Longmore Hall about an hour after dusk had fallen.

Turning her head to the side, Abigail blinked. A hazy pyramid of light—the long, drawn-out evening twilight—expanded from the western horizon. She narrowed her eyes as she gazed into the distance, squinting a little. Surely it wasn't possible? She had observed the rosy light of dusk disappear some time ago through this very window. So why was the night sky lit up once again? She looked at her aunt. "May we stop, Great-aunt?"

"Stop?" Her great-aunt's voice quavered. "But we're nearly home, Abigail."

"I wish to observe the light." Abigail pointed out of the window. "The sky is most unusually bright tonight."

Her aunt turned her neck stiffly. "Oh! I see what you mean, dear. Good heavens. It does look quite remarkable. I suppose we can stop for a moment."

Grasping the umbrella which lay on the seat beside her, Abigail turned the contraption upside down and knocked on the coach's roof with the handle. The carriage halted a few seconds later, and Joshua, her uncle Longmore's middle-aged groom, opened the door. After asking him to let down the step, Abigail exited the carriage in one swift motion.

She pressed her teeth into her bottom lip as she stood immobile on the road for a moment. Drat! She still held the umbrella, having forgotten in her excitement to place it back on the seat. But she didn't want to waste a moment. Even now, she could hear the coachman speaking to Joshua in a murmur, no doubt asking him what was amiss. Time was limited.

Abigail gazed up at the moonless sky. Their journey had been delayed for hours this morning when they had come upon an overturned cart blocking their way. Joshua had helped the coachman, James, to move the vehicle, but much time had been lost, and it had seemed as though they might need to stay an extra night on the road.

But, although her aunt stated that she was nervous about completing their journey in the dark, after some deliberation, she had decided to continue to Longmore Hall. She was desirous of returning home after all their mishaps, which, in addition to that unfortunate obstruction in the road this morning, had included the Longmore family coach becoming stuck in the mud on the first day and the carriage's axle breaking on the second.

Great-aunt Mildred's determination to press on meant they needed to drive the last part of their journey after the sun had already set. But the older lady believed that the risk of staying at the last inn they passed far outweighed the danger of traveling in the dark. "Damp sheets, dear!" she'd tut-tutted. "Such a shame as, in all other respects, it would do very well for us. But I don't wish to risk an inflammation of the lungs."

Great-aunt suffered from a chronic wheezing cough, so her desire to avoid this hazard to her health was perfectly understandable. But Abigail, observing the turret-like bedchamber windows of the passing inn with widened eyes, had sighed wistfully. What a splendid observational spot a room in one of those towers would have made. To train her telescope on the night sky from such a vantage point would have been delightful, especially as there wasn't a cloud in sight.

Abigail had swallowed her disappointment, training her thoughts instead on all the astronomical pleasures in store for her when she arrived at Longmore Hall. She would be able to sweep the heavens from her uncle's observatory to her heart's content whenever she so wished. She'd hugged the knowledge to herself, rather like a squirrel hoarding a particularly precious nut.

In fact, Abigail had been mulling over the assistance her uncle had asked her to render him in his astronomical studies when she first observed the extraordinary column of light. Luminous on the horizon, the ray stretched up to an astonishing height.

Now, as she stood beside the carriage, gazing upward, she wished her brother, John, were here. He would, in all likelihood, be able to identify this strange phenomenon as his knowledge of astronomy far outstripped hers. Indeed, she had learned everything she knew about the stars and planets from John.

Abigail walked away from the carriage light in order to see the night sky more clearly and was gazing into the distance when a crunch sounded on the road, much like the scraping noise a booted foot made when disturbing loose stones. As she brought her attention back to her immediate surroundings, her eyelids fluttered a little as they adjusted to the darkness.

A figure stood in the road a few feet away from her, just beyond the circle of light cast by the carriage lamps. Her mouth went dry and her pulse quickened as she glanced from the coach to the oversized shape.

A poacher, perhaps? Certainly not a footpad, as this wasn't a public road. She took a tiny step back. The shape moved, a throat cleared, and the person came within the circle of light. He was enormous—a vast, beefy, great-coated fellow with massive shoulders.

The skin at the back of Abigail's neck prickled. She had placed her aunt and the servants in danger by stopping the coach on this dark, moonless road. She hugged the umbrella to her middle as her heart leaped in her breast and a frisson of fear ran down her spine. Heaven help her!

James the coachman called out, "Who goes there?"

The man took a giant step toward the carriage door just as Abigail fled in the direction of the coach, and she ran straight into him. It was rather like running into a boulder, and she froze as the hard edge of something that felt alarmingly like the barrel of a gun dug into her ribs.

Her breath caught in her chest. Now she was done for. She should never have exited the coach on this dark and lonely road. But she hadn't imagined that stopping within the confines of her uncle's estate could be dangerous. Abigail drew back, gripping her umbrella between her hands.

Her umbrella—not much of a weapon, but it was better than nothing. And she had the element of surprise. She swept her make-do sword in a semi-circle before plunging the pointed end into her adversary's middle.

The man gasped just as Joshua approached, holding the carriage lamp aloft. The brighter circle of light cast by the lantern showed the giant staggering back a few paces. Gaining courage, Abigail shoved the tip of her umbrella into the man's belly once again. She must have winded him as he grunted and stumbled back into the spiky arms of a nearby bush.

With a faint cry, Abigail sprang into the coach. Thank goodness Joshua had left the door open. Panting, she fell in a heap on the seat. Her aunt's face wasn't visible within the dark confines, but her voice resonated with concern. "What's amiss, dear?"

"Someone's in the road. A giant of a man." Abigail's breath came in gasps. "He must be a villain as he was creeping around in the dark holding a gun. I jabbed him with my umbrella. Twice. We must leave!"

Joshua approached the door, the light of his lamp now spilling into the coach. "Begging your pardon, Miss Longmore, but Lord Rochvale requests a lift back to the Hall."

"Lord Rochvale?" Her aunt sounded bemused. "Oh, of course. He must be out looking at the stars."

Abigail's gaze swept from her aunt's face to Joshua's impassive features. "Lord Rochvale, Aunt?"

"Our closest neighbor, dear. He works with your uncle. He is also an astronomer and often walks between the two properties at night."

"Oh!" Rocks seemed to settle in the region of Abigail's stomach. She bit her lip. "Is his lordship hurt, Joshua?"

The groom opened his mouth to reply, but before he could say anything, a calm voice spoke from behind him, "I am perfectly well, thank you. Good evening, Miss Longmore."

Great-aunt Mildred nodded. "Good evening, Rochvale. You haven't sustained an injury?"

"Only to my dignity," he said dryly. "I was observing the night sky when your carriage halted. I did not announce my presence at first as I did not wish to alarm the young lady or disturb her . . . er . . . privacy."

Abigail glanced at the telescope the man held. It had a wooden barrel, which must have been what she felt pressing into her ribs. She flushed as she met a pair of quizzical eyes. *Her privacy . . .* He must have assumed she was answering the call of nature rather than responding to the splendid call of the heavens. How mortifying.

He looked at Great-aunt Mildred. "Will you take me up with you, ma'am?"

"Yes, of course."

"Thank you. I'll retrieve my case." He walked away and returned within minutes, the telescope now packed into a mahogany box. "I've asked James to move at a smart pace as I wish to inform Longmore about the zodiacal light. He may be able to observe it himself if we return in time."

Lord Rochvale climbed into the coach with a lightness of movement quite astonishing for someone so large. Abigail sat in stunned silence, unable to find her tongue as he settled opposite her.

Thank goodness he was in the seat next to Great-aunt Mildred as Baker, her aunt's maid, filled the space beside Abigail with her ample form. However, Abigail's relief was short-lived as his lordship's limbs pressed against her skirts, the long wooden case lodged between his legs. His knees seemed to go up almost to his chin. Indeed, this space was too small for such a large man. Abigail clenched the inside of her cheeks with her teeth, her face heating at the enforced proximity.

Blessedly the light in the carriage disappeared with the groom as he shut the door after Lord Rochvale. Silence reigned for the first few minutes, and then Great-aunt spoke: "So you were observing the night sky when my niece . . . er . . ."

"I was."

Silence held sway once more until Abigail said in a low voice, "I beg your pardon, my lord. I believed you to be a villain."

"A most sensible conclusion to have drawn in the circumstances, Miss . . . er . . . ?"

Great-aunt coughed in the dark. "Abigail, may I introduce Viscount Rochvale to you? Lord Rochvale, Miss Abigail Grantham."

"Your servant, Miss Grantham," he murmured.

"Abigail has come to assist my nephew with his astronomical observations," Great-aunt continued.

"Ah, yes. Longmore told me."

Abigail leaned slightly forward. "You said something about zodiacal light, Lord Rochvale?" She drew her brows together and then released her breath in a slight hiss as she cast her mind back over John's teaching. "I remember now! My brother told me that it is a cone of light that results at or after the vernal equinox due to dust particles surrounding the sun."

"Indeed," Lord Rochvale said. "The Italian astronomer Giovanni Domenico Cassini posited that particular theory."

"I wondered what the light was. I'm so pleased to have seen it." Abigail smiled into the darkness.

"I suspected it might be present tonight. I only hope your uncle will have the opportunity to observe it before it disappears."

They drew to a halt five minutes later. Joshua opened the door, and after they descended from the carriage, Lord Rochvale made his excuses and strode ahead into the house. They all passed through a vestibule into the large manorial hall, and Abigail followed her aunt through an oak door into the breakfast room. A door near the fireplace of this apartment led into the brightly lit drawing room, where her uncle's wife, Aunt Longmore, awaited them. She rose to her feet with a welcoming smile when they stepped inside. "I am so pleased that you have arrived safely, my dears. I've been in something of a stew since the sun set and there was no sign of you. I was about to ask Longmore to send out a search party."

Abigail curtsied and sat on the well-upholstered armchair her aunt indicated just as her great-aunt lowered herself onto a sofa with a sigh. "We were delayed for some time this morning, Margaret, which resulted in our late arrival. Our journey wasn't smooth, I'm afraid. But we are safely arrived now, and that is all that matters."

"What happened?" Aunt Longmore tilted her round, pleasant countenance to one side, nodding her head occasionally in concern as she listened to her husband's aunt's account of their troubled journey.

"It does seem that circumstances were conspiring against you," she murmured sympathetically.

"This particular journey appeared doomed from the start. But I was delighted to have the opportunity to visit John and meet his charming bride, so I do not repine."

"Indeed! And how is dear John?"

"In excellent spirits and in good health. He sends you and Longmore his best regards."

Aunt Longmore opened her mouth to respond, but the drawing room door opened, and Uncle Longmore stepped inside with Lord Rochvale beside him. Abigail hadn't seen the viscount clearly in the confines of the carriage, and now she stared.

For some reason, she had expected him to be older, closer to her uncle's age. But he was quite a young man with nary a grey hair in sight. He was dressed neatly and, perhaps wisely for a man of his size, without any ostentation. And his closely cropped brown hair and simply-tied cravat gave him the appearance of an unpretentious country gentleman. It must have been his air of calm solidity that had deceived her into thinking he was of a different generation.

Lord Rochvale bowed in their direction just as Uncle Longmore said with a smile, "Delighted to see you, niece! I hope you had a good journey, Aunt Mildred?" He turned to his wife. "Forgive me, my dear. We are stepping out to see a celestial wonder. We shan't be long."

Aunt Longmore gazed at him from under lowered brows. "Hmm. Why do I not believe you, Longmore?"

"Never fear, my love. I am speaking the truth this time. The zodiacal light does not last long. In fact, it may have disappeared already. Rochvale kindly hastened to me at once to inform me of the spectacle. Most grateful to him. Only stopped to let you know in case you wondered where we'd gone."

Uncle Longmore was retreating toward the door as he spoke, readying himself for his escape. Abigail repressed a smile. She well knew the feeling. Turning her head, she met Lord Rochvale's eyes and stilled at their intent expression. But then a veil descended, masking their depths. Had she only imagined that curious light? The room was well-lit, but shadows could perform odd tricks.

She turned her attention back to her uncle, but he was already out of the door. Lord Rochvale, with another brief bow, followed him, leaving the ladies alone.

Aunt Longmore's resigned expression indicated that she was somewhat accustomed to this behavior. "Ah, well. I shall ask for dinner to be set back by at least another hour, which should thankfully not be a problem for our chef as he has been awaiting word of your arrival so nothing would spoil. I assume Rochvale will be joining us." She nodded in Abigail's direction. "I shall present him to you later, my dear . . . Longmore should have at least waited long enough to perform the introductions."

"Great-aunt presented Lord Rochvale to me in the coach."

"In the coach?" Her aunt stared.

"We gave him a lift back to the house when we . . . um . . . encountered him on the road."

"Oh! I see." Aunt Longmore gazed into the blazing fire before looking back at Abigail. "Lord Rochvale is frequently at the Hall as he and Longmore are working together on this project your uncle wrote to you about. I have agreed that you can assist them with taking down their observations on the condition that Susannah's governess accompanies you at all times. Fortunately, Miss Smith has very little to occupy her during the day now that Susannah is away at boarding school, so she should be up to the task."

Abigail's lips parted slightly. "I shall be assisting Lord Rochvale as well as my uncle?"

"Indeed. But your uncle will explain it all to you in due course. My only concern is for the proprieties, as Longmore can be quite careless of convention when he is caught up in his astronomical endeavors. And no matter how trustworthy Rochvale is, he is still a single man and must be treated as such."

Abigail nodded but made no reply as she dwelt on her aunt's revelatory words. How unfortunate that her acquaintanceship with her uncle's astronomical partner had begun with her stabbing him in the stomach.

CHAPTER TWO

ABIGAIL WENT UPSTAIRS a short while later to settle into her bedchamber. Baker was already there unpacking Abigail's things in the lamplight. The fire blazing in the grate lit up the room quite well, and Abigail walked across to the pitcher. Pouring out some water into the washbasin, she splashed water on her face and cleaned her hands before allowing her great-aunt's maid to assist her into a simple cream silk evening gown.

Extracting a gold shawl from the depths of her trunk, Baker handed it to her. "I believe you'll need this, miss. Rather chilly tonight."

Accepting the blessedly warm covering with a word of thanks, Abigail wrapped it around her arms and hastened out of the bedchamber and back to the drawing room, gripping the shawl a little tighter as it reminded her of her sister, Thea, who had made it for her.

As a young child, Abigail had traveled once to Longmore Hall with her family and remembered the visit fondly. However, arriving in the dark had been disconcerting. Quite disorientating, actually. Tomorrow she would get her bearings which would hopefully make her feel more at home.

How odd it was to come here on her own. Abigail had never previously traveled anywhere unaccompanied by one of her sisters or her brother. But now, for the first time, she had journeyed to a destination without an immediate family member. It felt rather like having a protective cloak stripped away. No doubt, she would grow accustomed to it, but she would miss the comfort and ease of their companionship.

When she entered the drawing room, Uncle Longmore and Lord Rochvale had not yet returned. As her stomach gave an audible rumble, Abigail hoped the zodiacal light would disappear sooner rather than later. She was starving, and a delayed dinner would be most unwelcome. Not even a celestial marvel could distract her from her hunger pangs.

Her cousin Henrietta, three years older than Abigail who was recently turned eighteen, was seated with Aunt Longmore and Great-aunt Mildred near the blazing fire. Abigail hastened across the room and greeted her warmly before turning to the middle-aged woman beside her on the sofa, whom Aunt Longmore introduced as Miss Smith, governess to her younger daughter, Susannah.

Miss Smith's brown hair was screwed up in a tight bun, and her dark brown evening gown was rather somber. But her face held a sweet expression as she rose to bid her good evening, and Abigail suppressed a sigh of relief as she sat down. A dour chaperone would be a most uncomfortable encumbrance, especially as she would be in close proximity to her for hours on end in the dead of night when no one else was around.

The door opened, and Uncle Longmore and the viscount made their appearance on the heels of the butler, who announced to the assembled party that dinner was served. Abigail made her way to the dining room, where Aunt Longmore seated her between Henrietta and Lord Rochvale.

White soup was served for the first course, and Abigail, trying not to gulp, focused her full attention on the welcome nourishment. She glanced to the side only when a footman removed her bowl from the table and encountered the viscount's gaze.

"When was your last meal?" he asked in a low voice.

"Oh, dear." She swallowed. "Is it so obvious that I haven't

eaten in a while?"

"Your restraint was admirable, Miss Grantham. It was merely your lack of conversation that made me wonder."

The footman laid china for the next course giving Abigail a moment to collect herself. She was about to speak when Lord Rochvale continued, "I must beg your forgiveness for my part in delaying your dinner. Would you care for a slice of roast beef?"

She jerked her head to look up at him. His grey eyes glowed once again with that strange light in an otherwise grave face.

"Thank you, my lord," she muttered, allowing him to serve her before turning to help herself from a dish of asparagus offered by a hovering footman.

Perfect. Now the man considered her not only violent but greedy, too. *This little pig had roast meat.* She took a dainty bite of the beef and, clearing her voice, turned her head to meet his eyes once more. "Was my uncle in time to see the zodiacal light?"

"He was. Fortunately."

"I am so pleased. I was amazed when I noticed what appeared to be a second dusk. Fortunately, my great-aunt allowed me to stop the carriage. Did you expect to see the light tonight?"

"I was hoping to, which was why I walked to the Hall."

She tilted her head. "What kind of telescope do you have?"

"A three-draw achromatic telescope made by Joseph Smith."

Her eyes widened. "How extraordinary! I have the very same instrument—my father gave it to me. I must say that I find it most useful that one does not always need to use the tripod when one is out and about with it."

"Indeed. My telescope was screwed to the branch of a tree when the zodiacal light appeared."

Abigail chewed on a piece of rather stringy asparagus for a minute. Then, after swallowing it, she glanced up at him again. "I mistook the barrel of your telescope for the barrel of a gun. That is why I . . . er . . . proceeded to defend myself."

"I suppose it must have felt very much like a pistol digging into your ribs." His voice was sympathetic.

"Exactly. I was mortified when I discovered I may have harmed you." She drew her brows together. "Are you certain you've sustained no lasting injury?"

The corners of his lips twitched. "It would take more than the tip of an umbrella to injure me, Miss Grantham." He spread open his hands. "As you may have noticed, I'm rather large."

"Yes, but I pierced your *belly*, my lord, the chink in every man's armor."

"Oh?" he said mildly. "I thought it was his heart."

She resumed the contemplation of her plate, studying the gravy on the beef with vast concentration. How young he made her feel. And unarmed. Or was that disarmed? She gave a tiny shrug. No matter. Time to speak to Henrietta.

She turned her head. Her cousin had soft brown hair, blue eyes, and a pale complexion. The sensitivity of her mouth gave her an air of gentleness belied only by her chin, which was firm bordering on resolute. "Grandmama said you will be traveling to London for the Season next year?" Abigail shifted slightly in her chair.

"Yes. But I wasn't sad to miss the Season this year as I'm quite content living in the country. Our neighbors are most sociable, you know, and scarcely a week passes without one invitation or another. And now that you're here, Mama will encourage even more entertainments."

"As long as Aunt Longmore doesn't have a penchant for breakfasts." Abigail pressed her lips together. "I shall sleep in late after I've stayed up at night working in the observatory. And it's quite difficult to rouse me—or so my family says."

Henrietta smiled. "I am sure Mama will take that into account. Is there anything in particular you'd like to do while you are here?"

"Well . . . I would be most interested in visiting any sites of architectural interest in the district. I like old buildings."

"Oh! Then, you must speak to Lord Rochvale." Henrietta nodded in the viscount's direction. "His lordship has a particular interest in architecture and antiques."

He inclined his head. "What particular style of architecture interests you, Miss Grantham?"

"I am intrigued by medieval buildings. They appear so mysterious somehow."

The corners of his eyes creased. "St Mary's Church in Chesham has a 12th century Romanesque window. Perhaps we could arrange an outing there one morning."

"Thank you, sir. I should like that very much."

Dessert was served a short while later, and after sampling a delicious jelly and a piece of nougat almond cake, Abigail pushed back her chair at her aunt's nod and rose to her feet alongside the other ladies as the gentlemen stood.

"Aunt Mildred and Abigail must be exhausted, so we will bid you good night, gentlemen," Aunt Longmore stated. "Until tomorrow night, Lord Rochvale. Are you still able to dine with us?"

Lord Rochvale bowed. "Yes, thank you, Lady Longmore." His gaze rested briefly on Abigail. "I shall be delighted to."

"Very well." Aunt Longmore's smile was warm as it encompassed both the viscount and her husband. "Good night."

Abigail retired to her bedchamber, relieved that the endless day was finally over, and within minutes of her head touching the pillow, sleep claimed her.

The next day she spent with Henrietta, as Aunt Longmore was seeing to her household accounts in the library. The cousins walked in the gardens, which were bursting with blossoms as April was nearly upon them, and caught up on their family news.

After the arduous journey it was lovely to stroll about without any claim on her time, although Abigail suspected that Uncle Longmore would ask her to work that night, especially as Lord Rochvale had been invited to dine once more.

However, after another delicious evening meal, where Abigail took especial pains to ensure she made polite conversation with the viscount during the soup course, her uncle informed her that he would not require her help.

"Not tonight, my dear," he said with a firm shake of his head after she put the question to him. "You must still be tired after your journey and only just getting settled in. I shall discuss your duties with you tomorrow." He rubbed his hands together. "I must say, I'm most grateful that you've come to our assistance, niece. It is quite a task we've set ourselves to create this star chart."

"You mentioned in your letter to John that you will be using Mr. Bessel's *Fundamenta Astronomiae* catalog, Uncle?"

"Indeed. Bessel's catalog is most useful as we shall use the position of the fundamental stars to measure the position of other stars."

Aunt Longmore cleared her throat, and Uncle Longmore looked across at his lady, raising his hands in brief apology, before turning back to Abigail. "Let us speak more about this in private, my dear." His eyes twinkled a little. "Not everyone shares our interest in astronomy, after all. I hope that your brother and his bride are well?"

"They are in excellent health and send you their best wishes. John says he hopes to bring Emily to Longmore to visit sometime."

"We shall be delighted to see them. I am sorry that I haven't met his young wife as yet."

The conversation turned to a more general discussion about various family members, and then the ladies retired to the drawing room, leaving the gentlemen to their port. The men joined them only a short while later, however, making Abigail suspect they hadn't sampled any after-dinner wines.

This was confirmed by her uncle, who said, "We decided to join you at once, my dears. Too much wine makes one nod off at far too early an hour. And that would be a crime on such a clear night as this."

Henrietta took her place at the pianoforte as Uncle Longmore seated himself near his wife. Henrietta's lips curved into a smile as

Lord Rochvale strolled across to the musical instrument to turn the pages for her. Abigail studied the pair with slightly narrowed eyes as the viscount stooped to examine the piece Henrietta had chosen to play. They seemed on easy terms. Perhaps they had an understanding of some sort?

As the first strains of music filled the air, Abigail's gaze wandered around the room. Pale blue curtains of rich damask softened the rather grand apartment, which contained gilt cornices and a handsomely-molded ceiling. The fireplace's mantelpiece was of carved white marble superimposed upon yellow, with a figure from Greek mythology Abigail couldn't identify on a medallion in the center.

Several mirrors and an array of paintings hung on the walls. The framed canvas above the fireplace was of yet another figure from Greek mythology. This time, however, Abigail managed to identify the character—Aurora drifting on a cloud just as the sun rose, one hand trailing a garland and the other grasping a flower. She sighed. How entirely free the girl looked. Wouldn't it be lovely to drift through life in just such a way, experiencing none of the griefs of an earthly existence? To smell the flowers and feel the wind in your hair without concerning yourself with weeds or turbulent gusts . . .

Abigail looked away from the painting as beautiful sounds emanated from the pianoforte Returning her attention to her cousin, Abigail smiled in appreciation. What an accomplished performer Henrietta was! As Lord Rochvale turned a page of music, he glanced up and met Abigail's eyes. Startled at their keen expression, so at odds with his placid demeanor, Abigail straightened her back a little, raising her brows. But then he smiled, and her defensiveness drained away. He appeared a nice enough gentleman and not in the least formidable.

She did not know why she had suddenly formed the impression that he was.

CHAPTER THREE

WILLIAM DREW HIS gaze away from Miss Abigail Grantham with some difficulty. When Longmore had told him that his niece would be arriving to assist them with their star cataloging project, William had imagined a quiet, bookish kind of girl, not this blazing beauty, trailing like a comet across the night sky.

Copper-red ringlets tumbled around Miss Grantham's dainty shoulders, contrasting strikingly with creamy skin and bright blue eyes that regarded the world with an air of charming frankness. Her open manners and lack of dissimulation were refreshing. Becoming better acquainted with her was a most attractive prospect.

He leaned forward to turn the page once more. Undoubtedly, he would be one of many gentlemen seeking to spend time with Miss Grantham over the next few months. But only William would be working with her. He drew his brows together. In some respects, this could prove more of a hindrance than a benefit.

Henrietta Longmore played the last few notes of the piece before turning in her seat, nodding slightly to acknowledge the applause. As an accomplished pianist, he knew she spent hours practicing every day. She nodded now at her cousin. "Would you care to play, Abby?"

Miss Grantham shook her head. "Oh no! The piano is not my

forte, I'm afraid."

"Would you like to sing then? I have some music. Do you know "O Mistress Mine" from *Twelfth Night*?"

Miss Grantham nodded and rose to her feet.

Henrietta smiled up at him. "Would you care to join my cousin in song, my lord?"

"Very much so."

The red-haired young lady trod over to the pianoforte, and within moments, their accompanist began playing a tune from Morley's *Consort Lessons*. She said in a low voice: "You begin, Rochvale."

As the notes filled the air, William sang:

O Mistress mine, where are you roaming?
O, stay and hear, your true love's coming,
 That can sing both high and low:
Trip no further, pretty sweeting;
Journeys end in lovers' meeting,
 Every wise man's son doth know.

He paused, and then Miss Grantham took up the tune, singing in her pretty soprano:

What is love? 'Tis not hereafter;
Present mirth hath present laughter;
 What's to come is still unsure.

In delay there lies no plenty,
Then come kiss me, sweet and twenty,
 Youth's a stuff will not endure.

As the song came to an end, their audience gave a smattering of applause before Henrietta raised her fingers from the pianoforte and invited her fellow musicians to sing a couple of glees with her. Miss Grantham's cheeks were slightly flushed and her eyes bright as she participated enthusiastically in the short concert.

William's gaze rested on her bent head. How animated she was! That was what struck him most about her. Miss Grantham brimmed with energy as if life depended upon her full participation. No half-measures for this young woman. He leaned against the wooden instrument as they launched into a new song, his body shifting slightly so that she was in his direct line of vision. Unusual to have such vitality in a young lady. More often than not, governesses or strict boarding school regimes dampened that sparkle somewhat. His own sisters had visibly dimmed as they'd grown older, consciously assuming the mantle of refined dignity Society expected of women hoping to marry men in prominent positions.

Yet Miss Grantham was irrepressible.

What made her so? He had heard her uncle speak of the Grantham branch of his family, but he had not paid close attention to the older man's discourse as these were strangers to him. But now he trained his mind to recollect his astronomical partner's words. Longmore had mentioned that the entire Grantham family had a scientific bent and that his deceased sister's children had studied various branches of natural philosophy.

If he recalled correctly, the older sister, who was now married to the Duke of Stanford, was interested in horticulture. The second sister had a particular aptitude for chemistry. And Miss Abigail Grantham and her brother, Sir John, were fascinated by astronomy.

He met Miss Grantham's eyes now and smiled. Perhaps it was her constant star gazing that made them so luminous? His lips wryly twisted as Henrietta played the last notes and lifted her hands from the keyboard. Miss Grantham's dazzling effect on him must be making him think in metaphors.

Henrietta rose from the pianoforte, nodding in a friendly way. "You and my cousin sing beautifully together, my lord." She shut the lid of the instrument. "Your voices are perfectly attuned."

He raised his brow. *"That can sing both high and low?"*

She laughed. "Precisely. That song I chose was prescient, I do believe."

He narrowed his eyes as he met her bland gaze. He'd known Henrietta Longmore since the cradle as she had virtually grown up with his younger sister, Jane, who was now married. His sister's childhood friend rarely made idle statements. He suspected the strong impression Miss Grantham had made on him was evident to others.

Prescient indeed.

William followed the ladies to their vacated chairs in front of the fire. Who else had noticed his perturbation?

As he resumed his seat, Henrietta spoke in a low voice as Miss Grantham went to sit beside her aunt Longmore, who was patting the place beside her on the sofa. "Fear not, Rochvale . . . she hasn't noticed."

"You did, though."

"Yes. But I know you very well."

He lifted his hands, palms up. "Am I making a fool of myself, Hetta?"

She eyed him in a considering way. "Not yet. But you may."

He gave a low laugh. *"A coup de foudre.* Unexpected, I must say."

"Not really." She folded her hands in her lap. "Those who fall last often fall the hardest. And your heart hasn't been touched before, has it?"

"No. But I don't believe in love at first sight. That's the ridiculous thing."

"The heart sometimes knows what the mind refuses to recognize."

His brows drew together. A heart-knowing . . . That was exactly what it felt like. But perhaps he was only attracted to Miss Grantham's beautiful face and figure? He leaned back in his chair, crossing his arms as he rested his gaze on her once more. No. He sighed. He had met many pretty girls over the years, and none had affected him like this.

He had fallen in love.

What an unsettling experience it was.

He lowered his chin into the folds of his cravat. *How am I going to work with her?*

CHAPTER FOUR

ABIGAIL WANDERED DOWN the grand oak staircase the next morning, occasionally stopping to rest her hand on the smooth surface of the polished wooden banister. Several small, carved statues of characters from Greek and Roman mythology stood to attention at regular intervals on the raised pedestals along the railing. Abigail stopped to observe a Roman marshal armored in *lorica lamminata*, terminating halfway to his knees, before gazing at a plumed soldier holding a sword aloft.

Picking up her pace a little, she hastened along. If she stopped to examine every figure on display on the staircase, she would be late for the meeting with her uncle in the library at eleven. She had already lingered too long over breakfast in the company of Henrietta and Miss Smith, where she had nibbled a morsel of toast and drunk some chocolate.

She entered the spacious book-lined room beside the dining room and gazed around in delight. The morning light, pouring through an enormous bay window, illuminated several bookcases meshed with brass wire, stretching almost to the ceiling.

She made her way across the room to the white marble fire-place on the west side. In the center of the mantelpiece was a medallion of Galileo Galilei. As Abigail stepped closer to examine the image of the famous astronomer mulling over a problem, she smiled at the baby cherubs surrounding him. One was taking off the covering of a globe while his twin mischievously removed the cap of a telescope.

Turning away, she strolled to the bookshelves to examine the large selection of mathematical and philosophical works on display, written in English and other languages. Many of the books seemed very old and rare. She removed a copy of *A Table of the Longitude and Latitude of Various Places* and was paging through its contents when her uncle entered the library.

"Ah, so you've found my books." He rubbed his hands together. "If you need a reference for anything to do with astronomy, my dear, you'll find it here."

"What an extensive collection you have." Abigail replaced the volume. "I see some of the books are in foreign languages."

"Indeed. I had the opportunity a few years ago to travel to the Levant, where I bought works in Arabic, Persian, and Turkish. The titles were translated, with excellent commentary by a good friend of mine, the Reverend George Cecil Renouard. So, if you would like to examine those texts, pray do."

"Thank you, sir. I shall be delighted to."

He indicated a nearby trio of armchairs placed around a low, mahogany table. "Please sit down. We have much to discuss."

Abigail was lowering herself onto the comfortable-looking chair when the library door opened, and Lord Rochvale entered the room. She transformed the movement into a curtsy as he bowed in her direction. "Good morning, Miss Grantham. I trust you had a restful night?"

"Thank you, Lord Rochvale. I did."

Her uncle nodded at the viscount. "I invited Rochvale to our conference as we shall all be working on the star chart together."

The gentlemen took their seats, and for a moment, no one spoke. Abigail glanced from Lord Rochvale's calm countenance to her uncle's beaming one. The difference in appearance between the two gentlemen could not be more marked. Although of small stature, her uncle seemed to fill the room with his presence, while Lord Rochvale, although physically imposing, appeared quite content with the role of spectator.

Her uncle spoke: "My dear, I cannot tell you how grateful we are that you've arrived to help us. A trained astronomical assistant is most difficult to find."

"I hope that I will be of some use to you, Uncle." Abigail bit her lip. "However, I am still learning myself . . ."

"As are we all, my dear. As are we all. It is dangerous to believe that one can come to the end of learning." He creased his brow. "Indeed, half the problem with mankind is that humans believe they are omniscient. But studying the celestial heavens can certainly teach one humility."

"And patience," Lord Rochvale murmured. "Infinite patience is required for the task we have set ourselves."

"I hope you have that quality in abundance, Abigail." Her uncle released his breath in a puff. "Otherwise, you might as well cry quits at once."

Her lips curved into a half-smile. "I have learned a measure of patience in my astronomical work. But I am afraid the characteristic does not come naturally to me."

Uncle Longmore chuckled. "I suppose it doesn't come naturally to most young people, which is why it is counted as a virtue." His expression sobered. "Your aunt Longmore has impressed upon me the importance of allowing you sufficient leisure time. She does not wish you to become so fatigued from staying up late that you fail to enjoy the social activities she is planning for you. I assured her that even if I were a harsh taskmaster, which I am not, the British weather would ensure ample time for you to catch up on your sleep as cloudy nights are more common than not at this time of year."

Abigail nodded. "We were fortunate that the sky was clear a couple of nights ago."

"Indeed! Rochvale mentioned that you encountered each other on the road when you stopped the carriage."

She met the viscount's eyes and blushed. "Er, yes. Unfortunately, I thought his lordship was a villain as he was skulking about in the dark."

"Skulking, Abigail?" Uncle Longmore glanced at Lord Rochvale with raised brows before turning his attention back to his niece.

"If Lord Rochvale had called out that he was there, I might not have suspected him of nefarious intentions."

The viscount smiled. "It is one of the hazards of our occupation, I am afraid. To . . . ah . . . skulk about in the dark sometimes."

The amusement in his eyes caused the color to rush to Abigail's cheeks once more, and she swung back to her uncle. "May I see your observatory now, sir?"

"Yes, of course. It is next door. But first, let me explain the nature of your duties to you." He leaned back in his chair, glancing at the viscount. "Lord Rochvale has charted those stars listed in Bessel's catalog, and now we plan to add our own observations, measuring them down to the magnitude of nine. We thought it best to work together, in pairs, with one observer measuring the longitude and brightness of a star while the other measures the altitude. To ensure that our measurements are synchronized, we shall communicate our findings to one other before stopping for intervals to reduce them."

He drummed his fingers on the table, frowning a little. "It is painstaking work as we aim to measure up to three hundred stars in the next few months. I have agreed to do this as a trial for Bessel. He wishes to see how many stars astronomers in a private observatory can chart in a four-month period as he hopes to open up this project to other people and observatories in the future. Our work will give him a clear idea of what can be expected within a specific time frame. Therefore, it will be best if we divide the labor between the three of us."

"So I shall work with you on some nights, Uncle, and with Lord Rochvale on others?"

"Precisely, my dear. And Rochvale and I will work together, too. This arrangement will allow us a little freedom so that we aren't chained to the observatory at all hours. Although, this arrangement will only begin in a fortnight or so as Rochvale is writing a paper for The Royal Society at the moment, which is taking up most of his time. However, he will try to join us tomorrow night so that we can establish a working rhythm."

"Are you writing a paper on astronomy, my lord?" Abigail asked politely.

Lord Rochvale bowed his head. "On nebulae."

"How interesting. I look forward to reading it."

"As do I," Uncle Longmore said. "As do I." He leaned back in his chair, studying her with a pleased expression. "I must say that I am delighted to have a female family member who shares my interests. Although, as your aunt frequently reminds me, there are other important aspects to life." His tone, however, implied quite the opposite.

Abigail creased her forehead. "Will we be doing any other astronomical work, sir? I have a particular interest in comets.

"Perhaps you will see one, my dear, during the course of your observations. But our focus will necessarily be on the star chart."

Abigail attempted not to show her disappointment, but she must have been unsuccessful as her uncle added, "I know it is rather tedious work, my dear. But it is so necessary. I'm sure you're already aware how incomplete and inaccurate all our current star charts are. Bessel hopes that the creation of better charts, which could take years, to own the truth, may even help us discover more planets and asteroids, but I confess I just want to know the sky better, more completely." He smiled. "Think of the wonders others will discover after us with the knowledge we pass on to them."

"Yes, of course." Abigail looked away from him and encountered the viscount's measuring gaze. She straightened her spine. Perhaps he didn't think she was up to the task. But she was made of strong enough stuff even though her delicate appearance belied it. Frequently gentlemen alluded to her fairy-like qualities, saying things like, "Oh, Miss Abigail, do take care. Let me relieve you of the heavy weight of your shawl."

Well, not quite as bad as that. But a couple of would-be suitors she had met in Bath when she had visited the spa town last year had delighted in comparing her to a fragile flower or an ethereal sprite. Little had they known that their comments, far from pleasing her, had caused her considerable dismay. She had no wish to be seen in such an ineffectual light.

Fortunately, Abigail was quite tall, so that helped a bit with the fairy comparison nonsense. And at least she could look most men straight in the eye. But not the viscount. Oh, no. In order to meet that steady regard, her gaze was required to travel up to quite a heady height. And she had never been particularly fond of heights.

"Let me show you the transit room now," her uncle said as he stood. "Although we shall not use it for our star chart project, it is worth a look."

Abigail rose too, and when Lord Rochvale politely indicated that she should go before him, she followed Uncle Longmore to the eastern bay of the library, which led to an ante-room. "This is where the lamps are kept and trimmed." He nodded in the direction of a flight of stairs. "And those steps lead up to the roof. I frequently go up there to use my five-foot achromatic telescope."

"May I do so as well, Uncle?"

He smiled. "Of course."

He made his way into the adjoining transit room. It was an irregular octagon in shape and was divided in the middle by window openings on the north- and south-facing walls that extended up to the ceiling and were joined to each other by a slit in the roof that spanned the whole distance. Altogether it formed a wide gap through which a fixed telescope could easily sweep the sky. Coming to a halt, he pointed at the gap in the roof. "This is the *chax*. I open and close it using this weight-operated shutter."

But Abigail barely glanced at the mechanism. Instead, her attention fastened on a magnificent fixed transit instrument in the middle of the room, supported at its center by two cones ending in pivots made of bell metal connected to stone plinths.

"Ah! You're transfixed by my astronomical partner's pride and joy," Uncle Longmore said with a friendly nod in the viscount's direction. "When Rochvale inherited this telescope from his uncle a couple of years ago, I was delighted to accommodate it."

"What a beautiful instrument!" Abigail breathed.

"Its focal length is sixty inches, and the telescope's circumference is . . . what, twenty-five inches, eh, Rochvale?"

"Yes." His eyes smiled. "You're welcome to use it whenever you wish, Miss Grantham."

"Thank you, my lord! How very kind you are."

A slow tide of color appeared above the line of his cravat. Surprising. Perhaps he was one of those people who struggled to accept compliments.

Her gaze returned to her uncle, who was now leading the way out of the transit room. "And now on to the observatory portico." His voice boomed in the enclosed space as he passed through another room housing three telescopes, a clock, a brass sextant, a quadrant, and various other astronomical equipment. This chamber led outside onto a columned portico, and Abigail edged past her uncle to study a tripod mounted on a pedestal.

"We'll set up a telescope there," her uncle stated. "And this is where the second one will be positioned." He walked over to a nearby stone pier. "I am afraid it will be quite cold at night, so you must dress warmly, Abigail."

"I hardly feel the cold when I'm investigating the heavens, Uncle. Aunt Eliza always tells me I'll fall ill, but I rarely do."

"Carried away with inspiration, Miss Grantham?" Lord Rochvale murmured.

"Very much so. I am always at my happiest when looking through the lens of a telescope."

She gave him a friendly smile just as the door to the astronomical equipment room opened again, and a gentleman strolled outside. Abigail blinked at the newcomer's handsome appearance. Dressed in yellow pantaloons and a green coat, he gave the impression of an upside-down daffodil. An extremely well-turned-out upside-down daffodil.

"Lady Longmore informed me that you'd probably be out here," the gentleman said. "Rochvale, Lord Longmore . . ." His gaze swung in Abigail's direction, and he bowed. "Ma'am."

Abigail caught her breath at the gentleman's bright green gaze. His eyes were like twin emeralds. Truly they were mesmerizing. She looked down, taking in his expertly tied cravat, his natty waistcoat, and the almost blinding shine of his Hessian boots. Glancing up again, she felt the color creep into her cheeks at the small smile curling his lips.

"Gerald." Lord Rochvale's voice was calm as he inclined his head before turning to Abigail. "Miss Grantham, may I present my cousin, Gerald Burnby, to you? Gerald, this is Miss Abigail Grantham, Lord and Lady Longmore's niece."

After Mr. Burnby bowed and expressed his delight at meeting Abigail, Lord Rochvale addressed him once more. "When did you arrive?"

"This morning." Mr. Burnby's teeth glinted in the sunlight. "I was surprised to hear you were already at Longmore, coz. Usually, you visit at night. For obvious reasons."

"I had business here this morning."

When Lord Rochvale did not elaborate, Mr. Burnby shifted his gaze to Abigail. "Ho! Naturally."

Uncle Longmore cleared his throat. "Shall we go inside, Abigail? Your aunt wishes to spend the rest of the day with you. I think you have seen enough to go on?"

"Yes, thank you. But I am sure I will have many questions."

"Yes, of course. Ask away. We shall be pleased to answer any questions as they arise." He spread his hands in an ushering motion, and Abigail turned to precede the gentlemen indoors.

Returning swiftly to the library, she puckered her brow. Mr. Burnby appeared to be what her Aunt Eliza defined as a "man about town." He looked around the same age as Lord Rochvale, but while the viscount had the air of a staid country gentleman, his cousin exuded town bronze. Perhaps he had just come from London?

Lord Rochvale's voice came from behind her. "Have you seen Grandfather yet, Gerald?"

"He was sleeping when I arrived."

"He will be pleased to see you. I'm afraid he hasn't been in prime form recently." The viscount's tone was a trifle clipped.

When Abigail emerged into the book-lined room, her aunt was standing near the door. "Ah, there you are, Abigail. Come with me, my dear. We have much to discuss."

Abigail dipped into a slight curtsy as the gentlemen poured into the library after her. Encountering Lord Rochvale's contemplative gaze, she gave him a slight smile before turning to Mr. Burnby. She shook her head in faint bemusement as she studied his classical features.

Truly, he was the most handsome man.

CHAPTER FIVE

A UNT LONGMORE LED the way into the drawing room and indicated an armchair near the blazing fire. "Do be seated, my love. Henrietta will join us once she's finished her walk."

Her aunt settled herself on the sofa as she contemplated her niece. "You know, you're far too beautiful for your own good, Abigail. We shall have gentlemen descending on us in droves once I take you out and about with me. And you haven't even had your first London Season yet."

Abigail's cheeks warmed. "Um . . ."

Her aunt leaned forward. "I did not mean to embarrass you, my dear, but a chaperone must always take the appearance of her charge into consideration. And you are truly lovely. Quite out of the common way." She pressed her lips together. "I would be quite beside myself with anxiety if Henrietta weren't here to help keep an eye on you, too. She is most sensible and as she has known most of the young gentlemen in the district since her babyhood, they shan't misbehave when she's around." She sighed. "I must say that I am almost thankful that you have such a marked interest in astronomy. You will be safe at home most nights if Longmore has anything to do with it."

"I hope to spend most of my time in the observatory, learning from my uncle, especially as I shall have all the time in the world to attend parties when I travel to London next year." She smiled.

"However, I'll be pleased to partake in any social activities during the day. And on cloudy nights, of course."

"Yes. And there are many such nights at this time of year."

The door opened, and Henrietta came in. "Oh, there you are, dearest," her mother said. "I was just telling Abigail that I'll need your assistance looking after her. Your gaze is quelling enough to keep the more ardent gentlemen at bay."

Henrietta laughed as she sat on the sofa beside her mother. "Abigail will believe me to be a veritable dragon, Mama."

Abigail shook her head. "Not at all! You remind me of Alexandra and Dorothea, truth be told. And my sisters aren't dragons at all. Quite the opposite, in fact—they're more like mother hens."

"Older sisters do tend to have that air." Henrietta smiled a little. "It must come from the concern they have for their brothers and sisters."

"Indeed. Poor Alexandra was always getting me out of scrapes when I was a little girl. I have quite a spirit of adventure, you see."

Her aunt looked alarmed. "Well, I hope you won't adventure too far while you're under my aegis, my dear."

Abigail sat up a little straighter in her chair. "I've outgrown my youthful misdemeanors, I believe."

"I certainly hope so."

"We all make missteps in our younger years," her cousin said. "It is all part of growing up, after all."

"Indeed," Abigail murmured. But as her aunt asked Henrietta about the clemency of the weather, Abigail contemplated the older girl with curious eyes. A slight air of aloofness hung about her even though she was always very kind. Perhaps she was simply a person who did not like to reveal too much about her thoughts. Whatever it was, she was not easy to read, unlike Abigail herself. She well knew that her own emotions tended to spill out on her features in a most annoying way. Her family always guessed exactly how she was feeling. Frequently she'd wished for a cloak of anonymity to add an air of intrigue to her demeanor. But, alas, it wasn't meant to be. She would never be a lady of mystery.

The door opened, and Lord Rochvale and Mr. Burnby entered. The viscount bowed. "Forgive me for disturbing you, Lady Longmore, but before I leave, I would like to arrange an outing to Chesham. Miss Grantham expressed an interest in visiting St Mary's Church." His gaze rested on Abigail. "We could take my coach."

Mr. Burnby stepped forward, bowing in Henrietta's direction, before shooting a glance at his cousin. "I have an even better plan, coz. Why don't we take the ladies out in our curricles? It isn't too far for a day's expedition."

"And so it begins . . ." Lady Longmore muttered under her breath. However, collecting herself, she inclined her head. "Very well. When would you like to go?"

Lord Rochvale glanced out of the window. "It would be wise to take advantage of the fine weather. I doubt it will last very long." He turned to Henrietta. "We could travel there tomorrow if that suits you and Miss Grantham?"

The older girl inclined her head. "When I was walking in the Italian garden this morning, old Ned told me that he believed the clear weather would last until the end of the week. He is rarely mistaken in his predictions, so it sounds like a good plan."

"Miss Grantham?" Lord Rochvale raised his brows.

"I should like that very much. Thank you, my lord."

"Excellent. We shall see you tomorrow after breakfast."

Her aunt's brows knitted as she studied the gentlemen's retreating forms. When the door closed behind them, she looked at her daughter. "I suppose Gerald Burnby's come to stay because his grandfather is unwell." She glanced across at Abigail. "Mr. Burnby is Lord Rochvale's cousin, my dear. Their grandfather is the Earl of Barcombe, our closest neighbor. Rochvale, his heir, is in permanent residence at Barcombe Manor, while Burnby occasionally pays his grandfather a flying visit. We've hardly seen him these past few years as he is more at home in London."

"He does look like a London beau," Abigail observed.

"Yes, indeed. Mr. Burnby is a buck of the first stare." Her aunt lifted her shoulders. "But with expensive habits, I'm afraid. His grandfather is generous, and Burnby owns a snug property bordering Barcombe, which he inherited from his father, so he always comes about when he is in the neighborhood. But word has it that he is drawing the bustle a bit too freely these days." She cleared her throat. "I trust you won't set too much store by any attention he may give you, Abigail. He's a trifle wild."

Abigail's eyes widened. "Oh? In what way?"

"Er . . . in the usual way of young men." Her aunt waved a vague hand. "I doubt he will settle down for some time. He is quite a favorite with the ladies, though, so be on your guard. I doubt your grandmother would approve of his suit. In her last letter, she wrote that you need to marry a sensible man as you have a tendency toward impetuosity."

When Abigail frowned, her aunt smiled kindly. "Most girls your age do."

Abigail pressed her lips together but did not reply. She had grown up rather a lot during the last couple of years. But unfortunately, as the youngest child in her family, it was hard not to be labeled as green and immature. And although she wanted her future husband to be a man of sense, it rankled somewhat to be informed that she needed to marry one.

Unfortunately, when she thought of "sensible men," the image of gentlemen of her uncle's generation, not her own, came inexorably to mind. And honestly, they sounded a trifle dull.

However, she did not voice her annoyance to her aunt. The best course of action open to her would be to ignore it. After all, older people were always telling younger people to be more sensible.

When the gentlemen arrived the following morning, Mr. Burnby instantly claimed Abigail as his traveling companion. He stepped into the drawing room and offered her his arm, leading her straight to his curricle after they exited the house.

Lord Rochvale was just behind him, escorting Henrietta. As he drew his equipage alongside his cousin's a short while later, he said, "Shall we swap companions for the return journey? I wish to speak to Miss Grantham about our astronomical project."

"I should like that, my lord," Abigail said. "There is much I need to know." She looked at her cousin. "Henrietta?"

The older girl nodded stiffly in Mr. Burnby's direction but did not echo Abigail's pleasure in the arrangement. And neither did the gentleman seated beside her.

As Lord Rochvale drove off ahead of them, Abigail stole a glance at Mr. Burnby. There appeared to be some coolness between him and Henrietta. Abigail had been too preoccupied yesterday to notice the strain, but now as she cast her mind back, she recalled that Henrietta had not addressed a single word to him in the drawing room. How very awkward.

Abigail would keep an eye on the situation and perhaps offer to travel back with Mr. Burnby in Henrietta's stead. She nibbled her bottom lip with her teeth. Unfortunately, it would be difficult to withdraw her acceptance of Lord Rochvale's invitation now without appearing singular. But she might need to if Henrietta did not enjoy Mr. Burnby's company. His free and easy manners might not combine well with her cousin's more formal approach.

They were delayed for some five minutes as Mr. Burnby's groom ran back to deliver a message to the stables. When the youth eventually returned, her companion drove off fast. Abigail caught her breath as they bowled along the road, the Buckinghamshire scenery whizzing past her. When they eventually caught up with Lord Rochvale, Mr. Burnby attempted to pass him numerous times without success.

Eventually, he slowed down, giving a short laugh. "I do like speed, Miss Grantham. Unfortunately, my cousin is less inclined to travel at a spanking pace. Makes a journey a trifle dull, but it's too difficult to pass him on this stretch of road." He smiled at her. "But I shan't repine. It allows me the opportunity to savor the company of my charming passenger. Are you enjoying being my passenger, ma'am? You have a distinct sparkle in your eye, I must say. Most ladies tell me to reduce my pace."

Abigail's lips curved into a smile. She had been enjoying the sensation of the wind whipping through her hair. It reminded her of the joy she had experienced when she had ridden her pony as a young girl. She had always gone far too fast, according to her aunt Eliza, but Abigail had never been able to resist the temptation of galloping along. It had given her an amazing feeling of flying through the air. She had simply felt free. So free.

She had been experiencing that same sensation now, but the surface of the road wasn't smooth, and her teeth were soundly rattled. Perhaps it was a good thing that he had slowed down a bit. "I'm enjoying the drive very much, thank you, sir."

"And are you enjoying your visit equally?"

"Well, I have only just arrived, Mr. Burnby, but am I looking forward to a wonderful stay. Everyone is very kind."

He raised an eyebrow. "Of course they are! Who wouldn't be kind to such a pretty girl as you?" His green eyes glinted in the sunlight as he gazed down at her. Abigail swallowed, her pulse fluttering a little. The intensity of his expression was disconcerting, and she drew in a quick breath as he spoke again: "You have no idea how pleased I was to discover you at Longmore. The countryside can be a dead bore, at times, but it won't be now."

"Um . . . You plan to stay long?"

"For the next few months or so. Occasionally, I grow tired of London but fortunately never of life." He gave her another of his quick smiles before returning his attention to his horses.

Lord Rochvale proceeded at a steady pace in front of them. He did not drive too fast, perhaps because he and Henrietta appeared to be having a serious discussion. Their *tête-à-tête* was evident from the rigid set of Henrietta's shoulders and the way the viscount tilted his head in her direction to listen to what she was saying.

Mr. Burnby must have noticed their familiar posture as he

said with a frown, "I do wish our cousins would stop conversing. It's slowing us down."

Abigail turned her head. "There's no hurry, though, sir, is there? We have plenty of time to get to Chesham."

"I've grown accustomed to the faster pace of the Metropolis, I fear. It always takes me some time to adjust to country living."

"But you do eventually adjust?"

"Oh, yes. Once I've found something . . . or someone"—he shot her a swift glance—"to occupy my time."

A more expansive stretch of the road gave Mr. Burnby the opportunity he sought. He overtook the other carriage, passing it by a hair's breadth, and they traveled swiftly on, arriving in Chesham within the hour. Based on the viscount's sedate traveling pace, Abigail expected Lord Rochvale and Henrietta to arrive much later.

She climbed down from the curricle with Mr. Burnby's assistance and turned to look at the church, a flint building with light stone dressings. She was just beginning to feel a trifle uneasy about being in a strange place with a strange gentleman and no chaperone in sight when Lord Rochvale came trotting up at a far-from-slow pace.

The viscount drew his chestnuts to a halt beside Mr. Burnby's vehicle just as his groom sprang down to attend to the horses. After assisting Henrietta to alight, they approached them.

Mr. Burnby bowed, grinning. "My congratulations, coz. It appears your plodders just needed a little . . . er . . . prodding to speed up to an acceptable pace."

His cousin studied him calmly. "I never spring my horses at the start of a journey."

"Only at the end?"

"When I am satisfied that they won't do themselves an injury, I allow them their heads."

"Always so considered!" Mr. Burnby scoffed.

"And considerate," Henrietta said in cool tones. She turned to Abigail. "Should we go on ahead, Abby dear?"

Abigail nodded swiftly. Her cousin was bristling with disapproval.

"Although the church is in use, be aware that the tower is structurally weak," Lord Rochvale called out as she and Henrietta walked away.

Abigail turned back and met the viscount's eyes. Somehow she had the impression that he wasn't merely warning her about the tower.

Chapter Six

ABIGAIL LOOKED AT the church spire, rising high above a porch with Gothic perpendicular windows.

"The remains of a section of a Norman window is visible in the wall of the north transept." Henrietta glanced over her shoulder at the two gentlemen who were still conversing. "Let me show you."

Abigail followed her cousin inside, shivering at the slight chill in the air. She gazed around at the light interior of the church with its English Gothic aisles and stained glass windows. After carefully examining the Norman Romanesque window Henrietta pointed out, Abigail walked over to a carving of a girl wearing robes and a hood, kneeling beside a coffin in a mourning position, her head in one hand. Abigail read the inscription underneath the monument, which commemorated the deaths of a husband and wife. Looking back at the tragic pose of the girl, Abigail imagined her to be a daughter mourning both her parents—an orphan just like her.

Abigail turned away, gripping her hands together. She had lost her mother when she was ten years old and her father more recently. And although she had grown accustomed to grief, the sad expression on the girl's face brought back her own bereavement in an almost tangible way, knocking the breath out of her chest.

Abigail sensed someone beside her and blinked the moisture in her eyes away. Fiercely. How embarrassing to be discovered weeping in a church like this. Although, out of all buildings, a church was probably the most acceptable vessel for tears.

She kept her gaze averted as Lord Rochvale spoke, "St Mary's was built on a puddingstone circle dating from the Bronze Age and has a range of architectural styles."

Thank goodness he did not comment on her lachrymose appearance. Her nose always went bright pink when she cried, clashing hideously with her red hair. She cleared her throat, still not looking at him. "Why is the tower unstable, my lord?"

"It was widened in the 13th and 14th centuries, which weakened it. And on that already shaky arrangement were added bells and a belfry and a spire that I believe is even covered in lead. The increased weight along with the increased number of burials, both inside and outside the church, has caused many problems for the parish."

Abigail shivered. "I now have a horrid image in my mind of the tower collapsing on our heads."

"Fear not." She heard the smile in his voice as she peeked at him out of the corner of her eye. He was pointing in the direction of the south transept. "That arch was blocked up during the last century and a large hollow pillar that was a stairway to the rood loft was also filled in—both to help shore up the structure."

"Be that as it may, my lord, I would appreciate a breath of fresh air." Abigail needed to escape that mournful figure, reminding her of all she had lost.

"Perhaps a wise idea," he murmured, ushering her to the entrance. "Seven years ago, six more bells were placed in the tower."

She came to an abrupt halt. "More bells were added? I'm surprised the tower is still upright."

"Iron bands were set around it for extra support."

As they stepped outside, Abigail glanced up at the distinctly bandless tower. "What happened to them?"

"They snapped off and caused even more cracks to appear." His voice was apologetic. "These were duly filled in and plastered over. But it is an ongoing problem."

Abigail shook her head. "Why would anyone decide to add even more weight to an already shaky foundation?"

"I suppose the lure of shiny new bells was difficult to resist."

She laughed at the dry intonation in his voice. Looking over her shoulder, she spotted Mr. Burnby conversing with Henrietta just beyond the oak door. They spoke in hushed voices, but it did not look like a friendly discussion. Not in the least. Oh, dear. Instability all around . . .

As they walked on, Abigail released the breath she had been holding, relief permeating her limbs. Her imagination had always been too active. "At least I no longer feel as if I am in Jericho."

"As long as you are not wishing me *at* Jericho for suggesting this outing?"

She shook her head, smiling. "Not at all, my lord."

"I am relieved." He offered her his arm before leading her across the grass. "Is your interest in architecture limited to the medieval period?"

"I'm interested in all eras. I was recently in Bath and had a wonderful time exploring the Roman Baths."

"Have you heard of the recent discovery of a Roman villa in Oxfordshire? Henry Hakewell excavated the ruins not long ago. What's left of the mosaic floor is of particular interest."

Abigail clasped her hands together. "Have you visited the site, sir?"

"I have."

"How fortunate you are!"

He gazed down at her. "Indeed. I believe I am." After a pause, he continued in a brisker voice, "The Duke of Marlborough kindly allowed me to spend some time there recently. Unfortunately, the mosaics aren't what they once were, even at the time of their discovery. Souvenir hunters have carried away much and destroyed much of the beauty that was there."

Abigail shook her head. "It amazes me how some people

have no respect for antiquity."

"Many have a great deal of respect for its monetary value, though."

Abigail pulled a face. "What a horribly mercenary world we live in," she said as Henrietta and Mr. Burnby came up to them.

"Should we head off now?" Mr. Burnby's restless energy seemed to emanate from his pores. "The George provides excellent refreshments, and breakfast was some time ago."

"The proprietor is expecting us within the hour," Lord Rochvale said quietly.

"Is he, indeed?" Mr. Burnby rubbed his hands together. "What a fellow you are for thinking ahead. Excellent, excellent."

"Our horses are resting at the George. It is only a step away."

Mr. Burnby offered Abigail his arm. "Miss Grantham?"

She placed her hand on his coat sleeve as Lord Rochvale strolled ahead with Henrietta. Abigail frowned at her cousin's stiff back. What had happened to vex her? She seemed most unlike her usual calm self. Abigail stole a glance up at her escort. His brow was slightly creased as if he were miles away, but then his expression lightened, and he smiled down at her. "Did you enjoy your visit to the church? Best that my cousin explained its history to you as he enjoys such things. Find that kind of thing rather dull myself."

"Didn't you sense the history all around you, Mr. Burnby? I always feel it in old buildings."

He glanced up at the cloudless sky. "The only thing I sensed in there was the chill. Glad to be out in the sunshine again."

Was he remarking on the frigidity of the building or on Henrietta's manner? Best not to inquire too closely. Abigail breathed in the fresh, crisp air as she gazed around at the budding vegetation. Spring was here! She had never enjoyed winter's long, gloomy days, and her heart leaped now that the sap was rising.

Lord Rochvale and Henrietta stopped outside the inn, waiting for Abigail and Mr. Burnby to join them. They entered the low-ceilinged building, and Abigail surveyed the interior, dominated by heavy exposed beams and paneled walls.

A rotund little man hastened up to them then and bowed deeply. "Welcome, my lord," he said to Lord Rochvale in a cheerful voice before leading them upstairs to a comfortably furnished private parlor, where a table had been set.

A fine selection of food was on offer, including a delicious-looking pie, sliced roast beef, bread and cheese, fruit, and a selection of puddings. Abigail's stomach rumbled as she took her seat, and she gave a small cough to disguise the embarrassing sound. However, meeting Lord Rochvale's eye, she flushed. Her trick must have failed as there was a decided twinkle in his eyes as he offered her a slice of beef. Snapping her brows together, she concentrated on chewing. *This little pig had roast meat* yet again. She cleared her throat. "Does this inn have an interesting history, Lord Rochvale?"

"It is one of the oldest buildings in Chesham. Purportedly, there is a priest hole in one of the chimneys."

Abigail's eyes widened. "It appears you are a fount of knowledge about everything ancient, my lord."

"Lord Rochvale is a Fellow of the Society of Antiquaries, as is his grandfather, Lord Barcombe," Henrietta said. "There is an excellent museum at Barcombe Manor."

"Would you care to visit it, Miss Grantham?" Lord Rochvale set his cutlery on his plate and leaned back in his chair, observing her through half-closed lids. "One of the glass cases contains astronomical instruments such as astrolabes, quadrants, some primitive telescopes, and even some old-fashioned drawing tools."

Abigail set down her fork. "I should be delighted to visit."

"Once you've explored the museum, I'll take you off to the puzzle maze." Mr. Burnby popped some cheese into his mouth before saying in slightly thickened accents, "It's a good one."

"The cheese?" Abigail raised her brows.

He laughed. "The maze. I used to become hopelessly lost in it until I learned the secret to getting out."

"I am sure *we* shall enjoy exploring it," Henrietta said coolly.

Abigail smiled. "I love mazes—as long as they aren't too

difficult to exit."

Mr. Burnby's boyish enthusiasm for activities such as these matched Abigail's. She listened with pleasure as he told her about his recent visit to a maze on the Earl of Stanhope's estate.

"I like this sort of thing more than my cousin here." Mr. Burnby nodded at Lord Rochvale. "His mathematical brain solves puzzles far too quickly to derive any real enjoyment from them. It shows how being too clever can ruin your pleasure in the simple things in life."

Abigail inclined her head, suddenly realizing why the viscount's presence put her slightly on edge. Those grey eyes saw too much. Such people were always disconcerting as one never quite knew what they were thinking—unlike Mr. Burnby, whose manners were open and genial. His youthful demeanor and daring spirit appealed strongly to her sense of adventure.

And when I'm around him, I don't have to feel.

She drew herself upright at the odd thought. Lowering her gaze, she stared at her plate. That experience in the church had upset her equilibrium more than she realized. Seeing that young girl leaning over the coffin had reminded her of life's brevity and how nothing was certain. After mourning the early deaths of her parents, Abigail now had an almost feverish desire to live life to the full before it was snatched from her.

The strange, superstitious belief persisted that she would not live beyond the age her mother had died. She knew it was illogical, but the idea endured no matter how much she told herself she was being foolish. And perhaps that was why she sometimes embraced risk.

She wanted to seize the day—*carpe diem*—or at least seize the moment. She met the viscount's eyes and raised her chin at their contemplative expression. Lord Rochvale's archaeological interests might make him inclined to dig below the surface, but she hoped he would refrain from a deeper exploration of her motives and desires.

They were not open to excavation.

CHAPTER SEVEN

A FTER THEIR MEAL, they strolled around the town, stopping to observe a medieval house framed in timber with a red brick chimney in Church Street before returning once more to the coaching inn. Abigail spoke in a low voice to Henrietta as they approached the gentlemen's curricles. "Would you like to travel back with his lordship, Henrietta? I received the impression that you didn't much care for Mr. Burnby's company."

Henrietta shot her a sharp look. "Not at all, Abby. Lord Rochvale wishes to discuss his astronomical project with you. I shall return with Mr. Burnby."

"But . . ."

Lord Rochvale approached Abigail at that moment, and as Henrietta trod briskly away, Abigail allowed him to help her up into his curricle.

"I hope you enjoyed our outing," he said as they drove off down the street.

"I did, thank you. It was very kind of you to suggest it." She paused, still conscious of her lack of composure in the church. Although her nature was quite gregarious, Abigail hid her deeper feelings from everyone except her nearest and dearest. For Lord Rochvale to have witnessed her acute distress earlier was not to her liking. But the anxiety this provoked lessened somewhat when he kept their conversation to generalities and did not probe into personal matters.

Stealing a glance at his rather stern profile, Abigail suspected Lord Rochvale was quite a reserved person. And those who valued their privacy tended not to poke their noses into other people's affairs.

Although Abigail expected Mr. Burnby to come up behind them at any moment and pass them, he did not. He and Henrietta must have been delayed. Or perhaps her cousin had insisted on a more sedate pace.

Lord Rochvale looked down at her. "The weather is so clear today that it would be foolish not to begin our work tonight. It is rare to have so little cloud cover. Does that suit you?"

"Yes, indeed. I am looking forward to it."

"I was concerned you might still be tired after your long journey."

"Oh, I'm rarely fatigued for long." She stretched out her hands, interlinking her gloved fingers. "Besides, I have boundless energy for astronomy."

"The work will become monotonous after a while. Once the novelty has worn off, completing our chart will require perseverance."

She gave a sage nod of her head. "Which is why I am trusting that the odd comet will fly across my lens as a distraction."

"One can live in hope, I suppose."

She turned to look up at him. "But isn't that why we observe the heavens, my lord—with the hope and expectation that something magical might happen?"

He remained silent for some time. "Hope must be tempered by the knowledge that such occurrences are rare."

"But they do occur. Just think about Caroline Herschel's successes as her brother's astronomical assistant. She has discovered eight comets so far!"

"Indeed. But that was many years ago."

"A Great Comet was discovered in 1811."

"That is true. But nothing has been observed since which is

why I sound a word of caution."

"All that means is that we're overdue to discover another one—especially as we will be observing the night sky at every opportunity."

He glanced down at her again. "I appreciate your unshakable optimism."

Which was probably his polite way of saying she was a silly dreamer, but no matter. Abigail was not about to stifle her abiding hope of seeing a comet one day.

For the rest of the journey back to Longmore, they spoke about the methods they would employ to record their stellar observations. "We'll use our telescopes to follow the movement of the stars we wish to record and add them by eye as Bessel recommends," Lord Rochvale explained.

Abigail tilted her head. "Add them by eye?"

"It is when we estimate a star's position and mark it on the chart using the naked eye."

She frowned. "But is this accurate?"

"More so than you might think. We relate these estimated positions to stars whose positions we know precisely—stars in the catalog that have already been measured and marked. The level of accuracy we are therefore able to maintain is more than sufficient for our purposes. And it helps us sustain a quick pace which is important in this endeavor."

"I see. A clever technique."

"It works well."

They swept around a bend in the road, and Abigail blinked in the dappled sunlight as she gazed at the surrounding countryside. What a lovely day it was, and how splendid it was to be alive! She breathed in the spring-scented air as they passed peaceful sheep grazing in a nearby pasture.

Longmore Hall was situated in a fertile valley along the northern side of the Chiltern Hills in the middle of the county of Bucks, just over forty miles to the northwest of London. As they entered the local parish with its neat cottages and well-tended gardens, Abigail smiled and nodded at a woman cultivating a small vegetable patch who straightened and bobbed a curtsy.

They passed a schoolhouse and a church before leaving the village and traveling along a winding road through meadows and arable land. White poplars, so pale they appeared to be covered in snow, came into view as they ascended a hill. Finally, they reached the Lodge, which served as the main entrance to the grounds of Longmore Hall.

Abigail caught a glimpse of the house as they descended the hill and drove under the protective branches of an avenue of elms. She sighed. "I adore this time of the year when the trees and shrubs are budding, and the fields are brightest green. It is such a season of promise."

"Indeed. It is reassuring that spring unfailingly arrives even after the bleakest of winters."

"Yes." She hesitated a moment as she turned to meet his eyes, those shrewd grey eyes. Although she was of a naturally cheerful disposition, perhaps she was putting on a show of being a little *too* positive to make up for her display of vulnerability earlier. And although her companion hadn't said anything, she suspected he knew.

As she had reflected earlier, Lord Rochvale saw too much.

The horses clip-clopped over an arched stone bridge, and a spacious lawn stretched around them to the north and the east, terminating in the distance where the ground sloped upward. Abigail glimpsed an aviary, a flower garden, and the serpentine walk she remembered from her previous visit to the estate before Lord Rochvale drew the curricle to a halt at the front of the mansion.

Handing the reins to his groom, Lord Rochvale jumped down from the curricle and assisted Abigail to descend. He studied her face for a moment before offering her his arm and leading her inside. When they entered the drawing room, Aunt Longmore and Great-aunt Mildred were seated in front of the fire, working on their embroidery.

"Ah, there you are, my dear," Aunt Longmore said. "Did you enjoy your visit to the church?"

"Very much so, thank you." Abigail sat on the sofa opposite the older ladies. "Lord Rochvale is very knowledgeable about old buildings, which made the outing a pleasure."

Aunt Longmore set her embroidery frame aside and smiled at his lordship. "Pray sit down. You know, I was hoping you could enlighten me about the antiquity of some of our family heirlooms. Of special interest is a marble urn I found in the attic the other day. I've had them placed in the butler's pantry for safekeeping. When you have a moment, would you please examine them for me? I believe some of them could be of value."

As Lord Rochvale questioned his hostess more closely about the items, Abigail glanced up and saw Henrietta and Mr. Burnby standing together in the doorway. She smiled at her cousin. "Oh, there you are, Henrietta! Did you have a good trip back?"

Henrietta did not look at Mr. Burnby as she advanced into the room. "Driving in an open carriage on a clear spring day is always enjoyable," she murmured.

Davison, the butler, entered the room with the tea tray as Henrietta and Mr. Burnby took their seats. When Lady Longmore had poured out for everyone, the conversation returned to the balmy weather they had been experiencing.

"The cold will come back, no doubt, but I am enjoying these bright days, although it is still chilly inside." Her aunt stretched out her hands to the grate. "You will be working in the observatory tonight, no doubt, Rochvale?"

"Yes. We must make hay while the stars shine."

Abigail chuckled at the joke, and the viscount gave her his slow smile, which lightened his expression, making him seem quite approachable.

"Miss Grantham has informed me that she wishes to assist us this evening," Lord Rochvale continued, turning back to Aunt Longmore.

Her aunt inclined her head. "Very well. I shall inform Miss

Smith. She will chaperone Abigail whenever she is working in the observatory. Although Longmore has informed me that my niece will work with you only on alternate days, I have arranged for Miss Smith to be present at all times so that you will be free to visit the observatory whenever you please, as has been your wont."

Lord Rochvale bowed. "Thank you, ma'am."

Aunt Longmore looked down at her hands before raising her head and saying in an airy voice, "My dear Rochvale, while you are working on the star chart with Longmore and Abigail, please come as often as you'd like to break bread with us. We shall be delighted to welcome you at our table." Aunt Longmore smiled brightly at Abigail as she said these words before returning her attention to his lordship. "Indeed, I am sure my niece will have a thousand questions to ask you about the work you will be undertaking together, and you will be able to discuss it with her when you dine with us. From what Longmore tells me, you will not have many opportunities to discuss more . . . er . . . ordinary topics of conversation while looking through telescopes."

Lord Rochvale bowed. "Indeed, ma'am, our attention will be strictly on our work."

"Hmm. Well, I am eager for her to meet other young people in preparation for her Season next year, and so I have told Longmore, Abigail must enjoy some leisure time as well."

Mr. Burnby flashed a smile at Aunt Longmore. "I am delighted to hear that, your ladyship, as Miss Grantham has expressed an interest in exploring the Barcombe Maze. May I take her there one afternoon this week?"

Her aunt nodded before turning to Abigail. "You will enjoy exploring that maze, my dear." Her gaze traveled on to her daughter. "Would you care to join the outing too, Henrietta?"

Her cousin studied Mr. Burnby, her gaze steady. "Nothing could keep me away."

"It is a difficult maze," Great-aunt Mildred said in her quavering voice. "I became lost in it for hours when I first attempted it.

For some reason, the right-hand rule did not work."

"The right-hand rule?" Abigail creased her brow.

"It is when one places one's right hand on the wall upon entering a maze, keeping it there until one reaches the center. But the trick failed, and eventually, a gardener was dispatched to help me find my way out."

"My grandfather's maze contains independent hedge islands that are not attached to the main hedge wall," Lord Rochvale explained. "Therefore, the method you employed would not work, ma'am, as it leads you to the entrance time and time again."

"Oh, I see." Great-aunt shook her head. "It was a little frightening, I must say, as I went in on my own." She turned to Abigail. "My advice to you, dear, is to ensure you enter the maze with a companion. Then, should you get lost, you will not be stranded."

"Should we arrange the outing for tomorrow afternoon?" A small smile curled around Mr. Burnby's lips as he glanced at his cousin. "I, too, wish to take advantage of the good weather."

"It sounds like an excellent plan," Aunt Longmore said. "And how reassuring to know that when my niece is with you and Lord Rochvale, I can be assured that the good weather is the only thing that will be taken advantage of."

Although Aunt Longmore had directed her comment to both gentlemen, her gaze rested rather pointedly on Mr. Burnby. However, instead of looking chastened, he gave her such a charming smile that Aunt Longmore's expression softened, and she turned the conversation, speaking about the upcoming fair in the village. After elaborating on her plans for ensuring the stocking stall was a success, she returned her attention to the viscount, asking him when he believed he would be able to come up to the Hall to look at the antiquities she wanted him to value.

When the gentlemen left, her aunt shook her head. "Gerald Burnby is far too handsome for his own good, I must say! No wonder he has such a devastating effect on young ladies if he can disarm me at my great age. I hope you won't have your head turned by him, Abigail."

Abigail lifted her shoulders in a half-shrug. "Mr. Burnby is certainly very attractive, ma'am. However, I can see that he is the kind of gentleman who can easily make himself agreeable to young ladies. I shan't take his attentions too seriously, never fear."

"I am pleased you have a sensible head on your shoulders, my dear."

"A sensible head that isn't too easily turned is a very useful combination in a young lady." Great-aunt Mildred nodded sagely.

Abigail folded her hands in her lap, frowning a little. As Aunt Longmore had said, Mr. Burnby was disarming. Perhaps it had something to do with his boyish manner. However, there was nothing boyish about the broad set of his shoulders or the wicked glint in his eyes.

He looked like he had broken many a young lady's heart.

CHAPTER EIGHT

ABIGAIL MADE HER way to the observatory with a light spring in her step. Although Lord Rochvale had warned her of the tedium of their upcoming task, she couldn't help but be excited about the project as it was the first time she had worked independently with someone besides her brother. And, as Abigail had informed the viscount, there was always a chance they might discover something extraordinary in the night sky. A comet, nebulae, an asteroid . . . She hugged her arms around her middle. The possibilities were endless.

Her mood dampened, however, when she reached the observatory. Miss Smith was already there, ensconced in a chair on the portico, and although Abigail gave her a warm smile, she couldn't help but be a trifle concerned. The poor lady was doomed to sit outdoors for hours and hours every night merely to maintain the proprieties.

Abigail only hoped Miss Smith did not succumb to an inflammation of the lungs or something similarly horrific. Fortunately, the governess was wrapped in a cloak, and a thick blanket covered her legs. But still. It smacked a little of cruelty to companions.

Uncle Longmore was already there as well, fiddling with a telescope on the tripod. However, there was no sight of Lord Rochvale, whom her uncle had told her would be joining them for their first session.

Her uncle glanced up. "Oh, there you are, Abigail. Rochvale is in the butler's pantry, having a look at some family heirlooms. We shall start without him, and he can take over from me later."

He indicated a piece of paper nailed to the top of a tilted drawing board. As Abigail stepped closer, she saw that some stars had already been marked on the chart, illuminated by a couple of oil lamps.

"All the fundamental stars have already been added," her uncle said. "We will now begin the task of adding the missing stars. I'll work over there." He nodded at a telescope on the stone pier. "I shall call out the longitude and the brightness of each star while you measure the altitude. Do you think you will manage?" He regarded her with a beady eye.

"I hope so, Uncle. I've assisted John in measuring stars before."

"Hmm. I hope we won't go at too fast a pace for you. I don't like to dilly-dally, you know."

Abigail nodded before hastening to take up her position at the telescope. When her uncle returned to his telescope and indicated his readiness, they began to voice their measurements to one another, each recording notes as they went.

After working in this manner for some time, Uncle Longmore called a halt and left his telescope to join Abigail at the chart to reduce the data they'd gathered. They worked quietly together, plotting their observations, before her uncle finally stood back to observe the chart as a whole. "Excellent, excellent." He turned to Lord Rochvale, who was standing just beyond the circle of light. "Come and see what my clever niece and I have been doing. Have you been waiting long?"

"A short while. I did not wish to disturb you and throw out your synchronism." He strolled closer to observe the star chart. "Neat work, Miss Grantham. I commend you on your precision."

"After we have reduced all the measurements, you can take my place, Rochvale."

The viscount bowed and walked over to converse with Miss Smith as they finished their work.

After half an hour, her uncle gave a satisfied nod and stepped back. "On a clear night such as this, it would be a crime not to continue working. I only trust your aunt doesn't take me to task for keeping you up so late, Abigail."

Abigail looked over at Miss Smith, still chatting to Lord Rochvale. "I'm managing perfectly well, Uncle. But I do wonder about Miss Smith."

Uncle Longmore glanced at the lady as if seeing her for the first time. "Indeed." He trod over to where the governess was seated. "I'm retiring for the evening, Miss Smith, but my niece will continue working with Lord Rochvale. Can you stay to chaperone her?"

"Yes, of course, my lord," the governess breathed.

"Good, good."

After bidding them good night, he returned to the house, and Lord Rochvale stepped across to her uncle's telescope. "Should we begin, Miss Grantham?"

The next hour passed in a blur as the viscount communicated his observations in low, measured tones. Oddly enough, for someone with such a placid demeanor, Lord Rochvale worked much faster than his older partner. Indeed, Abigail had trouble keeping up with him.

Eventually, he called a halt and walked across to study her chart. "All's well, Miss Grantham?"

"Yes. Although you go at quite a pace, my lord."

He met her eyes. "You should have told me to slow down."

"I didn't wish to throw you off your stride."

"Impossible, I'm afraid."

Her eyelids fluttered just as his lordship glanced over her shoulder. "I've kept you and Miss Smith up far too late. Would you like to retire now?"

Abigail turned to observe her companion, who was nodding off in her chair. "Yes, of course. Miss Smith looks quite exhausted." Then, as she stepped away from the drawing board, Abigail dipped into a slight curtsy. "Good evening, Lord Rochvale."

"Good evening, Miss Grantham." His voice was grave, but a thread of laughter lightened its level tenor. *Just what did he find so amusing?*

Abigail dismissed the viscount from her mind as she approached the governess, who rose from her chair, stifling a yawn behind her hand.

"I trust you are not too chilled, Miss Smith?" she asked.

"I was snug enough under that blanket, thank you."

With a nod in Lord Rochvale's direction, Abigail accompanied Miss Smith inside the house.

CHAPTER NINE

WILLIAM STUDIED MISS Grantham's retreating back with narrowed eyes before turning away. Collaborating with her on this project was even more challenging than he'd anticipated. Frowning a little, he moved the two-inch Dolland telescope, which Miss Grantham had used, back to the astronomy equipment room before packing up the 750mm Fraunhofer instrument he had been looking through.

The problem with this arrangement was that he was desirous of courting Miss Grantham. But while he labored with her on this star chart, it was almost impossible to do so. He needed to wait until they had completed their work. Then, if she rejected his suit, he would not place her in an awkward position.

William was under no illusion that Miss Grantham would be interested in receiving his addresses. He was a quiet man, and someone with Abigail Grantham's lively nature might seek a less reserved suitor. However, he would do everything within his power to win her heart—just not while they worked together.

He gave a faint sigh. Perhaps that was why he had worked so speedily this evening. He wished to complete the task they had set themselves as soon as possible so he would be free to concentrate on an even more important goal.

His jaw tightened when he thought of Gerald's proposed outing to the maze tomorrow. His cousin flirted with every female he encountered, and he had already attempted to charm Miss Grantham. But William wasn't too concerned about his cousin's intentions toward Miss Grantham. For years he had declared that he had no wish to marry, and William doubted he would change this position now.

And, although he had always lavished his attention freely upon the young ladies in the district as a gentleman, he was well aware that he could not be too open in his affections without raising certain expectations within their breasts. Therefore, he spent much of his time with women of a distinctly different class.

He reflected, however, that Miss Grantham did not know of Gerald's stance regarding wedlock, and she might well succumb to his cousin's easy address and engaging manners. And then William would have his work cut out for him.

He carried his telescope to the equipment room and set it carefully inside before locking the door. He paused for a moment, his mouth set in a straight line. What a deuced frustrating situation this was turning out to be. He would need to observe which way the wind was blowing with Abigail Grantham.

And for the first time in his life, William's interest in meteorology had nothing to do with astronomy and everything to do with matrimony.

CHAPTER TEN

THE NEXT DAY dawned bright and clear, and Abigail rose from her bed and made her way to the window, staring out at the grounds of her uncle's estate. Unfortunately, after her first foray into the garden on the day after her arrival, she had not had any time to explore the beautiful gardens further. Spotting Henrietta walking on the lawn, Abigail rang the bell for her cousin's maid, Winnicott, whom her aunt had designated to look after her niece's sartorial needs while at Longmore Hall.

Five minutes later, the middle-aged woman entered the room and assisted Abigail into a simple cambric muslin gown. Resisting the dresser's attempts to arrange her hair, Abigail flung a warm shawl around her shoulders, shoved a bonnet on her head, and hastened outdoors.

She walked across the lawn in the direction of the ornamental shrubbery which her cousin had entered. A variety of shrubs, flowers, and trees were planted in informal groupings rendering the impression of natural woodland. Breathing in the dawn-scented air, Abigail passed through a forest thicket and looked around. No sign of Henrietta.

She stopped to admire a patch of ground bursting with prim-roses and early-blooming daisies before wandering across the lawn to the more formally laid-out flower garden.

Abigail eventually found Henrietta in the circular rosarium, where she was plucking the petals off a rosebud with an air of absent-mindedness. She glanced up with a smile as her cousin approached.

"Good morning, Abby dear. You're up early."

"I thought I would sleep in, but I woke at my usual hour."

"Your work went well last night?" Henrietta flung the now bare stem into a nearby wheelbarrow before returning her attention to Abigail. "Lord Rochvale told me all about the star chart project on our drive to Chesham."

Abigail pressed her lips together. "I managed to keep up with your father and Lord Rochvale."

"You doubted you would? Let us walk on."

Abigail shrugged as she fell into step beside her cousin. "I've only ever worked with John, you see."

They left the rosarium and strolled across the lawn in the direction of the stream with its picturesque stone bridge. "Well, I'm glad it went smoothly." The older girl hesitated. "Did you enjoy working with Lord Rochvale?"

Abigail tilted her head to one side, knitting her brows. "He is very efficient. In fact, I battled to keep up with him, which is surprising as Lord Rochvale has such an unhurried manner."

"He is a man of many parts."

"I suppose he must be if he's an expert in not only one but two fields: astronomy and antiquities. And we're only on the first letter of the alphabet."

"Henrietta chuckled. "He also has a great interest in botany."

"Dear heavens! And churches are the next item on the list. What does the letter 'd' stand for?"

"He is an excellent dancer. Unusual in someone so large."

Abigail was about to reply when she caught sight of a male figure walking in front of a belt of trees at the far edge of the lawn. Squinting a little, she recognized Mr. Burnby. He waved a hand and changed direction.

"Ladies!" He swept them a magnificent bow as he came up to them. "You're up with the larks, I see."

"As opposed to coming back from a lark?" Henrietta raised her brows.

"Ho!" His eyes glittered in the early morning sunlight. "No, no, Miss Longmore, I wasn't up all night. I rose early because I couldn't sleep. I thought an early morning stroll might blow away the cobwebs."

"You walked a very long way." Henrietta's tone was cool.

"I was following the course of the river." He turned to Abigail. "Are you looking forward to exploring the maze later today, Miss Grantham?"

"Very much so. I only hope the weather will hold."

Mr. Burnby peered up at the sky. "Well, there's not a cloud in sight, so it should be a fine day." He glanced back at Abigail. "In more ways than one. I am eager to spend the afternoon with such a delightful companion."

Warmth flooded Abigail's cheeks. "You flatter me, sir."

"Mr. Burnby is known to be a great flatterer." Henrietta's tones were clipped. "Should we walk on?"

Mr. Burnby's eyelids flickered, but his expression did not alter. "Don't pay her any heed, Miss Grantham."

"But I do wish to walk on," Abigail said innocently.

"Ho!" he said again, his bright gaze sweeping from Henrietta's reserved features back to Abigail. "I shall accompany you."

As they proceeded, Abigail wracked her brain for something to diffuse the uncomfortable silence that had settled upon them. Waves of disapproval emanated from Henrietta, although she maintained an impassive expression.

"I am a great walker too, Mr. Burnby," Abigail said eventually. "You mentioned that you were following the course of the river. It is an attractive path?"

"Most attractive." His gaze lingered on her upturned face. "Perhaps we could arrange a walk one day."

Henrietta came to an abrupt halt. "Mazes, walks . . . you seem intent on keeping us busy."

"But of course." He bowed. "It is my neighborly duty, is it

not, to welcome newcomers to the district?"

"You speak as though you're a permanent resident when you are hardly ever here."

"A man's restless days do not last forever, Miss Longmore. I have decided to set Burnby Place in order. It has been neglected for too long."

Henrietta's jaw tightened. "You're residing there now?"

"No. A bachelor's residence is always dreadfully uncomfortable. I'm staying at Barcombe Manor, as usual. But I am looking my property over with an eye to doing some renovations on it."

"What sort of renovations?" Henrietta's tone was suspicious.

"Well, the garden has become a bit of a wilderness, although that seems to be the fashion these days. And the roof of the stable needs repair. And, of course . . ." His gaze rested on Abigail's face. "The nursery must be set in order."

"The . . . nursery?" Henrietta's eyes all but popped out of her head. Then she released her breath in a hiss. "Oh. You plan to plant some trees."

A smile hovered about his lips. "Your original supposition was correct, Miss Longmore."

"You plan on setting up your *nursery*?"

"That usually happens once one gets married."

Henrietta began to pace again. "You're betrothed?"

"Not yet. But I hope to be. Soon."

Her cousin came to a halt once more. "Do we know the favored lady?"

Mr. Burnby placed his hands behind his back. "You do. But I cannot reveal her name as yet."

Henrietta studied him with a narrowed gaze. "I am sure we wish you very well, Mr. Burnby." She turned her head. "Don't we, Abigail?"

"Yes, indeed."

Henrietta's smile appeared somewhat brittle. "How strange, since for years you declared you would never marry."

He raised his shoulders. "Circumstances change, men mature,

and suddenly one's own hearth and home gain greater appeal."

Her cousin folded her arms. "I didn't think a leopard could change its spots."

"Ah, but it is never too late to turn over a new leaf." He rocked back on his heels. "And how suitable that I should say this in a garden."

Abigail wrinkled her brow. "I always thought that idiom referred to the leaf in a book."

"Perhaps, perhaps." He smiled at her before placing his hand in his coat pocket and removing his watch. "It's later than I suspected." Placing the ornate timepiece back in his pocket, he bowed. "I bid you good morning, dear ladies."

As he retreated rapidly out of view, Henrietta jerked her head. "Should we return to the house, Abby?"

Abigail nodded. "I'm feeling quite chilled."

Henrietta walked on in silence for some time before stopping abruptly. "Forgive me, Abby. But Gerald Burnby and I do not see eye to eye. I'm sorry if I made you feel uncomfortable."

"It is clear that you don't like him. Why is that so?"

Her cousin frowned. "I dislike his treatment of women."

"But if he has decided he needs to change, that must mean he has seen the error of his ways."

Henrietta shook her head. "I fear this change of heart has only taken place since he met *you*, Abby."

Abigail's mouth dropped open. "You believe I'm the lady he wishes to marry? But I've only just met him. He couldn't have made up his mind so quickly."

"I believe he has."

They walked on in silence before Henrietta turned her head and said, "Do you like him, dearest?"

"I find him quite amusing." Abigail bit her bottom lip. "But I don't know him, of course, so I have no knowledge of his character. I sincerely doubt he has any serious interest in me, though. He is a dreadful flirt."

As they walked on, Abigail realized that the only firm opinion she had of Mr. Burnby was of his striking good looks. Somehow his handsome face seemed to overshadow everything else about him. But it was a bit like staring at the sun. One immediately blinked and looked away.

CHAPTER ELEVEN

ABIGAIL, HENRIETTA, AND Great-aunt Mildred traveled to Barcombe Manor later that day in the Longmore family coach after consuming a light luncheon of meat and fruit. Abigail was relieved that she would not arrive at the Barcombe estate in need of sustenance, as she had embarrassed herself enough already in front of Lord Rochvale with her urgent victual requirements.

However, upon their arrival at the Earl of Barcombe's magnificent home, a gabled manor house in extensive grounds, they were ushered into a paneled dining room, where an array of dishes had been laid out on the dining table.

The viscount strolled into the room just as Abigail was surveying the mouthwatering spread. Queen cakes, a syllabub, fruits and nuts, bread with butter and jam, and a delicious-looking roast chicken made her feel hungry all over again.

She dipped into a curtsy in response to Lord Rochvale's bow. "I thought you might require some nourishment before entering the maze, especially as some people get lost in it for hours," he said.

Although the viscount's expression was bland, Abigail could not mistake the gleam in his eyes when they met hers. She tilted her chin, but when he merely smiled, she took her seat at the table with everyone else and tucked into the generous meal. No use cutting off her nose to spite her face by refusing to partake of anything merely to illustrate she wasn't always hungry. The luncheon Aunt Longmore had provided *had* been very light. And hours of exploration lay ahead of her after all.

Gerald Burnby hastened into the room just as they rose from the table. "Forgive my tardiness, dear ladies. I had some urgent business to attend to this morning." He studied the food laid out on the table. "Well, well, what do we have here?" He glanced at his cousin.

"Merely some refreshments for the ladies before they enter the maze."

"Good thing I had a meat pie at the village inn. Otherwise, I'd be tempted not to leave the dining room."

"I shall take the ladies to the maze if you prefer to remain here." Lord Rochvale leaned against a mahogany side table and folded his arms.

"Wouldn't hear of it, coz. This was my idea, after all." His voice was faintly challenging as he offered Abigail his arm, leading her out of a massive oak door into the hall.

"The maze first, and the museum later?" Lord Rochvale said as he ushered Great-aunt Mildred and Henrietta out of the room.

Mr. Burnby's brows snapped together. "I'd forgotten Miss Grantham wanted to see the museum, too."

Abigail looked from one gentleman to the other. "I shall be happy to explore the museum after I've completed the maze. I am in need of some fresh air after such a hearty meal."

Lord Rochvale bowed. "Very well, ma'am. I shall find you later."

Mr. Burnby escorted them out of the house, leaving Lord Rochvale alone in the hall. Abigail glanced over her shoulder and gave him a fleeting smile before turning her attention to the matter at hand.

The hedge maze was situated right near the house. Mr. Burnby explained that this was deliberate as those who became lost in the confusing web of passages could be directed to the exit by the simple expedient of someone yelling directions from an upper floor of the mansion.

"I shall not go off alone this time as I have no desire to repeat my last experience," Great-aunt Mildred said.

"Indeed, Great-aunt. I do believe it will be best if we all remain together." Henrietta gave Mr. Burnby a pointed look, but he was brushing a speck of dust off his coat sleeve and failed to notice.

Before entering the maze, Abigail stopped beside a monument, which had the following inscription engraved on a metal plate:

Along tortuous paths he ambles.
Pursuing twisted walks, he rambles
The misleading, confusing, perplexing ways
Of true-false choices in a winding maze.

Abigail squinted at the inscription before turning to her cousin. "Walking in a maze mirrors life's twists and turns and dead ends. Perhaps that is why humans enjoy the experience so much."

"Indeed. Although in a maze, you can retrace your steps and find the correct way. In real life, one wrong turn can have serious consequences."

Henrietta's tone was so grave that Abigail blinked at her. Before she could respond, however, Mr. Burnby gave a flourishing bow and invited them inside.

The eight-foot hedge walls loomed high on either side, cutting them off from the outside world as they began to navigate the intricate paths. They were covered in tan, and the crushed oak bark was soft under Abigail's shoes as she walked along. She breathed out a sigh of relief. Her slippers were thin, and with a maze of this size—Great-aunt had told her in the carriage that the Barcombe maze covered half an acre—her feet would have become quite sore if gravel had been the chosen material.

For the first fifteen minutes of traversing the paths, Great-aunt and Henrietta trod directly behind their younger relative and Mr. Burnby. But then they fell back a few feet, although still keeping Abigail within their line of vision.

Abigail wrinkled her brow. Her aunt and cousin took their chaperonage duties very seriously. However, in a maze, it was understandable, perhaps—a young lady needed to be careful not to be left accidentally alone with a single gentleman. Reputations were at stake, after all. And Abigail wasn't even officially out as yet. Her presentation would take place only next year when Dorothea had completed her Season.

Initially, Abigail had hoped her grandmother would allow her to be presented alongside her older sister. But, after receiving Uncle Longmore's invitation, Abigail was grateful Grandmama had decided her debut should take place the following year instead. Opportunities to work in the field of astronomy did not come along very often, after all, and Abigail was determined to make the most of the opportunity.

They came to a cul-de-sac, where Abigail admired an intricately cast bronze statue of a Roman goddess set within the niche of a hedge wall. As she turned around, Great-aunt Mildred and Henrietta lowered themselves onto a conveniently located bench, no doubt placed there as solace for frustrated walkers disappointed at discovering a blind alley.

Abigail tilted her head to one side. "Do you wish to rest for a moment?"

Henrietta rose to her feet. "No, no. Let us go on. Unless you wish to tarry a while, Great-aunt?"

Their aunt rose to her feet. "I am pleased to continue if you will lead the way, sir?" She nodded at Mr. Burnby. "You must know this maze like the back of your hand."

Abigail smiled. "We have just reached a cul-de-sac, Aunt, so Mr. Burnby cannot know it as well as all that."

He laughed. "You've found me out, Miss Grantham. Truthfully, I do know all the paths, but where would the fun be if I led you straight out of the maze?" He smiled into her eyes. "Turning the wrong way upon occasion adds some excitement to an expedition, don't you think?"

Abigail raised her shoulders. "For me perhaps . . . but isn't it rather dull for you, Mr. Burnby?"

He walked on. "Nothing is dull in your enchanting company, Miss Grantham."

Henrietta, right on her cousin's heels, cleared her throat somewhat loudly, and Abigail felt the color rush to her cheeks. Mr. Burnby seemed determined to put her to the blush with his lavish compliments. She changed the subject. "Did your grandfather design this maze, sir?"

"He did. It has always been his pride and joy. But, unfortunately, he can no longer stroll in Barcombe's pleasure grounds as ill health confines him to his bedchamber most days."

"How very sad."

"Indeed. I visit him as often as possible."

They walked on in silence, following numerous twists and turns, before eventually coming to an open space with a pavilion surrounded by flowering roses. Abigail clasped her hands together. "Oh, how lovely this is! Are we at the center of the maze?"

"We are." Mr. Burnby bowed. "I hope it measures up to your expectations."

"It more than measures up. What a charming spot to escape to." Abigail wandered over to an ornate fountain where water cascaded into a pool from a series of descending basins.

Great-aunt and Henrietta took their ease on a garden bench placed strategically under the shade of some trees while Abigail stepped into the pavilion. The sound of trickling water combined with the hushed murmur of conversation put her into an almost hypnotic state, and she gave a shake of her head to break the spell when Mr. Burnby followed her into the open-air structure.

"Daydreaming, Miss Grantham?"

"A little. It's so peaceful here. Is it difficult to find one's way out of the maze?"

"Not with me as your trusty guide."

She glanced at him out of the corner of her eye. Was he trusty? He seemed far too dashing to fit that descriptor. His cousin, on the other hand . . . She wrinkled her forehead. Why had her thoughts turned to him? She cleared her throat. "I am looking forward to exploring the museum later."

"Oh, that old place. Full of dusty relics." He took her arm to lead her out of the pavilion. "Stay here with me in the fresh air, Miss Grantham, I beg of you. It's far better for your constitution."

"I don't mind a little dust, Mr. Burnby," she said mildly.

"Well, I do. Particularly the dust my cousin kicks up if anyone so much as touches anything in that precious museum of his. I don't know why he's so particular about it."

"You aren't interested in antiquities, sir?"

The corners of his eyes creased. "I've always preferred the living to the dead. Far more intriguing, don't you think? Andrew Marvel was correct when he stated, *'The grave's a fine and private place / But none, I think, do there embrace.'*" His voice was quite carrying, and Abigail bit her lip. But she was saved from having to answer as they stopped just then at the bench where Great-aunt Mildred and Henrietta were seated. However, Abigail's cheeks were warm from Mr. Burnby's reference to Andrew Marvel's poem "To His Coy Mistress."

Abigail had stumbled across the verses, penned in 1678, in the Grantham Place library a couple of years ago and had been shocked at the frank sentiments expressed therein. Her governess would never have allowed her to read such poetry at that age, and Abigail had hastily set the book back on the shelf. However, the words *"But at my back, I always hear / Time's wingéd chariot hurrying near . . ."* had remained emblazoned in her mind. Even then it had added to a feeling of urgency within her, a sense that she needed to experience life at a heightened level before it was snatched from her hands.

"Ready to go on, Abby?" Henrietta rose to her feet.

Abigail nodded. "It would be easy to while away the afternoon in this lovely place, but I don't wish to keep his lordship waiting."

"Oh, Rochvale won't mind if you take your time," Mr. Burnby said. "He's the most patient fellow alive. The dullest of dull dogs, in fact." Somehow his mischievous smile robbed the words of any malice.

"His lordship is expecting me, though, so I should like to leave now."

"Your wish, dear lady, is my command. If you would follow me . . ." Mr. Burnby indicated a path behind the bench that led away from the central enclosure.

Henrietta stepped onto the path after him, and Abigail followed Great-aunt Mildred, who started limping a short while later.

"Would you like to stop, Great-aunt?" Abigail asked.

"No, no, dear. Let us continue. After my last experience of becoming lost in this maze, I confess I am quite eager to quit it."

When they eventually exited the endlessly intersecting paths, the older lady looked quite pale, and Mr. Burnby stepped closer to assist her to a nearby bench.

Henrietta sat beside the old lady, chafing her hands. "Would you like to return to Longmore now, ma'am?"

"No, no, dear. It is merely a twinge. I shall walk inside and rest in the museum. I don't wish to deny dear Abigail her treat."

Abigail gave a tiny shake of her head. "I shall be quite happy to return to visit the museum another day, Aunt, if you need to go home."

"I won't hear of it, dear. Let us go inside now. I can recover there just as easily."

Abigail observed her great-aunt with concern as Mr. Burnby assisted her to the house. Fortunately, her limp was not too marked. And when they entered the hall and passed through a door a footman flung open, her aunt sank onto a sofa near the museum's entrance with a reassuring smile. "I shall be quite well after reposing here a while. Thank you, Mr. Burnby."

Their escort bowed just as the door opened again, and Lord Rochvale stepped inside. His gaze encompassed the tableau for a moment before coming to rest on Abigail. "Ready to begin your next exploration, Miss Grantham?"

CHAPTER TWELVE

WHEN ABIGAIL HESITATED, her aunt said, "Run along, dear. I am perfectly comfortable here."

Lord Rochvale's brows drew together. "You are unwell, ma'am?"

"No, no. It is merely my knee. I'm afraid it creaks a little when I exercise it too much." Her hands fluttered in her lap. "But, as I informed my nieces, I am quite content to rest here while Abigail explores the museum."

Henrietta lowered herself onto the sofa. "Do go, Abby. I'll stay here."

Mr. Burnby raised a mobile eyebrow. "But that leaves no one to keep an eye on Miss Grantham."

"We can do that perfectly well from this position." Henrietta raised her chin. "The whole room is in our line of vision, after all, Mr. Burnby. And Lord Rochvale is always a perfect gentleman."

Mr. Burnby's eyes gleamed, but before he could respond, Lord Rochvale said quietly, "Will you be joining us, Gerald?"

"No, no, coz, I'll leave you to it." A smile curled his lips. "Indeed, I must take my leave of you all. I have some business to see to on my estate. Farewell, dear ladies. What a relief that I leave you in the care of a perfect gentleman." He gave another of his elaborate bows. "I thank you for gracing me today with your fair presence."

As he strolled out of the room, Lord Rochvale said, "Time limits us, unfortunately, Miss Grantham. You will need to return another day to explore the museum fully. Is there a section you would like to see?"

Abigail switched her gaze from Mr. Burnby's retreating back to a carved Greek statue of a woman holding a torch on a mahogany library table near the window. "The classical era interests me."

As Lord Rochvale led the way to the table, he indicated a series of pictures hanging on the wall between some intricately worked tapestries of famous battles. "Gobelins tapestry. This used to be where all our family portraits were hung, but my grandfather's collection of antiquities grew so large that he decided to transform the old Gallery into a museum to house them. So now it functions as a gallery museum." A smile tugged at the corners of his mouth as he halted in front of the window. "Being sixty feet long and twenty feet wide, it just about provides us with enough space."

The spacious apartment, well-lit by three prominent Elizabethan windows, was the perfect place to store such a vast collection of ancient items. Abigail stepped forward to observe the statue of the woman more closely.

"That statue was discovered amongst the ruins of ancient Tyre in 1811," the viscount said. "My grandfather bought it from a Greek, who sold it to him after receiving permission from the local Patriarch."

"How beautifully it's made." After admiring it thoroughly, Abigail finally moved away to examine an exquisite silver patera, some terracotta pottery, and a chaplet, before wandering over to the far end of the table to study a seven-inch statuette of a Roman goddess.

"Venus, the goddess of love," Lord Rochvale murmured in her ear.

She met his eyes, and something in their grey depths made her cheeks warm. "How lovely this is." She cleared her throat, but the urge to chatter could not be repressed. *Why do I always do this around him?* "This figurine is very similar to one I saw earlier in the maze. This statue is just in miniature." When he remained silent, she felt compelled to continue talking. "It truly is the most wonderful design. Mr. Burnby told me your grandfather constructed the maze?"

When Lord Rochvale still did not answer, she drew her brows together. But then he appeared to collect himself, focusing his full attention on her. "My grandfather is a mathematician. He enjoys logical problems and designed the maze in the hope that it would be difficult to solve."

"It certainly is. I doubt I would have found my way out if Mr. Burnby hadn't accompanied us."

"I am sure you would have contrived somehow, Miss Grantham."

"Perhaps." She tapped the edge of the wooden table upon which the statuette stood. "But only after hours and hours of traipsing about." She turned away abruptly. "I might panic in such a situation. I hate the feeling of being trapped."

"Is that why you like studying the heavens?"

"Perhaps," she said again. "The vast expanse of the night sky is full of endless possibilities, epitomizing true freedom."

"As opposed to untrue freedom?"

She spun back around, peering up at him. She would develop a crick in her neck at this rate. "Untrue freedom exists," she said slowly. "It comes from the lies we tell ourselves to make ourselves feel better about the world."

"You're young to have discovered that." His eyes searched her face. "Truth or kindness. Which would you say is more important?"

"When I am interacting with those I love . . . truth. However, with strangers . . ." She shrugged. "Good manners have very little to do with honesty, I'd say."

He gave a low laugh. "You're full of surprises, Miss Grantham."

Abigail approached a cabinet containing a selection of medals. One of them had the face of Julius Caesar etched upon it. As she examined the round object, she noticed a comet also engraved on the brass.

She looked up. "Do you know anything about the history of this medal, my lord?"

He came up beside her, bending his head to study it. "That is Caesar's Comet. It is believed to have appeared shortly after Julius Caesar was assassinated in 44BC, causing a great stir amongst the Romans."

Abigail took a step back. "Of course. I believe it was mentioned in Shakespeare's *Julius Caesar*, was it not?"

"Yes. Humans have always been fascinated with comets, seeing them mostly as harbingers of doom."

"While today we see them merely as objects of scientific interest."

He leaned against the cabinet, folding his arms as he looked down at her, his expression teasing. "Merely, Miss Grantham?"

A smile curved her lips. "I must admit, despite my best intentions, that I would not be able to contain a sense of mystic wonder if I ever saw a comet despite my primary astronomical interest in it."

Henrietta came up to them then. "Forgive me, Abby, but I have ordered our carriage to be brought around. Great-aunt isn't looking at all the thing. She isn't accustomed to walking such distances, I'm afraid, and is very fatigued."

Abigail glanced across the room at the figure of her aunt, who sat slumped on the sofa. "Yes, of course, Hetta."

Lord Rochvale bowed. "You must return another day, Miss Grantham."

"I should like that. Thank you, sir." Abigail hastened back to her aunt's side. "I am sorry you are feeling unwell, Great-aunt."

"It came upon me suddenly . . . the faintness. I shall be better directly." She looked from Abigail to Lord Rochvale, who had come up behind her. "We needn't leave."

"But you are not well, ma'am. Of course, we must go home." Abigail assisted her older relative to her feet just as Lord Rochvale approached them and offered the lady his arm. He led Great-aunt Mildred outside and helped her into the Longmore coach.

After Abigail and Henrietta had settled into the coach, he took a step back and bowed, "Ladies."

Abigail's smile was distracted as she bid him farewell. As the carriage rolled away, Great-aunt Mildred said, "I'm dreadfully sorry to cut short your time with his lordship, dear. We are all very fond of him, you know." She cleared her throat. "Indeed, I believe your aunt will be quite vexed that we've had to leave early."

Abigail wrinkled her brow. "Vexed?"

Henrietta, who sat beside their great-aunt, put a hand on the older lady's arm, but she continued speaking, "Well, yes, dear . . ." Pressing her arm yet again, Henrietta shot her a warning glance, which caused her to sink into silence.

Understanding suddenly dawned on Abigail as she glanced from one to the other. They wanted her to wed Lord Rochvale! The truth was written all over Great-aunt Mildred's guilty face.

Abigail wasn't sure why she was so surprised. As her uncle's close friend, she hadn't even considered the viscount in the light of a potential suitor. Now, however, it all made sense. Lord Rochvale would be an excellent match for most young ladies.

Just not for her.

Matrimony was not something Abigail wished to give her attention to at the moment. She had other, more important things to focus on during her one precious year of freedom. There would be time enough next year to turn her attention to finding a husband when her grandmother presented her. But now what she wanted—no, *needed*—to do was give all her attention to learning, as she would have very little opportunity to further her astronomical studies once she arrived in London and was caught up in the dizzy whirl of the Season.

And although the astronomy tasks she was performing were

objectively dull, the repetitious nature of the work had a soothing quality to it that already appealed to her on a fundamental level, even in the short time she'd been doing it. Indeed, the work calmed her emotions, which could be difficult to settle, tethering her to a project that was rapidly absorbing her full attention.

The trip back wasn't long, but they returned to Longmore only to discover the usually calm household in an uproar. Abigail followed Henrietta and her great-aunt into the drawing room, where the butler stood in conversation with Aunt Longmore while anxious servants hovered in the hall.

"I cannot believe it!" Aunt Longmore wrung her hands. "Are you sure it's no longer there, Davison?"

"I am certain, my lady. When I entered the pantry this morning, the urn was missing."

"Oh dear, oh, dear." Aunt Longmore twisted her hands together again. "It's worth a small fortune."

Henrietta hastened across to her mother. "What happened, Mama?"

Aunt Longmore swept her fingers across her forehead. "The marble urn has been taken from the butler's pantry."

"Oh, no!" Henrietta sank onto a nearby armchair. "But how?"

"We're not sure what happened. Davison locked the pantry last night after inspecting the items there as always."

"I shall question the servants, my lady. As you know, I keep the key in my room. Someone must have entered while I was out. I never thought . . ." The butler stared at the floor, his hands clasped behind his back.

"It isn't your fault, Davison." Aunt Longmore's voice was reassuring. "I know you always take the utmost care."

Henrietta tapped her fingers on the arm of the chair, a crease between her brows. She turned suddenly to her mother. "Is the key missing?"

"That's the odd thing. It's in Davison's room. It must have been replaced after the urn was taken," Aunt Longmore replied.

"I wonder who it was," Henrietta mused. "Most of the servants have been here for years. I can't imagine them turning thief. Are any of the windows broken, Davison?"

"No, miss. But the door to the kitchen wasn't locked when I made my inspection this morning. And I most definitely locked it last night before I retired to bed. There were no signs of a forced entry, either."

"So someone let the thief into the house," Henrietta said.

"Indeed," Aunt Longmore said. "But who?"

CHAPTER THIRTEEN

A THOROUGH INVESTIGATION was launched into the mysterious theft of the stone urn. However, no new information
was uncovered, and Uncle Longmore finally decided to call in a
Bow Street Runner to hunt down the missing heirloom.

A middle-aged man named Watkins arrived a couple weeks
later from London to interrogate all the servants, conducting his
investigations in the library. Abigail, seated on the far end of the
room, reading *On the Art of Finding the Zenith in Every Altitude*,
listened with one ear as he questioned the servants about their
movements on the day of the crime.

Watkins took detailed notes, but no new evidence came to
light. When the Runner concluded his final interview, he
informed Lord Longmore, who had entered the library just as the
last servant trailed out of the room, that he would alert his fellow
thief-takers of the loss of the urn in order to discover if any
attempts had been made to sell the stolen item in criminal circles.
He rose to his feet. "Fortunately, it's a very distinctive artifact,
milord, so that should aid us in our quest to retrieve it."

"I certainly hope so," Uncle Longmore said, ushering the
investigator out of the library.

Abigail set her reading material aside and stared out of the
window. A pall had settled on Longmore Hall since the robbery,
the air of suspicion hanging over the place casting a blight on

what was once a happy household. Things would return to their previous peaceful state only when the guilty party was apprehended, but it seemed increasingly unlikely. That urn appeared to have vanished into thin air.

A footman opened the door once more, and Lord Rochvale stepped inside. When his gaze alighted on Abigail, he strolled across the room to the window seat where she was ensconced. "Good afternoon, Miss Grantham."

Abigail rose. "Lord Rochvale."

"I trust you are well?"

"As well as can be expected, I suppose." She lifted her shoulders. "The mystery of the stolen urn has cast everyone into the suds, I'm afraid."

He bowed his head. "An odd occurrence, especially at Longmore, where so many servants are faithful retainers. Do you know if any of the servants have been recently employed?"

"I believe a couple of the housemaids have not been in service here for long. And there is a new footman and a scullery maid. However, all the servants submitted to searches of their rooms, and the vase wasn't discovered. Therefore, we suspect that a thief entered the house from outside."

"With the assistance of an accomplice from inside."

"Yes. The kitchen door wasn't locked when Davison made his inspection in the morning."

Lord Rochvale narrowed his eyes. "An intolerable situation for everyone. That urn is valuable, so this isn't a matter that can be easily dismissed."

Abigail sighed. "I need to change for dinner now, my lord. If you will excuse me?"

She went to the library door, which stood open, before turning around at the last minute. "Will you be working in the observatory later, sir? I thought I was working with my uncle tonight."

"He asked me to work this evening as I have completed my paper."

Abigail inclined her head and then exited the room, her gaze on the marble-tiled floor. Ever since it had become clear that her aunts and Henrietta had lined up Lord Rochvale as her ideal suitor, she had felt uncomfortable at the idea of seeing him again. Fortunately, Abigail had worked exclusively with her uncle this past couple of weeks, so she hadn't seen his lordship since her visit to Barcombe Manor. But now he was back, and she didn't quite know how to handle the situation.

It wasn't as if he had done anything to embarrass her. Indeed, he had not indicated in any way that he might be interested in courting her. However, the fact that her female family members were eager to throw them together made her wish to avoid him at all costs.

And if Lord Rochvale sensed that her aunts were eager for a match between them, he might suspect that Lord Longmore and Abigail were in on their machinations as well. She went hot and cold at the humiliating thought as she marched up the stairs to her bedchamber. How mortifying it was.

Winnicott helped Abigail change into a delicate gauze over-dress worn over white satin with a bodice of cerulean blue. The maid carefully arranged Abigail's copper tresses, allowing ringlets to fall on either side of her face while pulling her hair back on the crown of her head into a bunch of curls. She wore a pearl cross around her neck, matching drops in her ears, and several pearl bracelets. After flinging an embroidered white silk scarf around her elbows, Abigail pulled on her white kid gloves and left the room with a word of thanks for the dresser's assistance.

When she walked into the drawing room, Lord Rochvale was the sole occupant. She froze for a moment before advancing inside.

"My lord."

"Miss Grantham." He bowed and then studied her for a moment. "Is there anything amiss?"

"Amiss?"

"You appear ill at ease." He leaned back against the mantelpiece, folding his arms. "Or am I mistaken?"

Something about that perceptive gaze compelled Abigail to open her mouth. "I confess I am a trifle disturbed."

"If you need a listening ear, I am very discreet."

"Well, it does happen to concern you." She closed her eyes. *Why did I let that slip?*

"Me?" He straightened. "Well, in that case, please feel free to keep your counsel."

At the teasing note in his voice, she smiled. Perhaps being frank about her concerns would be best. So, taking a deep breath, she said, "My aunts . . . Well, they seem eager to . . . throw us together." Heat flooded her cheeks. "I don't wish you to think I am a party to any matchmaking schemes, especially as we will be working together."

"I see." He studied her face, his expression impassive. But then the corners of his eyes creased. "There is no need to concern yourself about any discomfiture I might feel. I am not easily embarrassed. Besides, your nature does not lend itself to scheming. Plotting to entrap a gentleman in matrimony is not quite your style, I would say."

"No, indeed! The very thought of it . . ." She pressed her hands to her hot cheeks before dropping her arms to her side and straightening her spine. "Besides, I have far better things to do with my time."

The corner of his mouth twitched. "Indeed?"

Her eyes narrowed a little. Perhaps she had hurt his feelings? "Not to say that there aren't a dozen females who wouldn't think it a very worthwhile thing to do."

"Just not you."

She inclined her head, feeling suddenly out of her depth. But then Lord Rochvale smiled, and that odd feeling she had of being suspended above a very great height disappeared. "You are enjoying our astronomical work?" he asked.

"Very much so. Being part of such a worthwhile project is most satisfying."

The door opened, and Henrietta came into the drawing room. "Oh, there you are, Abby. I stopped at your bedchamber, but you weren't there." Her gaze rested on the viscount. "Good evening, Rochvale . . . Is Mr. Burnby joining us tonight?"

"He cried off. He's spending most of his time at Burnby Place these days."

"Ah yes, preparing his nursery." Henrietta's tone was dry.

"His nursery?" Lord Rochvale's brows shot up.

"Hasn't your cousin told you of his intentions? He informed Abigail and me that he plans to wed soon and therefore needs to set Burnby Place in order."

When Lord Rochvale remained silent, Henrietta continued, "I was equally surprised."

"Do you know the lady he intends to marry?"

"No. Mr. Burnby would not tell us her name. But I have my suspicions."

Abigail felt the heat rising in her cheeks once more when Henrietta's gaze settled on her significantly. But then the door opened again, and her aunt and uncle's entrance into the room eased the awkward moment.

After Great-aunt Mildred joined them a short while later, they repaired to the dining room, where Abigail took her place at the table beside Lord Rochvale. However, she paid scant heed to the conversation as the first course was served. She'd quite forgotten about that encounter in the garden with all that had been happening at Longmore lately, but it all rushed back now in great detail. Could Henrietta be correct in her supposition that Mr. Burnby was interested in marrying her? He appeared fond of a good joke, and Henrietta, quite a serious-minded person, might not have realized that her neighbor was merely funning when he made those comments. Perhaps he *was* merely planning to plant some trees.

Lord Rochvale said in a low voice, "May I offer you a slice of gammon, Miss Grantham?"

"Thank you," she murmured, taking a dainty bite. "I hope the sky remains clear tonight. It is frustrating how we are always subject to the whims of the weather."

"The curse and blessing of all of us astronomers."

Abigail nodded, exceedingly pleased that he referred to her as an astronomer. It meant so much to be considered as an equal. She had had a taste of working with him upon her arrival at Longmore, and Lord Rochvale did not patronize her or assume she was ignorant because she was a woman. Indeed, it was refreshing to meet a man who did not think she was an oddity for being passionate about this branch of natural philosophy.

She was about to respond when her gaze settled on the butler, who was speaking with an air of urgency to her uncle at the end of the table. After the manservant stepped back, Lord Longmore said to the table at large with a shake of his head, "How extraordinary! Davison has just informed me that the urn has been returned."

CHAPTER FOURTEEN

"THANK HEAVEN!" AUNT Longmore said before turning to the butler. "It is back in the pantry?"

"Yes, my lady. I locked the room up after discovering it there."

Her brows drew together. "How odd that the thief decided to bring it back."

"Once an investigator from Bow Street becomes involved in a matter, my dear, it places a different complexion on things," Uncle Longmore said. "I am relieved we can call off the search. Whoever the culprit is has evidently learned his lesson."

"Or hers," Aunt Longmore said.

He shrugged. "We have no way of knowing. But I, for one, wish to put this disagreeable business behind us."

"But it is such a mystery," Aunt Longmore said. "I find it puzzling that the urn was taken instead of that silver vase with the naval emblems. It was right next to it on the shelf, you know, and is a far more likely object for a thief to set their sights on."

"Perhaps he or she had a particular interest in acquiring antiquities," Lord Rochvale said. "That marble urn has a unique bird and floral motif, which sets it apart."

Aunt Longmore sniffed. "Well, silver usually holds the most appeal for dishonest servants."

Abigail glanced at the butler and the two footmen, standing

to attention on either side of the table, and felt sorry for them. After they removed the second course, a selection of cakes, sweetmeats, nuts, cheese, custards, and flavored ices was set on the table. Abigail was studying some delicious-looking preserved cherries a footman placed in front of her when Henrietta said, "What did you discover about that urn when you examined it, Rochvale?"

"It is from the Roman era." He turned to his hostess. "I am surprised that something of such value was discovered in one of your attics, Lady Longmore."

"Oh, those rooms upstairs are overflowing with discarded items. Of course, I should set them in order, but it has always appeared a rather thankless task, especially as I suffer from sneezing fits the moment I step inside."

Great-aunt Mildred fluttered her hands. "Let me assist you in the endeavor, dear niece. The attics are filled with furnishings and ornaments which have gone out of fashion. My own dear mama no doubt placed that urn there when she redecorated the reception rooms when I was a child. But now that Roman and Greek artifacts are *à la mode*, we should probably search the attic for discarded ornaments to find out if any more classical items have been stored there."

Aunt Longmore inclined her head. "Would you care to assist us, Rochvale?"

"I would be pleased to do so, ma'am. As Miss Longmore pointed out, other treasures may be hidden up there, too."

"I do believe you're right," Aunt Longmore said. "I only came across the urn because I was looking for an old chest filled with clothes that I want the girls to try on for Lady Flinton's masquerade ball."

Abigail's eyes opened wide. "We've been invited to a masquerade ball?"

She nodded. "It is an annual affair to cheer up all the young people who haven't gone to Town for the Season."

"Of course, the rule is that everyone must unmask at midnight to maintain a certain standard of conduct," Henrietta said. "Some of the gentlemen have been known to be a little too free and easy with their attentions while in disguise."

"Probably due to the fact that they're a trifle disguised in quite another sense of the word," Lord Rochvale said dryly. "Sir George always serves the finest of wines."

"What kind of costumes do you have in the chest, Aunt?" Abigail asked eagerly.

"I shan't tell you that now, my dear." Aunt Longmore gave Lord Rochvale a somewhat arch look. "We don't wish to spoil his lordship's fun, now do we? It is more enjoyable when everyone's identity is unknown."

"I will show you the costumes tomorrow, Abby," her cousin said. "Then you can make your selection. The ball is next week, so Winnicott should have time enough to make the necessary alterations to your gown."

Abigail selected a cherry and nibbled on it. "I never expected to attend a masquerade ball. Aunt Eliza disapproves of them."

Aunt Longmore nodded. "I shouldn't like either of my daughters to attend a public masquerade ball in London, as it only courts trouble for unmarried young ladies. And even if a masquerade is private, far too many unknowns exist about another hostess's guest list. However . . ." She tapped her fingers on the table. "Here in the country, the ball can be far better managed. There is rarely any doubt about the identity of any of the gentlemen." She smiled in the viscount's direction. "Lord Rochvale has a particularly difficult time disguising himself."

"I've given up trying." He looked down at Abigail. "In fact, I have worn the same costume for years."

"And what may that be?" Abigail tilted her head.

"I believe I shall keep that knowledge to myself." His smile was wry. "Then, at least, I will present a vague air of mystery to at least one person at the party."

When Abigail made her way to the observatory later, she worked quietly alongside Lord Rochvale while Miss Smith huddled in her chair. However, their session was cut short by some cloud cover, and Abigail retired to her bedchamber earlier than usual, battling a feeling of unease. Whenever she worked with the viscount, his clarity of mind and incisiveness of thought were vastly apparent. He might assume the mien of a sleepy giant in company, but his mind was as sharp as a needle. An unsettling combination.

It seemed that she had been correct in her initial belief that he was rather formidable.

After breakfast the following day, Abigail accompanied Henrietta upstairs to her bedchamber, where a footman had placed the trunk of costumes unearthed from the attic.

Winnicott had laid some garments on her mistress's bed already, and she was in the process of sorting through a selection of bonnets that looked a little the worse for wear. Henrietta bent down to pick up a crown, which had fallen onto the floor. "I am sure we will find something here. Do you have an idea what you'd like to wear, Abby?"

Abigail studied the vast array of clothing, including a very well-sewn Queen Elizabeth costume.

Henrietta nodded at the regal gown. "Your hair would go so well with that costume."

Abigail wrinkled her nose. "But it wouldn't be much of a disguise, would it, if my red hair is on display for all to see?"

"True."

Abigail trailed her hand over a gossamer silk gown that looked like something a princess might wear before her gaze came to rest on a quaint shepherdess ensemble. "The idea of going as a princess or a shepherdess doesn't appeal to me either, I'm afraid." She studied the crown in Henrietta's hands, which had a delicate crescent moon attached to the front. "Isn't that the crown for Selene, the Greek moon goddess?" At her cousin's nod, Abigail clasped her hands together. "That would be a perfect costume for a lady astronomer if I wear this silk gown with it." She pointed at one of the dresses on the bed.

"Yes, indeed," Henrietta replied. "Only . . ." A line appeared between her brows, but then she shook her head. "I am sure you will look lovely in it, Abby. Winnicott will see if it needs to be taken in."

Abigail picked up the silk robe on the bed. "What do you plan to wear, Hetta?"

"Last year I went as Cleopatra, but this year . . ." Her cousin's gaze alighted on a delicate mask a sprite might wear. "I think I will go as a naiad. We have the costume somewhere."

"Here it is, miss." Winnicott pulled a costume out of the trunk. While her cousin examined it carefully, Abigail slipped the silk gown over her head. It settled in beautiful folds around her ankles, and she stepped in front of the glass to examine it more closely. It would do. But she was determined to find a wig. Otherwise, she would be identified the minute she stepped into the ballroom, which would be no fun at all.

CHAPTER FIFTEEN

THE MORNING OF the ball, Abigail was sitting up in bed drinking her chocolate when a knock sounded on the door, and Henrietta entered the room. "I'm glad I didn't wake you, dearest. Did you sleep well?"

"Yes, very well, thank you. For once, I was quite grateful that there was cloud cover last night so I could go to bed early. It would have been awful to be tired at the ball."

"Yes . . . the ball." Her cousin pressed her lips together. "I wasn't going to say anything to you about this as Lord Rochvale wanted his costume to remain a surprise. But, I cannot rest entirely easily about it as I am concerned that if I don't tell you, you might be put to the blush."

Abigail blinked. "The blush? But why?"

"Well . . ." Henrietta sank onto the silk counterpane. "Lord Rochvale always goes to the masquerade ball dressed as Endymion, you see."

Abigail frowned. "The Aeolian shepherd-king?"

"He dresses in Endymion's guise as an astronomer."

"Endymion was also an astronomer?" Abigail frowned. "But of course! Now I remember. Pliny the Elder wrote that Endymion was the first human to study lunar movements."

"And he loved Selene, the moon goddess," Henrietta said quietly.

Abigail sucked in her cheeks. "Oh! Oh, dear." She sat up straighter against her pillows. "You were correct to tell me, Hetta! I *cannot* wear that costume tonight. Thank you ever so much."

"But what will you wear then? I'm not sure if anything else in that trunk will fit you. Most of the gowns would need taking in as you're so slender."

Abigail placed her head on one side as she considered her cousin. "Perhaps we could swap costumes? We're about the same height and size."

Henrietta hesitated. "I suppose we could. But I don't want to wear that moon crown, either. So I will choose a different goddess."

"Thank you ever so much," Abigail said, smiling in relief.

When she dressed for the ball later that day, Abigail surveyed her reflection in the glass with a critical eye. She had managed to slip on the Naiad costume without Winnicott's assistance, as the softly draped muslin garment with its green and white cord was easy to pull over her head. And, instead of wearing a wig, Abigail had decided to powder her red tresses.

Great-aunt Mildred still used hair powder even though it had gone out of fashion many years ago. She acceded to her niece's request, sending her maid, Baker, to assist Abigail with the extremely untidy task. The dresser covered Abigail in a voluminous apron before drenching her hair with pomade, to which the powder adhered. As Abigail surveyed her pinned-up snow-white curls in the mirror, she twisted this way and that before turning around and peering over her shoulder to ensure that Baker hadn't missed a single strand of her distinctive hair.

Satisfied with her inspection, Abigail left her room a few minutes later and made her way downstairs to the drawing room, where everyone had already gathered.

"Oh, you look charming, my love!" Aunt Longmore said, stepping forward. "I predict you and Henrietta will be the belles of the ball."

And indeed, as Venus, the goddess of love, Henrietta looked beautiful in her luminous silk gown. She'd flung a rose-colored shawl around her shoulders and wore a tiny silver Cupid in her hair. However, it was the wand topped with a heart that she held in one hand which served as the biggest clue to her identity. After complimenting her cousin on her appearance, Abigail turned to study her Aunt and Uncle Longmore's costumes. They had dressed up in the guise of Robin Hood and Maid Marian, and Abigail's lips curved into a smile when she set eyes on her uncle's bow and arrow. "Surely the Cupid in Henrietta's hair should have that bow and arrow, Uncle?"

"What?" He squinted a little as he observed his daughter's headdress. "Yes, indeed, niece. I would gladly relinquish it to her if it would aid her in the pursuit of matrimony." He gave his daughter a meaningful look. "Henrietta is far too nice in her requirements, I fear, and most men do not measure up to her high standards."

His daughter laughed. "I cannot strike myself with Cupid's arrows if he is resting in my hair, now can I, Papa?"

"Very true, my love." He gave a little grunt. "Not but what we are delighted to have you at home still. But you must have a care that you don't end up an old maid. Time passes quickly, you know."

"It does, indeed," Great-aunt Mildred said. "Within a blink of an eye, in fact. And so speaks a true old maid."

Uncle Longmore's brows snapped together at his aunt's words, but her eyes twinkled in her lined face, so evidently she hadn't taken offense. The older lady wore the shepherdess costume Abigail had spotted in the trunk the other day and looked quite sprightly, with her hair arranged in neat, white ringlets and a staff in one hand.

Davison entered the room at that moment to inform them that the carriages awaited them in front, which resulted in a flutter of activity as the members of their party gathered their masks and dominoes and made their way to the hall before heading outside to the two coaches.

Abigail traveled in the same carriage as Henrietta and Great-aunt Mildred, who seemed to shed a dozen years in as many minutes as she chatted in quite an animated fashion to her great-nieces, who sat across from her. "I always did enjoy charades," she said as they bowled along. "Somehow, when one dresses up in character, it frees one from the role one assumes in everyday life. Last year I went as Anne Boleyn. I confess I was quite tearful by the end of the evening as I contemplated her imminent beheading. So, this year I decided it would be best to go as a shepherdess so that I could mind my own business . . . and my sheep of course." She nodded in their direction.

"We're your sheep, Great-aunt?" A laugh trembled in Henrietta's voice as she looked across at the old lady.

"Well, more like my lambs, I suppose. But definitely in need of minding so pretty as you both are." She turned her somewhat myopic gaze on Abigail. "In fact, your dear grandmama has asked me to ensure that you do not fall into any scrapes, dear, and I have assured her that I shall shepherd you to the best of my ability." She appeared suddenly struck. "*Shepherd* . . . that must be why I chose this costume. It has been in the back of my mind all along." She gave a slow nod. "Do assure me, Abigail, dear, that I shan't end up as Little Bo-Peep by the end of the evening. Naiads may be free spirits, but I cannot have you drifting away."

Abigail chuckled. "I shall do my best not to go astray, Great-aunt."

"I am pleased to hear that, dear."

The conversation turned to a discussion of the theme of the evening, which was always kept a secret. Last year, Henrietta said, the ballroom had been decorated as a Roman temple, and the food and drink served was the type of fare one might have found at a Roman festival many centuries ago. "Loads and loads of grapes," Henrietta said. "There were bunches everywhere. A sight to behold."

As they drew into the gates that led into Flinton Place half an hour later, Abigail clasped her hands in anticipation. What a splendid evening it was for a party! The weather was fine, and the air almost balmy, for which she was very grateful. There was nothing worse than shivering all evening in a too-thin gown. And her muslin draperies would not ward off the chill.

When Abigail exited the coach, she followed her great-aunt and Henrietta to the other carriage. After Aunt and Uncle Longmore alighted from the vehicle, they walked to the entrance of the grand-looking mansion, joining the mass of people waiting to enter.

Eventually, it was their turn to walk past Sir George Flinton and his lady, dressed as Hermes and Aphrodite, which hinted at the evening's theme, Henrietta told Abigail in an aside. And sure enough, when they entered the enormous ballroom, it had been decorated as a Greek temple with numerous paintings on the walls of scenes from Greek mythology.

Abigail gazed around in wonder. Splendidly lit by three massive chandeliers, the room was bright and welcoming. Glancing down, she saw that the floor had been expertly chalked with figures from Greek mythology. She chuckled. "I fit the theme perfectly!"

"You do indeed, my dear," her aunt said as Henrietta and Great-aunt Mildred wandered off. "Indeed, it is the perfect setting for you."

"Oh, Aunt!" Abigail shook her head in wonder. "I am delighted to be here. Thank you so much for bringing me with you."

"Why, of course, my dear. Your grandmother is quite eager for you to participate in social engagements while you are here in preparation for your upcoming Season. And I do hope you will enjoy yourself tonight, although I shall be keeping a close eye on you." She glanced around the room a trifle uneasily. "Sometimes youthful high spirits can lead to rowdiness at affairs such as these."

A deal of care had evidently gone into the preparations for the ball. Wrinkling her brow, Abigail said in a low voice, "Why have Sir George and Lady Flinton stayed in Bucks rather than going to

London for the Season? A party of such a splendid nature seems to be more in keeping with the Capital than the country."

"Well . . ." Aunt Longmore lowered her voice. "The Flintons are not accepted into the highest circles in London as Sir George made his fortune in trade. So . . ." She gave a little shrug. "Perhaps they are more comfortable staying at home. And we are certainly most grateful that they do! Lady Flinton hosts the most wonderful entertainments every year, quite livening up our sleepy valley. And with a husband like mine who cannot bear to leave his observatory for more than a few weeks at a time, I am sorely in need of such distraction!"

Her aunt stepped away then to greet an acquaintance, and Abigail gazed around the room, free to gawk from behind the protection of her silken mask. A certain buzz of excitement seemed to permeate the air, created no doubt by the fact that everyone's true identity was hidden. People were at liberty to behave in quite extraordinary ways at a masquerade ball as all the usual rules and regulations of Polite Society could be forsaken, at least for a few hours.

A gentleman attired as a shepherd came up to Abigail and pressed a beautiful posy into her hands. Abigail took a startled step back, but before she could say anything, he spoke in a low voice:

Come live with me, and be my love;
And we will all the pleasures prove
That hills and valleys, dales and fields,
Woods or steepy mountain yields.

And I will make thee beds of roses,
And a thousand fragrant posies;
A cap of flowers, and a kirtle
Embroider'd all with leaves of myrtle.

If these delights thy mind may move,
Then live with me, and be my love.

The words were spoken in an impassioned tone, and Abigail recognized the poem at once. *The Passionate Shepherd to His Love* by Christopher Marlowe. But who on earth had recited it to her? Abigail glanced down at the posy of Damask roses and stilled. This was no accidental meeting. Resting atop the beautiful floral arrangement was a delicate cap of flowers.

The shepherd lifted the garland and set it carefully atop Abigail's head. A fabric covering concealed his face, but as Abigail gazed into his eyes, she recognized him at once. That bright emerald gaze was unmistakable.

It appeared Henrietta was correct in her supposition that Mr. Burnby regarded Abigail in a serious light.

But could he truly have fallen in love with her so swiftly?

Before Abigail could say anything, Great-aunt Mildred came up to them. She nodded and smiled at Mr. Burnby. "How delightful to meet a fellow keeper of sheep."

Mr. Burnby bowed, which looked quite strange in his long shepherd's robes, before gazing once more at Abigail and walking away.

"Was that young man making a nuisance of himself, dear?" Great-aunt Mildred asked. "I noticed he gave you some flowers."

"He merely quoted poetry to me." Abigail watched him pick his way through the crowd like a cat for the lithe grace of his movements.

"Oh. Well, here is Lord Rochvale approaching you now, Abigail. I know I can leave you quite safely in his company. Let me take those flowers from you, dear, so that you can dance with him if he asks you."

Abigail hastily removed the cap from her head and pressed the floral tributes into Great-aunt Mildred's hands. As the old lady stepped away with them, Abigail turned to observe the viscount, who was resplendent in a white robe with a crown atop his head, his face covered by a Grecian-looking mask. "Good evening, my lord."

He gave a faint sigh. "Am I so recognizable then?"

"Your height will always set you apart, Sir Endymion."

"You know your Greek mythology."

"Your costume is excellent. A shepherd-king with a crown of moon and stars . . . you are very clearly Endymion." Not desirous of giving Henrietta away, Abigail hastily changed the subject. "You recognized me, too. I thought my disguise was impenetrable."

His gaze rested on her hair. "You have hidden your most distinctive feature, so it took me longer to identify you. However, while speaking to your cousin and Lady Longmore, I deduced it must be you standing here with Miss Longmore. But, even if I hadn't that clue, you have a particular mannerism that gives you away."

Abigail tilted her head. "And what might that be?"

"Perhaps I will tell you one day."

"You cannot leave me in suspense, Lord Rochvale. You must know that curiosity is my besetting sin."

"Is it?" She heard the smile in his voice. "Why am I not surprised?"

The fiddlers struck up at that moment for the first dance of the evening, and Lord Rochvale bowed. "May I lead you into the first set, Miss Grantham?"

She felt a slightly hysterical giggle welling inside her as she was struck by the fact that yet another shepherd had approached her tonight. Except this one hadn't declared his love.

Accepting Lord Rochvale's arm, she allowed him to lead her into the set which was forming. As they waited for more couples to join them, Abigail glanced around at the disguised figures flocking to the middle of the room. It certainly changed the tone of an entertainment when one couldn't see anyone's face. Not that she would recognize any people in this part of the world anyway, even if she could view their hidden visages. However, it definitely added a certain frisson of danger to the evening.

The couple who stood at the top of the set began to dance. After the various ladies and gentlemen ahead of Abigail and Lord Rochvale had taken their turns, Abigail curtsied in response to her partner's bow and progressed down the line. She met him in a figure, and they moved down the center together, executing their steps in perfect harmony before retreating to their respective sides again.

Just as Henrietta had told her, Lord Rochvale was an excellent dancer. Somehow, it seemed out of character with his somewhat sober demeanor. Thinking about it more carefully, she would have supposed Lord Rochvale's cousin would be the more eager dancer. But, as she gazed around the ballroom, she couldn't see him anywhere. Just where had Mr. Burnby disappeared to?

Abigail smiled when she reunited with Lord Rochvale at the bottom of the set. "That was exhilarating, my lord."

The movement of the dance began once more, preventing him from responding. But, when they stopped to wait for the couple in front of them to complete a figure, Lord Rochvale said, "I see you dance with the same enthusiasm you lend to all the activities you undertake, Miss Grantham. You seem . . . happy."

Abigail opened her mouth to reply but then shut it again. Happy. She did indeed feel happy, dancing at this exhilarating ball with such a personable gentleman. In fact, she felt as if she were walking on air, which was breaking new ground as any happiness she had experienced in past years had been tinged with grief in the knowledge that her parents were forever lost to her. How strange for this deep sense of joy to flood her even so.

She swallowed a sudden tightness in her throat and turned her head, spotting Mr. Burnby in conversation with Henrietta over the viscount's shoulder. The somewhat rigid set of her shoulders suggested she was not in charity with him. Why did they dislike each other so? Was it merely a matter of the stark differences in their personalities, or had something more serious occurred to sour relations between them?

Lord Rochvale turned his head to follow the direction of her gaze. "Quite fitting for a shepherd to be in conversation with the goddess of love," he observed dryly.

The Passionate Shepherd to His Love . . . Abigail sucked in her breath. Was Mr. Burnby making advances to every woman in the ballroom tonight? Was that why Henrietta looked so furious? She craned her neck to see if he had given her cousin a cap of flowers and a posy as well. Perhaps he had a supply of them to present to all the single ladies at the party?

But, no. Her cousin's hands were empty. Then, as Abigail watched, Great-aunt Mildred approached her older niece and whispered something in her ear. The old lady indicated the floral tributes Mr. Burnby had given Abigail, and her cousin stiffened even more, if possible. When she turned back to Mr. Burnby, she said something to him which caused him to bow and leave her side immediately.

The rest of the evening passed in a blur of activity for Abigail. She did not sit out one dance, and her sandaled feet were aching by the time the bell eventually rang at midnight to signal it was time for the obligatory unveiling.

Abigail took her place beside her female relations at the side of the room just as Lady Flinton stepped onto the musicians' dais to request everyone to unmask. When all the guests had removed their face coverings, Abigail glanced around the room for Mr. Burnby. But he was nowhere to be seen.

She turned back to Henrietta, who was dangling her mask by its string, an abstracted expression on her face. Abigail was about to ask her about her evening when Great-aunt Mildred pressed the floral cap and posy into her younger niece's hands. "Have you discovered who that daring shepherd was, dear? I must say it was a trifle audacious of him to give you these."

Lord Rochvale, who had just come up to them, his fabric mask in one hand, glanced at the love tokens in Abigail's hands and raised his brows. And, for some utterly annoying reason, when she met his gaze, Abigail couldn't prevent the blood from rushing to her cheeks. Somehow, the viscount made her feel like a naughty child caught stealing sweets from the pantry.

A most ridiculous feeling. What did it matter what he believed?

CHAPTER SIXTEEN

U PON THEIR RETURN to Longmore Hall, Winnicott awaited Abigail in her bedchamber. "Rather go and assist Miss Longmore, Winnicott." Abigail yawned. "My clothes are easy to remove, and I just want to fall into bed."

"Very well, miss." The maid scrutinized Abigail's hair. "It *is* a little late to remove all that hair powder. But I'll place a cover on your pillow so that it doesn't spread everywhere."

"Thank you." Abigail sank onto the silk counterpane. "I must say, I am very grateful to live in this century and not the last one. Powdering one's hair is a difficult business, although it was worth disguising mine for the masquerade."

Winnicott placed a cloth over Abigail's pillow. "You must have been unrecognizable, miss."

"Most of the guests were strangers to me, of course, but Lord Rochvale knew me."

"An observant gentleman, that."

A note in her voice made Abigail tilt her head. "You know Lord Rochvale?"

"I worked for many years at Barcombe Manor as a nursery maid, helping to look after his lordship and Mr. Gerald."

"Oh, I see. So they were raised as brothers, then?"

"Just about. Mr. Gerald's mother, Lady Helen, came back to live at Barcombe after her husband died. Mr. Gerald was still quite small, and she didn't wish to live at Burnby Place as she was an invalid, poor lady."

"And Lord Rochvale? Did his mother and father live at Barcombe too?"

She nodded. "Until the influenza took 'em when his lordship was but thirteen. A sad loss for us all. The boys were away at school at the time."

Abigail stared. "How tragic."

"It came as a shock to us all as they were both in good health."

Abigail shook her head as she rose to her feet. "How terrible for his lordship."

She allowed Winnicott to help her out of her Grecian robes.

"Always had his nose in a book, even as a boy. Scholarly, that's what he is, although he's fearless on a horse. And he always took care of Mr. Gerald, rescuing him from scrapes. Close they were, even though they're so different."

After slipping into her nightgown, Abigail slid under the bedcovers. "Thank you, Winnicott."

"Good night, miss." Winnicott blew out the candle on the table beside the bed before heading to the door with her own. "I'll help you with your hair in the morning."

Abigail woke up quite late the following day and had her breakfast in bed before Winnicott began the lengthy process of returning her hair to its natural state. But eventually, the task was completed, after which the maid helped Abigail don a simple cambric morning gown.

"Do you know if my cousin is awake?" Abigail glanced back at the maid as she opened the door.

Winnicott looked up from folding the powder-stained cover she had removed from the pillow. "When I looked in on Miss Longmore earlier, she was fast asleep, but I didn't wake her on her ladyship's instructions."

"We did retire rather late. Let me see if she is still in bed."

Abigail stepped across the corridor and knocked on her

cousin's bedchamber door, opening it only when a faint voice bid her to enter. Henrietta was still abed, but she didn't look as though she had slept a wink. Crescent-moon-shaped shadows stood out under her eyes, and her face was very pale.

"Are you unwell, dearest?" Abigail hastened inside.

Henrietta sat up against her pillows. "I'm well enough, thank you. I just feel tired after last night."

Abigail lowered herself onto the bed. "You enjoyed the masquerade?"

"It was well enough." Henrietta plucked at a loose thread on the coverlet before glancing up. "You had a great many admirers last night, Abby. Anyone you favor in particular?"

"No one. I enjoyed dancing with all the gentlemen but only knew Lord Rochvale. The rest were strangers to me."

"Indeed." Henrietta pulled the loose thread free. "And what did you think of the gentleman dressed as a shepherd who gave you that posy?"

"Oh, him!" Abigail frowned. "I do believe he was playing the part of the passionate shepherd in Christopher Marlowe's poem. That must have been why he carried those floral tributes—to hand them out to various ladies in his role."

"Did he speak to you again?"

"No. He must have left before the unmasking." For some reason, Abigail was reluctant to inform her cousin that she had recognized Mr. Burnby, having no wish to ignite a conflagration. Abigail had come to the conclusion that Mr. Burnby must be a dreadful flirt. He appeared to be one of those gentlemen who could not speak to a woman without flattering her. And he did it with such charm that it was difficult to remain indignant with him when he switched his attentions to someone else.

If Abigail had viewed him in a serious light, she might well have taken his tributes to be more meaningful. But after spotting him speaking earnestly to Henrietta after he'd left her side last night, she realized he must have been intent on reciting poetry to all the young ladies he encountered.

Henrietta, however, might see it differently. She had no doubt recognized Mr. Burnby last night; otherwise, why had she flown up in the boughs? He seemed to have the ability to upset her cousin's equilibrium like no one else.

Someone scratched on the door, and a young parlor maid put her head around it to inform Abigail that Mr. Burnby awaited her downstairs.

Abigail straightened. "Oh?"

"Yes, miss. He came in his curricle."

She frowned as she rose from the bed. "Thank you, Rosie. Please inform Mr. Burnby that I shall be with him directly." She turned to her cousin. "I shall see you later, Hetta."

Henrietta fell back against her pillows. "I trust you will be on your guard with Mr. Burnby, Abby. As I've said before, he isn't to be taken seriously."

"I know, dearest. Rest assured, I am in no danger of having my head turned by him."

"I am pleased to hear that. I'd hate for him to break your heart."

"Has he broken so many, then?"

"Enough to make him dangerous."

Abigail made her way to the still-open door and said with a quick smile. "Well, I have his measure, so I'm in no peril."

Upon Abigail's entrance into the drawing room, Mr. Burnby bowed. "Would you care to accompany me on a drive this morning to the village, dear ma'am? Nothing better than fresh air to blow away the cobwebs. I have seen your aunt Longmore and she has already given me her permission to take you."

"Oh!" Abigail hesitated. In truth, she had been about to inform Mr. Burnby that her aunt required her presence at home this morning. Now she didn't have that excuse. Unable to think of a polite way to turn him down, she said with a tiny lift of her shoulders, "Very well, sir. I should like that. If you would wait a moment."

Upon re-entering her bedchamber, Abigail located her favorite straw bonnet in the large mahogany wardrobe in the corner. She tied the yellow ribbons under her chin, snatched up a Paisley shawl, and returned to the hall, where Mr. Burnby stood, drumming his fingers against the wooden banister.

"That was quick!" he said with a smile, ushering her outside.

"I didn't want to keep you waiting."

The curricle and pair stood nearby, and Mr. Burnby helped her into the vehicle before climbing up beside her. As he directed the horses along the drive, Abigail observed the passing scenery. How lovely it was to be outdoors. She stole a look up at her companion. He was driving the curricle at a much slower pace than the first time he'd taken her out. Perhaps it had something to do with the fact that no one was ahead of him to overtake. Without the lure of a moving target, there was no need to speed along.

He glanced down at her. "Did you enjoy the masquerade last night, Miss Grantham?'

How to answer? Should she let him know that she had recognized him last night? "It was a delightful evening, thank you." She averted her gaze, concentrating on a nearby field filled with sheep. "I failed to see you at the unveiling."

The horses jerked forward momentarily, and her companion only answered once he had brought the spirited pair under control again. "I wasn't there."

"Oh!" Abigail stared down at her hands.

"A matter arose yesterday evening that required my urgent attention. I sent Lady Flinton my apologies this morning for my non-attendance."

So that was how he was playing it. For some reason, he did not wish to admit that he had been at the ball last night. How odd. She cleared her throat. "Her ladyship must have been disappointed. There always seems to be a shortage of gentlemen at country balls to partner the ladies who wish to dance."

"I doubt you lacked any partners, dear ma'am."

"I was fortunate not to miss any dances."

"What costume did you wear?"

"I went as a naiad."

"Ah! If I recall correctly, a naiad is some sort of nymph?"

"Yes." She cleared her throat again. "I had the oddest encounter with a man dressed as a shepherd last night. He declared his love to me, which I found vastly surprising. Indeed, I believe he was merely amusing himself by pretending to be Christopher Marlowe's passionate shepherd speaking to his love."

"No doubt. People assume dashed peculiar identities at masquerades."

"Hmmm. Now that I think about it, I should have responded to the shepherd with Sir Walter Raleigh's verses, which are most appropriate considering that a naiad *is* a sort of nymph."

He stared straight ahead. "And what might those verses be?"

She peeked at him. "Haven't you heard *The Nymph's Reply to the Shepherd*, Mr. Burnby?" She quoted:

"If all the world and love were young,
And truth in every shepherd's tongue,
These pretty pleasures might me move,
To live with thee, and be thy love."

Stillness reigned between them for quite some time before Mr. Burnby said, "There are a deuced number of sheep about today, aren't there, Miss Grantham? Indeed, I believe your unknown admirer should stick to tending his flock rather than attempting to woo the ladies. What, after all, could a simple shepherd offer a lady? You are very wise to spurn his advances."

"I believe so," Abigail said in a low voice, meeting his emerald gaze squarely.

He was the first to look away, and a strange silence settled between them, where what was left unsaid spoke just as loudly as the words that had just been uttered.

CHAPTER SEVENTEEN

M R. BURNBY DROVE through the village, turned around, and took Abigail straight back to Longmore Hall. He brought up various topics of conversation during their brief excursion, but his manner was more reserved than usual, and Abigail experienced a faint qualm at his somewhat dampened air. But she could not regret her frank words. Even if Mr. Burnby *had* fallen in love with her at first sight, his rushed declaration was not to her taste. Moreover, it was also extremely puzzling, considering Henrietta and Aunt Longmore's warnings about his wild, wicked ways.

When they arrived back at the house, another curricle stood in the drive. Abigail recognized Lord Rochvale's chestnuts at once, and when Mr. Burnby escorted her into the hall, the viscount was standing there, chatting to Henrietta.

He broke off his conversation and bowed. "Good morning, Miss Grantham."

"Lord Rochvale."

The viscount nodded at Mr. Burnby before turning his attention back to Abigail. "I see that my cousin has stolen a march on me. I hoped to take you to the village of Stone to visit the church of St John Baptist. It dates from 1135."

Abigail smiled. "I should dearly like to visit it. Thank you."

"May I take you now if you are not too weary from your drive?"

Abigail glanced at Henrietta, who stood silently beside Mr. Burnby. "Would you care to visit the church too, Hetta?"

"No, thank you. I've been there on numerous occasions. Besides, I have some letters I need to write. You go with Rochvale in his curricle, Abby. It's only a short distance away."

"Very well." Abigail murmured a word of thanks to Mr. Burnby for her outing before accepting the viscount's proffered arm and leaving the house with him.

"You are in great demand this morning," he said as he escorted her to his curricle.

"You know what they say, my lord—it never rains, but it pours." She settled into the passenger seat just as Lord Rochvale's groom, who held the horses, passed the reins to his master, and jumped onto the seat behind them.

Lord Rochvale gave his horses the office to start, and they moved off down the drive at a trot. Abigail blinked as they passed the sheep-filled pastures she had recently observed, stifling a laugh at the thought that yet another shepherd had asked her to drive out with him today. What was it about all things ovine that they kept popping up in her vicinity?

"I trust you will like the church, Miss Grantham. It was consecrated in 1273, although, as I said, part of the structure dates from the previous century."

"I'm sure I will."

Lord Rochvale concentrated on turning a corner, and Abigail sat quietly, her hands folded in her lap as he navigated the bend in the road. When they were on a straight stretch again, he looked down at her. "I won't ask you if you enjoyed the ball last night. It was evident that you did."

She sighed. "You make me sound dreadfully gauche."

"Not at all. Your expressiveness is charming."

"Hmm. Well, Miss Mason, the headmistress of the seminary I attended in Bath, instructed me to repress my enthusiasm in public. But at a masked ball . . ." She sighed. "Surely one can allow oneself a little more freedom from Society's dreary strictures?"

"Of course. However, danger sometimes arises when wolves in sheep's clothing allow themselves too much of that freedom."

Abigail blinked. Sheep again! "Fortunately, that is unlikely to happen at a private ball, my lord."

He glanced down at her. "You truly believe that?"

"Well . . . surely gentlemen must always behave in an honorable way when they are in the presence of ladies."

"Not always," he said shortly. "To believe that all people have inherently good intentions is dangerous."

"I don't believe everyone has good intentions. But I *do* believe people tend to comply with Society's conventions so that they aren't ostracized from their communities."

"Did everyone you encountered last night stay for the unveiling at midnight, Miss Grantham?" He stared straight ahead.

"Well, no."

"I rather think that proves my point."

"I suppose it does." She furrowed her brow. "I will be more on my guard in the future. Although I doubt I will soon find myself in any other social occasions where people will disguise their identities."

"People disguise their identities all the time in one way or another."

"Now we are moving into the realm of philosophical thinking, my lord."

He smiled down at her. "I quite enjoy entering that realm with you. What is the proverb? As 'iron sharpeneth iron; so a man sharpeneth the countenance of his friend.'"

His friend . . . The words were somewhat alluring. He was the type of person who would make a good friend. She dismissed the thought as she glanced around at the surrounding countryside. They had left Longmore Park by now and were driving through the local village.

"In a short while, we will enter the next parish, where Stone is situated," Lord Rochvale said as the horses continued to clip-clop along the road.

And indeed, in what seemed like the blink of an eye, they were approaching the neighboring settlement. Lord Rochvale drove straight to the church, situated in the middle of the village, and once his horses were in the care of his groom, he jumped down from the curricle and assisted Abigail to descend.

"The rise this church was built upon is not natural, so there is some speculation that a barrow from Roman times lies beneath." He indicated the church tower with one gloved hand. "That part of the sanctuary was built in the fourteenth century, while the south porch was constructed in the fifteenth." He smiled at her. "You'll be happy to learn that this particular church has excellent foundations."

She laughed. "A relief indeed."

When they entered the church, Lord Rochvale told her a bit more about its history before they came to a halt in the north arcade. "These three bays are Norman and were built around 1170." He indicated a doorway to the south. "And this is also Norman. Its construction hints at the advancing Gothic period, while the actual door is from the twelfth century."

As he spoke, someone stepped through the entrance. A young woman, dressed in the height of fashion, advanced inside. "Rochvale! I'd recognize those chestnuts of yours anywhere. When I saw your curricle, I instructed my coachman to stop." The lady's gaze settled on Abigail, and her brows rose in friendly inquiry.

Lord Rochvale stepped forward. "Lady Amelia! May I present Miss Abigail Grantham to you? Miss Grantham, this is Lady Amelia Netley, my childhood friend and neighbor who resides at Hythe Place. Lady Amelia is the eldest daughter of the Marquess of Hythe."

Abigail dropped into a curtsy. Lady Amelia looked to be around Lord Rochvale's age, in the late twenties, which made sense considering he had referred to her as his childhood friend. Evidently, they were on comfortable terms with each other.

Abigail wondered about the nature of their relationship. Although Lady Amelia appeared very agreeable, she had a watchful expression in her eyes.

"You had a good journey?" Lord Rochvale asked.

Lady Amelia gave him a speaking look. "If you come to Hythe later, I shall tell you about it."

Feeling a trifle uncomfortable, Abigail stepped away to study the chancel arch, but she couldn't help but hear Lady Amelia saying in a lowered voice, "You received my letter, William?"

Lord Rochvale replied in the affirmative, and the conversation became more general before Lady Amelia said, "I had better return to my coach. It was a pleasure to make your acquaintance, Miss Grantham."

Abigail dropped into another curtsy as Lady Amelia smiled and moved away. Lord Rochvale accompanied her to the church door, where they had a murmured conversation before the young woman stepped briskly away.

The viscount returned to Abigail, who was still studying the chancel arch. She glanced up at him. "Thank you for bringing me here, my lord. The sense of peace one finds in old churches is always so calming."

He leaned his shoulders against the stone wall and folded his arms. "You feel the need to seek out such peace?"

She gave a small shrug. "Sometimes. I do not experience serenity from within, unfortunately. I think my emotions are too turbulent. So, when I seek peace, I must look out of myself for it, finding rest in nature and places of worship."

"And the night skies?"

"Yes." Studying his calm face, she suddenly realized that his company also brought her a measure of tranquility. Lord Rochvale's rock-solid demeanor quietened the sometimes chaotic state of her mind. He exuded dependability and appeared to be the type of person one could turn to in a crisis.

As if reading her mind, he said, "You are so full of vivacity, Miss Grantham, that I imagine you experience life as a rushing stream rather than a restful pool."

She nodded. "Very much so. My sister, Thea, has a measure of serenity in her nature that I have always wished for. But I was not blessed with such a disposition."

He straightened. "A nature such as yours has its own rewards, I imagine."

"Perhaps." Her voice was doubtful. To experience life in vivid colors was exhilarating but also exhausting at times, which was why she needed external sources of tranquility to restore her equilibrium. How much easier it would be if those sources were within her! She sighed. "What I wouldn't give to be a calm expanse of water."

"Such water has its own problems—like the danger of growing stagnant."

She smiled. "I hadn't thought of it that way."

He strolled across to her. "If you have had your fill of looking at this church, I shall take you home."

Abigail inclined her head before placing her hand on his outstretched arm. As he led her outside, she couldn't help but wonder if his upcoming visit with Lady Amelia had anything to do with the sudden truncation of their outing. The viscount's friend appeared to have some urgent news to communicate with him.

Abigail wondered what it was.

CHAPTER EIGHTEEN

After taking Miss Grantham back to Longmore Hall, William drove straight to Hythe Place, which bordered Barcombe Manor on the east. As he drove up to the front of the Marquess of Hythe's country seat, built on the site of an old abbey, he frowned as he came to a halt and handed over the reins to his groom.

Why did Lady Amelia wish to see him so urgently? The appeal in her eyes had prompted him to abandon his initial plan to inspect Lady Longmore's attics for hidden ancient treasures in favor of discovering what had occurred in London to send his childhood friend home forthwith.

When he entered the drawing room, Lady Amelia sat in the window seat, staring out at the extensive grounds. As far as he knew, Lord and Lady Hythe were still in London, which made their daughter's sudden return to Buckinghamshire even odder.

She rose to her feet as he advanced into the room. "You've come! Thank heaven."

He frowned down at her. "I could scarcely make out what you wrote in that note you sent me. Did you return to Hythe alone?"

"Cousin Jane came with me. I . . ." She bit her lip. "I'm in a spot of trouble, I'm afraid, Rochvale. I wanted to let you know as soon as possible as it concerns you, too."

She waved at a nearby armchair, but William did not take the seat she indicated. Instead, he remained standing, studying her wan countenance. "What's happened?"

She sank onto the window seat, pressing her hands together. "Well . . . do you remember the pact we made a couple of years ago—that should we be single at the age of thirty, we would marry one another?"

"Yes."

Lady Amelia began to fidget with the fringe of a cushion. "Well . . ." she said again as she drew in a deep breath. "I was in a state about Sir Reginald. I do believe he's the most vexing man of my acquaintance. I thought he would offer for me this Season, particularly as I saw so much of him before we traveled to London. But instead . . ." She lifted her shoulders. "He went off to the British Museum every day and spent hours and hours looking at the polar exhibition. All he could talk about morning, noon, and night was John Ross's expedition to the Arctic last year and Barker's Panorama in Leicester Square. I declare if I hear one more word about the Crimson Cliffs or Croker Mountains, I shall scream." She shook her head in irritation. "Do sit down, Rochvale. I hate being loomed over."

He lowered his length into a nearby armchair. With a nod of approval, she continued, "The frustrating thing is that we spent so much time together before the Season began. He called on me nearly every day, and Mama and I assumed he would pay me his addresses once we arrived in Town, where the news could be announced to all our acquaintances. But, once we got there, I scarcely saw him. And then, last week, he called on me to take me driving in the Park. I asked him about his plans for the rest of the year. And do you know what he said?" Her bosom rose and fell in agitation. "He made some mention of wanting to join William Parry's expedition to the Arctic this year! Sir Reginald used to sail in the northern latitudes with Parry when Parry was a lieutenant on the frigate *Alexander*. I have no idea why he wishes to risk life and limb by joining this new expedition now."

William remained silent for a moment. "Sir Reginald left the Royal Navy only two years ago. And the call of the sea is very strong for a sailor."

"That may well be. But the call of children is even stronger for me! I am not getting any younger, and if I don't marry soon and start a family, it may never happen."

"Yes." William frowned. "The irrevocability of marriage for a man who has always been free to travel the world might give Sir Reginald pause, however. He never expected to inherit Markham Park from his uncle and put down roots."

"Well, he did inherit the baronetcy. And there is no use in wishing to escape his responsibilities now in favor of this hare-brained scheme." She released a forceful breath. "I am the last person to wish to clip anyone's wings. But, sometimes, a choice needs to be made! Sir Reginald spent last year virtually on my doorstep, raising expectations in my . . . er . . . maidenly breast. I have every right to be unhappy with his behavior now."

"I am in agreement, my dear."

"Thank you! I am pleased that we see eye to eye on this, which I hope may soften your displeasure when you discover what I've done."

When he raised an eyebrow in silent inquiry, she looked away. "Sir Reginald intimated that he wished for me to wait for him. He actually wants me to sit in England twirling my thumbs for months or even years while he goes off on this expedition." She shook her head and looked back at him. "But I cannot do so, Rochvale! It is too much to ask of me at my age. And insulting too! To pursue me with such dedication, only to decide at the last minute that his wish for adventure supersedes the importance of my feelings . . . Well, I confess, I lost my temper and informed him of our pact to marry should we both be unwed by the age of thirty—which age I might certainly be by the time he deigns to return to England."

"And then you left London."

She nodded. "I couldn't face him again. Mama agreed it might be a good idea for me to cool my heels here with Cousin Jane, as I've given him a deal to think about. It is best that I'm not in London, where one must always maintain an iron composure." She glowered at the Aubusson carpet. "I confess I am not at all in charity with the world at the moment, so it is best I vent my spleen away from prying eyes."

"Do you think he will follow you home?"

She raised her head. "I don't know. I suppose if he cares enough about me, he will follow me here. And if he does, I don't think it will do him any harm to think I might soon be betrothed to you. But I know it places you in an awkward position as you are his friend and fellow astronomer."

"That isn't my only concern, Emmy." He leaned back in his chair, frowning again. "I wish to marry Miss Abigail Grantham, the lady I introduced you to earlier."

Lady Amelia covered her mouth with her hand. "Oh, no, William. I had no idea. This is rather sudden, is it not?"

"Falling in love can be rather sudden, as I discovered when I met Miss Grantham." His lips twisted wryly. "I have no idea if she reciprocates my feelings, and I have been courting her with some circumspection as she is working with Lord Longmore and me on our star chart project, which casts an obstacle in the path of normal wooing." He leaned forward. "I am surprised you mentioned our old pact to Markham. We made it when we were both heart free."

They had made the decision to enter into a marriage of convenience should they never find anyone else they preferred to marry—William, for duty, and Amelia because she did not wish to become a spinster aunt, dependent on her family.

She looked away. "I know. Friendship seemed a good enough basis for marriage then."

"It isn't enough for me anymore, Emmy," he said deliberately.

"Nor me. Oh, Rochvale, forgive me . . . I've made such a mull of things."

He leaned back and tapped the wooden arm of his chair. "I'm more inclined to think Markham made a mull of things to favor traveling the high seas over marrying you."

She twisted a ring on her finger. "I wouldn't want him to give up what he loves if he married me. But for the first few years . . . I would not wish him to leave me, either." The words came out rather painfully.

"Did you communicate any of this to him?"

"No." She sighed. "I was in too much of a passion."

"Well, let's see if he follows you here. Then we can decide on how to manage the situation."

"Thank you for your understanding. I truly do not wish to cast another obstacle in the path of your courtship with Miss Grantham."

"Indeed. I must say I have never wished for an astronomical study to end so quickly. But the work cannot be rushed, so I have been biding my time. However, matters have been complicated somewhat by the fact that Gerald is also pursuing Miss Grantham."

She straightened her back. "Burnby is pursuing her? I thought he would never settle down."

"He is setting Burnby Place in order and has declared that he wishes to enter the state of matrimony."

"Good heavens!" Her expression became thoughtful. "Are you sure he isn't teasing you because he senses your interest in Miss Grantham? Your cousin can be as mischievous as a monkey, you know."

"I did consider that . . . but he is renovating Burnby Place as we speak. Perhaps he also experienced a *coup de foudre* upon meeting Miss Grantham."

"It seems I need to take some pointers from your young lady." She grimaced. "She has managed to bring two gentlemen to her feet within a short space of time while I struggle to pin down the affections of only one. I wonder what her secret is?"

"It may be because she isn't contemplating matrimony," he

said slowly. "Sometimes, when one is too focused on achieving something, one fails to attain it. Miss Grantham wishes to make her mark in astronomy before she is presented in London next year. This desire surpasses any thought of finding a husband, which makes her quite unselfconscious in her manner. Her work is her main focus at present."

"Then she has much in common with Sir Reginald," Lady Amelia said tartly.

"I am sure he will follow you here, my dear. It is probably just a case of shying at the final fence."

"You have a very unsentimental turn of phrase sometimes, my lord!"

He shrugged. "I wouldn't abandon hope. He will probably return home as soon as he comes to his senses. Besides, he cannot abandon Markham Park."

"Yes." She took a handkerchief from her reticule and blew her nose fiercely. "I trust you are right—you usually are. At times it is quite an annoying characteristic, but I would welcome it in this instance."

"Let us hope for the best." He rose to his feet and stood looking down at her. "Cheer up, Emmy. Things are rarely as dire as we think them to be."

"Indeed. It has just come as something of a shock as I've been dreaming of my wedding." She shook her head. "And who would have thought that you've been doing the same? I do look forward to getting to know your Miss Grantham."

"She's not my Miss Grantham yet."

"Oh, I am sure she will be. She looked very happy in the church when I met her. Maybe she was dreaming of her wedding as well."

"I certainly hope so. But one thing I've discovered about Miss Abigail Grantham—she can be unpredictable."

"Well, I predict a wedding very soon." She came forward and pressed his hands, smiling up at him. "You deserve to be happy, William. You truly do."

"Thank you, my dear. As do you. Let us hope that the course of true love will take a turn and start to run smoothly for both of us."

CHAPTER NINETEEN

WHEN ABIGAIL ENTERED the drawing room, Henrietta was there alone, working on some embroidery. Her cousin looked up with a smile as she approached. "Oh, there you are, Abby. That was a short outing. I have only just finished writing my letters. Did you like the church?"

"I did, thank you." Abigail slowly lowered herself onto a sofa. "I met someone there. A Lady Amelia Netley."

Henrietta set her embroidery frame to one side. "Emmy is back? Goodness, me! She usually spends the entire Season in London. Did she say why she'd returned?"

"No. She appeared a trifle agitated and asked Lord Rochvale to visit her as soon as he could."

"Did she, indeed?" Henrietta gazed into the middle distance. "She must have some important news to impart to him. Perhaps she is finally betrothed to Sir Reginald Markham. We have been expecting the announcement of their engagement for months."

The sense of relief that swamped Abigail at this news left her speechless for a moment. Finally, she said, "Who is Sir Reginald Markham?"

"He recently inherited Markham Park, a fair-sized estate on the other side of the village. Before that, he was an officer in the Royal Navy. He has a particular interest in nautical astronomy and comes here often to see Papa. He left for London at the same time as the Hythes."

"Oh! I wonder why Lady Amelia returned so suddenly. I received a letter from my sister the other day, and she said the Season has yet to reach its peak."

"I must say that I do not miss cutting a dash in Town myself. I always find it most fatiguing. I think I am a country person at heart, and I believe Lady Amelia to be the same. She went up to London for the Season for years and years and did not find a husband, even though she is the daughter of a marquess, and her portion is respectable. And, in the end, she met Sir Reginald right here in Buckinghamshire."

The door opened at that moment, and Uncle Longmore hastened inside. "Ah, there you are, Abigail. I have been looking all over for you. I have a task that requires your astronomical expertise."

She rose to her feet. "I should be pleased to help you, Uncle."

"Excellent, my dear. I was just in the village where I bumped into Sir Reginald Markham, who is back from London. He's considering joining Parry's polar expedition but has misplaced his copy of *Nautical Astronomy by Night*. He asked me if he could borrow mine, but I've learned the unwisdom of lending any books from my library! Too often, they are never returned. So I told Markham, instead, that he's welcome to transcribe any tables he might need for the expedition. *Nautical Astronomy by Night* contains a table of the right ascensions and the declinations of eighty principal fixed stars, adapted to the beginning of 1817. But Markham needs to correct them for 1819." He gave a firm nod. "This is where you come in, niece. I'd like you to assist Markham with calculating the annual variation."

"Oh!" Abigail stole a look at her cousin, who was staring at her father in surprise. "I should be happy to."

"Excellent, excellent."

Henrietta opened her mouth and then shut it. Finally, she said, "But I don't understand, Papa. Isn't Sir Reginald on the verge of offering for Lady Amelia? He has been very pointed in his attentions toward her."

Uncle Longmore waved a vague hand. "When I came upon Markham in the village, he was in conversation with Lady Flinton. She made some mention when Markham left of Lady Amelia's recent betrothal to another. But I didn't pay close attention to what she was saying. She does tend to chatter on so."

"Oh!" Henrietta's expression was quite blank.

At that moment, Aunt Longmore hastened into the room, holding a letter. "Ah, there you are, Henrietta. I have just received the most interesting communication from Lady Hythe. She writes that Lady Amelia has found the Season somewhat tedious this year and has decided to return to Hythe Place with Jane Netley."

Henrietta nodded. "I heard the news from Abby. Lord Rochvale took Abigail to see the church in Stone this morning, and they met Lady Amelia there."

Aunt Longmore sank onto a sofa. "What was Lady Amelia doing there?"

"She recognized Lord Rochvale's horses and came into the church to speak to him," Abigail explained.

"Ah, yes. Lady Amelia and Rochvale have always been good friends." Aunt Longmore looked down at the letter again. "Lady Hythe writes that she informed Amelia that she could spare Miss Netley. But she has since decided that she needs her cousin's assistance in London." She stared contemplatively into space. "I suppose Lady Hythe's constitution has never been strong, and chaperoning her youngest daughter during her first Season must be fatiguing—Lady Anna is quite a headstrong young lady, I believe." She set the letter down and looked across at her husband. "Lady Hythe has asked if Lady Amelia can come to stay with us for a couple of months to free Miss Netley to return to London."

"Well, it makes no difference to me, my love," Uncle Longmore said. "As long as it doesn't put you out too much."

Henrietta tilted her head. "Does Lady Amelia like the idea,

Mama?"

Aunt Longmore glanced down at the letter again. "Her mother hasn't broached the plan with her yet, as she was desirous of discovering first if I am amenable to the idea."

"Ah." Henrietta pressed her lips together before turning to her father. "How long do you think it will take Sir Reginald to transcribe the tables, Papa?"

"Eh?" Uncle Longmore drew his bushy brows together. "What has that to do with anything, daughter?"

"If Lady Amelia is betrothed to another gentleman, it might be awkward for her to encounter Sir Reginald here," Henrietta stated patiently. "He has paid marked attention to her this past year, and if she is now betrothed to another . . ."

Uncle Longmore scratched his head. "That's entirely between Markham and Lady Amelia. Shouldn't concern us at all. Besides, they're neighbors, so they'll need to meet sometime. Makes no difference if it's here or elsewhere."

Aunt Longmore's lips parted as she gazed at her husband. "Lady Amelia is *betrothed*?"

Uncle Longmore started backing to the door. "Lady Flinton said something of the sort when I met her in the village."

Aunt Longmore glanced from Henrietta to her husband. "Are you sure she's not betrothed to Sir Reginald, Longmore?"

He raised his hands. "It appears not. But I wasn't paying close attention to what Lady Flinton was saying. Thinking about Markham's polar expedition, y'know."

"His *polar* expedition?"

"Markham might be joining Parry's expedition later this year." He rubbed his chin. "Fortunate fellow."

"I . . . !" His wife stopped short. "I never was so surprised."

Uncle Longmore set one foot out of the door. "Well, my love, I must be going." And with that, he shot out of sight.

Abigail stared at the now-empty doorway before returning her attention to her aunt and cousin, who sat in stupefied silence. Aunt Longmore roused herself first. "I wonder who Lady Amelia has betrothed herself to? It doesn't make the least bit of sense. Although Sir Reginald took his time courting her, he did appear serious in his intentions."

"Perhaps Lady Amelia met a suitor she preferred in London," Henrietta mused.

"Yes. But why return home then?" Aunt Longmore shook her head. "I hope she isn't involved in some sort of scandal."

"I doubt it," Henrietta replied. "Lady Amelia is the last person I'd suspect of committing an indiscretion."

"Indeed. But as I have often said, young women can lose their heads when they fall in love. And Lady Amelia has been in Town these past few months." Aunt Longmore's eyes grew round. "For all we know, she might have been *forced* to accept an offer of marriage from another, and that is why she came back to Buckinghamshire."

"It could explain why Sir Reginald is eager to depart on this polar expedition." Henrietta frowned. "But I still can't see Lady Amelia landing herself in such a scrape. Of our set growing up, she and Rochvale were always the most responsible, and it *wasn't* just because they were the oldest."

Abigail looked from one to another with a growing sense of unease. She couldn't help but recall the watchful expression in Lady Amelia's eyes when she had met her earlier that day. And she had all but ordered Lord Rochvale to call on her this afternoon, which was a very odd thing for a single lady to do, even if she *was* the daughter of a marquess. Indeed, that was something that could only be excused in a betrothed lady.

But the biggest clue that Lady Amelia might be committed to Lord Rochvale was that she had written him a letter to advise him of her imminent arrival. Etiquette dictated that single ladies *not* write letters to gentlemen unless they were betrothed to them. Aunt Eliza had repeatedly drummed this into her nieces' heads over the years.

And she had called him William.

Desolation swamped Abigail at the weight of this realization, and she intertwined her fingers in her lap. This visceral feeling of loss was shocking, quite physical in its intensity. She released a slow breath. How could she not have recognized before how attracted she was to Lord Rochvale? She must have been aware of it on some level, but she had shoved the quiet knowledge aside, determined to avoid any romantical entanglements before her London Season.

And although she had been on her guard with Mr. Burnby, taking no heed of his blatant flattery, she had not even considered protecting her heart from Lord Rochvale. Perhaps because she had always sensed that he was utterly to be trusted . . .

And now he might be betrothed to somebody else.

CHAPTER TWENTY

AUNT LONGMORE WROTE back to Lady Hythe the same day she received her neighbor's letter with the assurance that Lady Amelia was welcome to stay at Longmore Hall for as long as she wished. The marquess's daughter was consequently installed at Longmore Hall a few days later, on the very day Sir Reginald came to the house to consult Lord Longmore's copy of *Nautical Astronomy by Night*.

"Written by Parry himself," Uncle Longmore said to Abigail as he removed the book from an upper shelf. He had summoned his niece to the library to meet the baronet, a tall, loose-limbed gentleman with dark hair and a slight air of restlessness about him. His face was long and thin, and his forehead very high, but his expression assumed an air of warmth when he smiled at Abigail, which made him seem most agreeable.

"Parry took advantage of his time on the *Alexander* when it was stationed so far north at Spitsbergen to study astronomy in that part of the world. This little volume will prove most useful for navigation on his latest expedition." Uncle Longmore turned to Sir Reginald. "I believe the Lord Commissioners of the Admiralty have agreed for the two commissioned ships to be equipped with provisions for two years. Do you think Parry will find a passage through the Arctic to the Pacific this time?"

"He certainly hopes he will manage to find the Northwest

Passage. I must say I agree with Parry that Ross turned back too soon last year."

Abigail opened the book her uncle handed her as he and Sir Reginald discussed the upcoming Arctic expedition. Glancing down at the book's first page, a quote attributed to someone called Young jumped out at her: "Stars teach as well as shine."

Stars teach as well as shine. She smiled. Such wonderful words to sum up her passion for astronomy, she thought, sitting down at the library table.

"Now, niece." Her uncle looked across at her. "I shall leave you with Sir Reginald. If you have any questions, pray let me know."

He nodded at Miss Smith, seated in the corner of the library in her role of chaperone, before leaving. Sir Reginald sat down at the other end of the table with a copy of *A Table of the Longitude and Latitude of Various Places* Uncle Longmore had found for him. However, he did not seem to be paying much attention to the book.

"When do you leave on your journey, Sir Reginald?" Abigail asked.

A slightly constrained expression crossed the baronet's face. "The expedition is due to leave England quite soon—they hope to set sail in the first part of May. However, I haven't made up my mind yet if I will be on it." He gave a slight shrug. "I promised Parry that I would arrange for the annual variation to be calculated, as he has so much to see to before his departure, but my plans are uncertain."

"Oh. I see." Abigail pressed her lips together. Could this mean Sir Reginald might yet hope to win back Lady Amelia's affections? "A two-year expedition is a serious commitment," she murmured.

"Indeed. And it has all been arranged within a short space of time."

Abigail nodded and looked down at her book once again. When Sir Reginald had gone up to London for the Season, he had no doubt met up with his friends from the Navy. Perhaps pressure had been brought to bear upon him to join the upcoming voyage, especially as the Admiralty would be seeking experienced officers for crew members.

Had Lady Amelia informed Sir Reginald that she was considering another offer of marriage to show him she had other matrimonial choices besides him? That was a distinct possibility, especially as the baronet had been courting Lady Amelia for some time.

Sir Reginald's statement that he had not yet decided to join the expedition gave Abigail a small measure of hope. But, as she stared unseeingly at the preface she had been attempting to read for the past five minutes, she realized it was cold comfort in face of the reality that, regardless of the gentleman's intentions, Lady Amelia might have already decided that she preferred Lord Rochvale's suit to Sir Reginald's.

Abigail's thoughts twisted this way and that until she eventually drew in a deep, calming breath. It was dangerous to indulge in unfounded speculation. Her agitation was serving no good purpose. If Lord Rochvale was indeed engaged to Lady Amelia, there was nothing Abigail could do about it. Only time would reveal the truth. Now, what she needed to do was focus her attention on the task before her. The calculations she was required to make should provide a welcome distraction from her madly racing thoughts.

On her way to the library earlier, Abigail had walked past the drawing room, where Lady Amelia was ensconced with Henrietta. Hopefully, her cousin would inform their guest of Sir Reginald's presence in the library so Lady Amelia could stay well out of his way if she so wished.

The door opened then, and Abigail raised her head as Lord Rochvale entered the room. She stole a glance at Sir Reginald before looking back at the viscount. He appeared as calm as ever as he advanced inside. Abigail suddenly felt foolish for her wild conjectures and gave Lord Rochvale a tentative smile, inordinately glad to see him.

He bowed as he came to a halt beside her chair. "Good morning, Miss Grantham. I see you're hard at work as usual." He turned to Sir Reginald. "You've returned to Bucks early, Markham."

Sir Reginald rose to his feet. "Rochvale! Just the man I wanted to see." Abigail's eyes widened as she wondered if he planned to bring up the matter of Lady Amelia's betrothal right then and there. But the baronet merely said, "I saw Parry just before I left London, and he expressed the hope that an optician will be able to develop a telescope much larger than the sort usually attached to a sextant. He believes it will better define the horizon at night at sea. I told him I would consult you on the matter."

Lord Rochvale nodded. "It would be of great use on the voyage he is about to embark upon. A pity there isn't time to manufacture one before he leaves. Unless he has already approached Thomas Harris & Son with the idea?"

"I don't know. I'll ask him when I return to London to deliver the calculations Miss Grantham is kindly working out for me."

"So you've discovered our treasure." Lord Rochvale's warm gaze rested on Abigail before he looked back at the baronet. "Lord Longmore says you might be joining Parry's expedition?"

Sir Reginald indicated the empty chair beside his, before sitting down again. "I am still making up my mind about it. It's not easy to leave Markham Park in a hurry."

Lord Rochvale sat at the table, and the two gentlemen discussed the upcoming polar expedition. Returning to her work, Abigail frowned a little as she attempted to block out their voices. She'd hate to make any mistakes. But try as she might, she could not help but overhear their conversation drifting down the table toward her. Perhaps her ears would have been trained in that direction in any case as she was curious if any clues might drop from Sir Reginald's lips about his intentions toward Lady Amelia.

But he failed to say anything, and Lord Rochvale did not mention her either.

It suddenly dawned on Abigail that Sir Reginald might not know that Lady Amelia was staying at Longmore Hall. That could create some awkwardness if he happened to bump into her when he left the library.

In the end, it was Lord Rochvale who brought up Lady Amelia. Standing up, he strolled across to the end of the table where Abigail sat, coming to a halt opposite her chair. "Miss Grantham, forgive me for the interruption. Your cousin would like to know if you'd care to accompany her and Lady Amelia on a walk in the grounds later today. I promised to give her your response on my way out."

Out of the corner of her eye, Abigail caught the look of shock on Sir Reginald's face. He must not have known that the marquess's daughter was resident here.

Abigail contemplated *Nautical Astronomy by Night* with great concentration. "I must work on these calculations for the next couple of hours, my lord. Please advise Henrietta that I should be pleased to join her and Lady Amelia after luncheon if that suits them."

"Very well."

He failed to move away, and Abigail eventually raised her head. When her eyes met his, she caught her breath. Could her recent discovery of the tender nature of her feelings for him be reflected in her eyes? Was it even possible to keep such sentiments hidden?

But his expression did not alter as he searched her face, and a sense of relief permeated her body. She hadn't given herself away. "Will you be joining us on our walk this afternoon, my lord?" she asked hurriedly.

"Not today, I'm afraid. I have a few matters I must attend to this afternoon." He looked back at Sir Reginald. "If you stop at Barcombe Manor later, Markham, I'll give you that copy of *The Nautical Almanac*."

"Thank you," the baronet said quietly.

Lord Rochvale bowed then and took his leave. As Abigail

gazed at his retreating form, she had the oddest sensation that her heart was leaving the room with him. Her brows snapped together as she stared down at the volume in front of her. This level of emotion simply would not do. Lord Rochvale could, at any moment, announce his betrothal to Lady Amelia. And, until she knew how the land lay, she must do her very best to keep her heart armor-plated.

Nothing would be more embarrassing to her or more mortifying to Lord Rochvale than the discovery that Abigail had developed a *tendre* for him if he did not reciprocate her sentiments. She needed to be on her guard, not just for her sake but for his. To place him in such a difficult position would be untenable.

Abigail stole a look down the table at Sir Reginald and stilled. The expression on his face was unimaginably bleak. Was this due simply to his discovery that Lady Amelia was here or was it sorrow that she had chosen another? A feeling of dread settled in the pit of her stomach, and she clenched her eyes shut.

Things looked distinctly unpromising.

CHAPTER TWENTY-ONE

AFTER A LIGHT luncheon, Abigail went upstairs to fetch her hat and shawl before joining Henrietta and Lady Amelia in the hall.

"I thought you might like to follow the course of the river today, Abby," Henrietta said. "It's a lovely walk."

Abigail smiled. "I should like that very much. Isn't that the walk Mr. Burnby wanted to take us on?"

"Yes. But I would prefer to go without him. He always speaks such nonsense." She directed a sharp glance at Abigail as she said these words, but Abigail pretended not to notice. Her poor cousin never ceased to warn her not to fall in love with the man. If only she knew that there was no danger of Abigail succumbing to him! Not when her heart was already half-lost to another.

As they walked along, Henrietta and Lady Amelia chatted about mutual acquaintances who had gone to London for the Season. With her head still full of the morning's calculations, Abigail welcomed the opportunity to clear her head. She breathed in the scent of damp soil as they passed through a screen of foliage, which led to a lawn sloping down to the river.

A majestic walnut tree with extensive branches came into view, and Abigail gazed at it in awe. "Do you know the age of that tree, Henrietta? It must be ancient to be so fully grown."

"Our old walnut is 180 years old."

"It's enormous!"

Her cousin nodded. "When I was a little girl, I adored coming to this spot, and this was my favorite tree. Back then it was nearly twenty feet around the trunk, but I suspect it's even more now."

Abigail craned her neck. "It shades most of this section of the park. A good place for a picnic when the weather is warmer."

"Yes, indeed. We've had numerous picnics under those branches. I'll ask Mama if we can arrange one for next month. Heaven knows there are enough of our acquaintances in the neighborhood to invite." She cleared her throat. "Did your work go well this morning, Abby?"

"It did, thank you." Abigail bit her lip. Did Lady Amelia know that Sir Reginald had been in the Longmore library all morning? Henrietta was surely aware of the fact, but perhaps she hadn't told her guest of his presence for fear of distressing her.

Lady Amelia turned to Abigail as they strolled on. "What sort of work were you busy with, Miss Grantham? I believe you have an interest in astronomy?"

"Indeed. My uncle asked me to do some calculations. I . . ." Abigail trailed off. She did not want to mention Sir Reginald or the polar expedition. "I have always found it quite interesting how astronomy has two distinct branches—measuring star positions, which is essentially mathematical work, and actually observing the structure of the heavens themselves, which is what William Herschel does to such great effect."

"Which one interests you most?" Lady Amelia asked.

"Oh, most definitely observing the heavens. There's something magical about that."

Lady Amelia shook her head. "But you are able to do both. You must be very clever, Miss Grantham. Very much like Lord Rochvale, in fact." She paused. "You even share his interest in old churches."

The look she bent on Abigail was quite speculative, causing the blood to rush to her cheeks. If Lady Amelia were secretly betrothed to Lord Rochvale, she would be wondering why he had been squiring another lady about that day. "Er ... yes," she murmured, quite unable to think of anything else to say.

"I believe you are involved in some sort of star chart project with Rochvale," Lady Amelia continued. "I trust it is progressing at a steady pace?"

Abigail sent her a sideways glance. Was Lady Amelia concerned about the time Lord Rochvale would be spending with Abigail over the next few months? "Fortunately, we have been making excellent progress, your ladyship," she murmured.

They had reached the bank of the river by now, and the calmly-flowing water soothed Abigail's somewhat ruffled feelings. As she felt her axis tilt back toward equilibrium once more, she released a sighing breath. Thus it always was with her—streams, rivers, lakes, and waterfalls could somehow still her soul.

They began to walk beside the river once more, taking a footpath that led to a kissing gate. Passing through this quaint contraption designed to keep sheep out but allow people through, Abigail traipsed behind Henrietta and Lady Amelia on a narrow path until they reached a simple stone bridge. Henrietta nodded at a field on the other side of the river, screened by a hedge. "That's Burnby Place, Abby. The river serves as a border between the two properties."

Her cousin frowned a little as she looked across at Mr. Burnby's land. But then she turned briskly away, leaving Abigail and Lady Amelia to follow. They skirted a meadow and came across some farm buildings and yet more fields filled with sheep before leaving the river path behind and passing through another gate.

As Abigail tracked across a meadow behind the other two ladies, she breathed a sigh of relief that she had decided to wear her sturdy half-boots today rather than a pair of delicate slippers—that sort of flimsy footwear would never have stood up to a walk like this.

Eventually, Henrietta stopped under an oak tree at the edge of an arable plot of ground and stretched out her arms. "How lovely it is to be out of doors! I was feeling quite crotchety before we set out, but now all seems right with the world." She sighed. "But we had better return home soon, or Mama will be sending out a search party."

Abigail smiled. "Oh, I think she's accustomed to your long walks, Hetta."

"Still, she won't be too pleased with me for dragging her guests out for so long."

They retraced their steps to the riverbank before making their way back to the Hall at a leisurely pace.

Abigail's feet ached a little, and a blister was forming on the back of her heel. Thank goodness they were nearly home. She bent her head to examine a smudge of dirt on the kid leather of one of her half-boots when Lady Amelia abruptly halted beside her.

Looking up, Abigail spotted Sir Reginald walking to a curricle at the front of the house. The marquess's daughter drew herself up to her full height as though preparing for battle as she walked on.

Sir Reginald came over to them then and bowed deeply. "How do you do?"

It was a good thing no answer was expected to that particular question, for if Lady Amelia had responded, she would no doubt have expressed that she did very badly indeed. Her displeasure at the encounter was evident in the rigid set of her shoulders and the way she avoided meeting Sir Reginald's eyes.

Henrietta jumped into the awkward gap and asked Sir Reginald how he had enjoyed his time in the Capital. After a quick glance at Lady Amelia's aloof countenance, he said, "I have never been one for parties, Miss Longmore, but my time was most profitably engaged in other activities. There is something to occupy everyone in London, fortunately."

"Yes, indeed," Henrietta said. "I tend to spend most of my time in the museums or at exhibitions when I go to Town."

"You share that in common with Sir Reginald then, Henrietta," Lady Amelia said in a low voice. "He spends much of his time there, too."

Sensing distinct undercurrents but not quite knowing what they were, Abigail waded into the lull. "What exhibitions are on at the moment, Sir Reginald?"

When he failed to answer immediately, Lady Amelia said, "At the Leicester Square Rotunda, there is a panorama about the recent polar expedition."

"How interesting." Henrietta's voice was bright as she turned to her friend. "Did you visit it, Lady Amelia?"

"No. But I heard all about it."

Henrietta nodded. "When I am next in London, I hope to see it. Although I will probably only travel to the Metropolis next year."

"Never fear, my dear," Lady Amelia said. "By that time, there will be no doubt be another exhibition to illustrate the triumphs of *this* year's exploratory voyage." Her gaze rested on the baronet. "When does your ship leave, sir?"

"Parry plans to leave in the next few weeks. But I am uncertain if I will join him."

"Oh!" Lady Amelia pressed her lips together. "I thought it was a certainty."

He bowed. "Nothing in life is ever certain, your ladyship. And now, if you will excuse me, I cannot keep my horses standing." He took a step away before turning back to Abigail and doffing his hat. "Until tomorrow morning, Miss Grantham. Thank you for your assistance."

Lady Amelia stood perfectly still as he strode away. And it was only when he had disappeared completely out of sight that she started walking again. "Were you working with Sir Reginald in the library this morning, Miss Grantham?" she asked as they entered the hall.

"Yes. My uncle asked me to assist Sir Reginald with some astronomical calculations."

"Ah." She looked straight ahead, her forehead slightly creased. "If you would excuse me . . ."

Lady Amelia hastened up the stairs, leaving Abigail and Henrietta together. Her cousin shook her head when her friend disappeared out of sight. "Perhaps I should have told Lady Amelia that Sir Reginald was here. But I didn't wish to distress her. And I thought he'd be gone by the time we returned from our walk. Perhaps Sir Reginald was waiting to speak to Papa—Mama said he meant to be out on the estate most of the day."

"Has Lady Amelia confided in you about her betrothal?"

"She hasn't said a word, which makes me wonder if Lady Flinton isn't mistaken. Why would Lady Amelia hide such a thing?"

Abigail knit her brows. Why indeed? It was all very strange. If only she didn't care so much! Waiting for the announcement of Lady Amelia's betrothal to Lord Rochvale was torture.

But one thing gave Abigail hope as she trailed up the stairs behind Henrietta. Lady Amelia did not seem in the least indifferent to Sir Reginald. Indeed, the tension between the two had been palpable, which meant that the rumor of Lady Amelia's engagement to another man might hold no water.

CHAPTER TWENTY-TWO

ABIGAIL SPENT THE next days closeted inside the library with Sir Reginald. She made good progress with her computations, concentrating hard on the task, as Sir Reginald wished to return to London as soon as possible.

"I was planning on calculating the annual variation myself at Markham Park," the baronet said toward the end of the week, "but when I couldn't find my copy of *Nautical Astronomy by Night*, I requested Lord Longmore's aid. It's a boon to have your help, Miss Grantham. You are far more accomplished at this kind of thing than I am. Who taught you?"

"My brother, John, and to some extent, my father. I was allowed to study alongside my brother because he was an invalid as a boy and educated at home. He had an excellent tutor, and my sisters and I shared his lessons in mathematics."

"Well, you are a credit to your teachers, Miss Grantham."

"Thank you." She smiled at him before returning her attention to the book before her. Knowing Sir Reginald planned to return to London as soon as Abigail completed her task put some pressure on her. But she welcomed the distraction from her thoughts, which were still shooting in all manner of directions whenever she had a moment to herself.

The feelings she had developed for Lord Rochvale had taken her utterly by surprise, as though she had been plunged into an ice-cold lake and come up gasping for breath. How could her life have gone from sailing on seemingly still waters to being rocked about by these waves?

Although Abigail had often dreamed of falling in love, it had always been a fantasy she expected to occur at some point in the future. Wishing for a grand passion, after all, did not necessarily mean one was ready for it.

Her reluctance to delve into more profound feeling had been reinforced when she observed the statue of the mournful young girl in St Mary's church. Abigail's losses had come crashing in on her then, striking her with such force that she had been left grasping for peace rather than passion. Passion meant she would need to embrace the disruption brought about by deep emotion yet again, and she hadn't felt ready for that. Consequently, she had not been looking for it.

When you nursed a broken limb, it needed to be held immobile for it to knit properly. And that was what Abigail had been doing these past few years—keeping her inner being motionless, hoping that time would bring the healing she so desperately needed.

To distract herself from grief, she had embraced living in the moment instead, appreciating life in all its richness and fullness, as though she had very little time left to enjoy it. This sensory approach had reaped its rewards, allowing her to exist happily with no danger of having her equilibrium disturbed, even if that disturbance would mean a change for the better.

But now, her calm had been shattered, and she was left with the feeling that the firm ground beneath her feet had turned into clouds. And Abigail was no Aurora from Greek mythology, able to float about in such a fashion. Instead, she liked to be firmly attached to the ground so that she could look up at meteorological phenomena. The last thing she had expected was to turn into one herself—for wasn't that what falling in love was . . . to become airborne?

She shook her head at her fanciful train of thought and tried to focus instead on the mathematical problem on the page in front of her.

If only love was something that could be solved as easily.

Abigail completed the calculations within the next two days, handing them over to Sir Reginald, who received them with a word of thanks. "Your assistance is much appreciated, Miss Grantham." He set the pages on the table and stared down at them briefly before looking up. "I leave for London tomorrow. I should like to take my leave of your aunt, Miss Longmore, and Lady Amelia before I depart."

"I believe they are in the drawing room."

He nodded. "Let me stop there to make my farewells."

Abigail rose to her feet too and walked ahead of him out of the library. Glancing back, she saw that Miss Smith, seated before the fire, had dozed off. Abigail had worked into the early hours for the past few days, so Miss Smith must be exhausted from the succession of late nights. After hesitating a moment, Abigail left the governess to sleep. They were experiencing an uncommonly fine spell of weather at the moment, and Abigail would be working alongside Lord Rochvale again tonight if the skies remained clear.

Henrietta was occupied with some embroidery when they entered the drawing room while Lady Amelia was conversing with Lord Rochvale. *Lord Rochvale!* Abigail came to an abrupt halt and glanced across at Sir Reginald. His shoulders were set in a rigid line as his gaze settled on the viscount and Lady Amelia. But then the baronet stepped forward and bowed, and the moment of tension was lost in the flurry of greetings that followed.

Abigail hesitated a moment before taking a seat beside Henrietta. Her cousin turned to speak to Sir Reginald, who sat across from her, while Lady Amelia picked up her embroidery and started stabbing at it. Abigail blinked in dismay at the disarray of the other girl's needlework and itched to remove the frame from her grasp. Although she did not list embroidery as one of her finer accomplishments, Abigail had at least mastered the art of neat stitchery. The hash Lady Amelia was making of the fine work made Abigail's eyes water.

"You are to be congratulated on the speed with which you completed those calculations, Miss Grantham," Lord Rochvale said. "I fear we all take advantage of you."

"Oh, I enjoy keeping busy, my lord," Abigail said. "Besides, hard work relieves my mind of anxiety." Only after Abigail uttered the words did she realize their unwisdom. She frowned at her clasped fingers. She really ought to learn how to guard her tongue. She glanced up, meeting the viscount's gaze for one unnerving moment.

"Are you anxious about anything in particular, Miss Grantham?" he asked.

Abigail was spared the necessity of responding by her aunt's sudden entrance into the room. The older lady surveyed its occupants, tilting her head when her gaze settled on the baronet. "I believe you are leaving us, Sir Reginald, in favor of more arctic conditions?" she said as she advanced inside.

Glancing across at Lady Amelia's frozen face, Abigail wasn't quite sure how much more arctic the conditions could be anywhere else. Sir Reginald and Lord Rochvale rose to their feet and bowed, resuming their seats once Lady Longmore had settled herself on the sofa. She kept her gaze fixed on the baronet, her brows raised in inquiry.

Clearing his throat, Sir Reginald murmured, "I am as yet uncertain if I shall join the voyage," he murmured.

"Oh! You're leaving it rather later to make up your mind, are you not?"

"My decision depends on a number of factors, your ladyship."

"Ah." Aunt Longmore's eyes narrowed as she surveyed him, and Abigail wondered if the interrogation the poor man was being subjected to might have something to do with the letter her aunt had received from the Marchioness of Hythe that morning. However, after a brief inclination of her head, her aunt turned away from Sir Reginald and addressed herself to Lord Rochvale instead. "Have you come to see Longmore, Rochvale? I'm afraid he's at the home farm, speaking to Selby."

"I've come to look through your attics, ma'am."

"Oh, excellent!" Aunt Longmore's face creased into a smile. "I asked Davison to tidy those rooms just yesterday to make your task easier. Would you care for some assistance?" She glanced across at Abigail. "Unfortunately, Henrietta and Lady Amelia are off to see the Vicar's wife this afternoon, but my niece has no plans. Would you care to offer your help to his lordship, my dear? I am sure he would welcome it."

"Well . . ." Abigail swallowed. Was it wise to spend even more time in his vicinity when she still knew so little of his true connection to Lady Amelia? "I should like that if you do not mind the help of an amateur, my lord."

"As long as you aren't too tired after toiling away all this morning, Miss Grantham."

She shook her head. "I would welcome the opportunity to explore those attics."

Miss Smith crept into the room at that moment with a somewhat sheepish air. No doubt she was dismayed at falling asleep while she was meant to be keeping an eye on her charge. Abigail gave the governess a reassuring little smile, and Miss Smith, meeting her gaze, bobbed her head in silent acknowledgment.

"Ah, there you are, Miss Smith," Aunt Longmore said. "We have been discussing the afternoon's plans. Please accompany Miss Grantham and Lord Rochvale up to the attics. They will be sorting through the contents this afternoon."

Miss Smith seated herself on a hard, upright chair far away from the blazing fire. "Very well, your ladyship," she said quietly.

Sir Reginald rose to his feet and bowed. "I must take my leave now. Thank you, Miss Grantham, for your invaluable assistance. Lady Longmore . . . Miss Longmore . . ." He turned slightly and bowed once more. "Lady Amelia." He turned to Lord Rochvale. "If I may have a word in the library about that telescope design?"

"Of course." Lord Rochvale stood and accompanied the other man out of the room. Four sets of intent feminine eyes followed their retreating backs.

Abigail sighed as the door closed softly behind them. How odd that those two gentlemen represented such a vast quantity of hopes and dreams.

CHAPTER TWENTY-THREE

S IR REGINALD PICKED up the pages Abigail had left on the table before turning around to face William, who had followed him into the library. "Would you write down the dimensions you recommend for that design?" The baronet found a pencil and a spare sheet of paper on the table and handed them across to him.

Seating himself at the table, William wrote down the requested information before leaning back in his chair and studying the other man. "You leave tomorrow morning?"

"Yes. But I'll need to return to Bucks for a flying visit if I join the voyage—to make final arrangements with my bailiff. Fortunately, we aren't too far from London."

"Indeed."

Sir Reginald studied the page William handed back to him with intense concentration. "I believe congratulations may soon be in order for you?" The words came out like scattered bullets.

"I hope so," William murmured.

Sir Reginald remained silent for some time before crumpling the pages in his hand. "She deserves more than a damned marriage of convenience, Rochvale."

"I'm in full agreement," William said coolly. "I don't intend to settle for such a marriage."

"But you don't love her."

William pushed his chair away from the table and rested his

arm on the back, twisting sideways. "Love has many faces—not all of them conducive to matrimonial happiness. A pair of partridges has a far greater chance of contentment in the domestic sphere than a swallow winging its way across the world."

Sir Reginald's expression was grim. "A brace of partridges more like." He strode to the window, swept the curtains aside, and stared outside. "Swallows return."

"To a much-changed land."

Sir Reginald remained silent for some time. "Oh, damn you, Rochvale. You can't marry Lady Amelia."

"I don't intend to."

The baronet twisted around. "What? But you've just admitted you plan to become a tenant for life."

"I do. But my . . . er . . . affections lie in quite another direction."

Sir Reginald's shoulders eased visibly. "I don't know whether to shake your hand, my lad, or plant you a facer."

William's smile was wry. "I'd say it's already bellows to mend with you."

Sir Reginald frowned. "Yes, dash it all. I've been a fool."

When William made no response, Sir Reginald paced back to the table. "Do you think I've blundered irretrievably?"

"I've always found Lady Amelia open to reason. What do you plan to do?"

"Sort things out with her. But first, I must go to London."

William studied his friend meditatively. "Don't take too long."

Sir Reginald smoothed out the creased papers. "I won't. I've taken too long already, I daresay."

"A rumor is circulating in the village that Lady Amelia is betrothed to someone else."

"What?" He stared. "How did that get about?"

"Did you mention your last conversation with her to anyone?"

"Only Gregory Flinton when he asked me if I planned to join Parry."

"He must have said something to Lady Flinton, as she's been spreading the news."

"Devil take it." Sir Reginald released a harsh breath. "I'd better make haste before the whole county knows about it."

William nodded as he rose to his feet. After wishing his friend a good journey, he returned to the drawing room, where he learned from Lady Longmore that Abigail and Miss Smith had gone upstairs already.

With a word of thanks, William retrieved the notebook and pencil he had left on a table before crossing the hall to the main staircase, which meandered to the top floor of the house. He halted and turned down a corridor toward an open door at the end, where he discovered the two ladies.

The sloping ceiling made it impossible for William to stand up fully, and he smiled as he bent his neck to one side. "I think it would be best if I sit out of the way at that table over there." He nodded at a wooden table near the door.

Abigail looked around the small, cluttered space. "I think that should work well enough. I can pick my way through everything like a goat and bring you the items to inspect."

"A goat, Miss Grantham?" Laughter threaded his voice.

"I am very sure on my feet, which one needs to be with all these things scattered about," she said with dignity.

"Yes, of course. It is just that you are the least goat-like person I have ever encountered."

"I am very tenacious." Her voice held a note of challenge.

"Hmm. You have persevered with our star chart project, which is admirable considering the repetitive nature of the work." He gave a small bow. "Therefore, I retract my last statement. You do have something in common with goats."

"Indeed. Once I have committed myself, I rarely draw back."

She studied him rather searchingly, and he wondered if the rumors from the village might have reached her ears. He was about to investigate further when she added, "Goats make me laugh, you know. They're so inquisitive and stubborn. I am afraid I share those characteristics with them as well."

A smile tugged at his lips. "Now that I think about it, in Greek mythology, Amalthea, considered the foster mother of Zeus, is strongly associated with goats. Sometimes she is represented as a goat and at other times as a nymph who fed goat's milk to the infant Zeus." He frowned in recollection. "In one story, the goat's horn broke off, so Amalthea took the empty horn and filled it with fruits that she also fed to Zeus. To honor her, he set the goat in splendor amidst the stars." He raised an eyebrow. "Another reason for your affinity with them, perhaps?"

Abigail laughed, the corners of her eyes crinkling up in such an adorable fashion that Willliam wanted to pull her into his arms. But at that moment, Miss Smith stepped into sight, reminding him forcibly that they weren't alone.

"How may I assist you, my lord?" the governess said diffidently. "Should I sort through that trunk in the corner? Miss Longmore and I went through it the other day, so I am familiar with its contents."

"An excellent plan. Thank you, Miss Smith."

She smiled fleetingly at him before crossing to an enormous trunk near the window. Abigail, meanwhile, brought William a dusty vase she hastily wiped down with a cloth she'd found on the windowsill.

He made a list of the various items, writing notes beside any object he wished to examine in a better light at a later stage. They worked steadily for a couple of hours, and he was about to call a halt when Abigail brought him a marble urn she had unearthed from a pile of crockery in a box near the door.

He stilled when he studied the familiar motif. "This is a replica of the newly returned Roman urn I examined before. It must be a matching set."

"Really?" Abigail leaned closer to examine the piece, so close that if she turned her head only a fraction, her lips would touch his. She drew back slightly, gazing into his eyes, and it was only Miss Smith's delicate throat-clearing that brought him back to earth.

Abigail stepped away. "So *two* urns were abandoned up here, my lord?" Only the slight tremor in her voice betrayed her lack of composure. "They are both such splendid pieces that they are difficult to ignore."

"It is odd." William returned his attention to the Roman antiquity. "Especially as the house was thoroughly searched the other day. I would have thought this second urn would have been discovered then."

Abigail turned her head to one side. "I wonder how it was missed?"

"A mystery. Let me take this downstairs to the butler's pantry. It'll be best to get Davison to lock it away, as well."

"Indeed." She looked at her chaperone. "Are you ready to leave, Miss Smith?"

"I shall come downstairs when I have tidied this room a little."

Abigail nodded and walked out of the attic ahead of William. The opposite door opened just as he followed her outside, and his old nursery maid emerged from her quarters. As she shut the door behind her, William smiled at her. "How are you, Annie? We haven't seen you in an age at Barcombe."

She curtsied. "Have a deal to keep me busy here, milord, but I plan to visit on Sunday." Her gaze rested on the artifact William held. "I hope there's no more trouble, milord?"

"There's none," he said quietly.

"We were right worried the last time." She turned to Abigail. "Do you need anything from me now, miss?"

Abigail shook her head. "Nothing, thank you, Winnicott. I'll see you later."

William carried the urn down the stairs, with Abigail walking a little ahead of him. Spotting Davison in the hall, William approached him and learned that Lord Longmore was still out on the estate. Delivering the Roman artifact into the butler's safekeeping, he turned back to Abigail. "Until this evening, Miss Grantham." He smiled down at her. "One way or another, we *are* putting your hand to the plough."

"As I said before, my lord, I like to keep busy."

He studied her quizzically. "Ah, yes, because it relieves your mind of anxiety. You never answered my question earlier, you know."

Her gaze faltered. "No."

"If I can assist you in any way, I am yours to command. I hope you know that, my dear."

Abigail nodded, but she failed to meet his eyes when he took his leave. As William walked out of the hall, he frowned, trying to pinpoint the subtle change in her demeanor. Something must have occurred to upset her equilibrium. But Abigail was keeping the matter to herself, locking him in a puzzle maze with no clear plan of getting out.

As he waited for his curricle to be brought around, he tightened his jaw. The best thing he could do was bide his time until the obstacles in his path could be removed. Forcing the issue was not his style. He sighed. It was a good thing astronomy had taught him patience, because keeping Abigail at a respectable distance was becoming more and more frustrating.

CHAPTER TWENTY-FOUR

ABIGAIL OPENED THE curtains in her bedchamber and, removing her telescope from its case, set it up with the ease of long practice. Everyone else was in the drawing room downstairs, but Abigail had excused herself after dinner, murmuring that she was in need of a little quiet time. Aunt Longmore, no doubt believing Abigail to be tired, had agreed that she should rest before the arduous astronomical work of the night began. And so she had sent her niece upstairs with an understanding nod and a smile.

But, in actual fact, Abigail's reason for retiring after dinner had nothing to do with fatigue but rather her very real need to escape from Lord Rochvale's perceptive gaze. She couldn't believe she had once considered him something of a slow top. Although the viscount wasn't a man of many words, when he did speak, his words counted. And those grey eyes seemed to penetrate her very soul. A most disturbing experience, especially as Abigail had secrets residing there that she had no desire for him to discover—not while she was as yet uncertain about his connection to Lady Amelia.

Lady Amelia. She sighed as she peered through the lens. Although it was evident that the marquess's daughter was deeply affected by Sir Reginald's presence, this did not mean that Lady Amelia was desirous of marrying him. For all Abigail knew, Lady

Amelia had decided that Lord Rochvale would make a much better husband than Sir Reginald, which could account for her distinct air of tension when she had come face to face with the baronet the other day.

The fact that Sir Reginald might soon be joining a voyage of discovery to a faraway land did not bode well for any possible marriage between him and the woman he had once courted, which left Abigail in the unenviable position of caring for a man who might at any moment announce his betrothal to a lady living under the same roof as her.

She released a sigh of frustration. So much for her desire to remain emotionally disengaged! Somehow, she had landed in deep waters while believing all the time that she had been paddling in the shallows.

She determinedly directed her thoughts in a more pleasant direction. This morning she had received a letter from her older sister, Thea, advising her that she was betrothed to Lord Castleroy. Abigail had been delighted to learn the news as she had become acquainted with Lord Castleroy and his sister, Anne, the previous year in Bath and liked them both very much. Lord Castleroy would make Thea a splendid husband.

However, an odd tone in her sister's words gave Abigail the feeling that Thea was keeping something from her. Her letter had not been in the least expansive, and Abigail longed to hear all the romantical details of the proposal. But on second thought, Thea was the last person to write openly about such things. Her sister kept her deeper feelings under lock and key and was not one to wear her heart on her sleeve. Abigail would need to wait until she saw Thea again to learn more.

She finished sweeping the heavens and rotated the telescope down, spotting a glow in the distance. Blinking a little, she trained the telescope on some flickering lights near the river bordering the Longmore estate. A shepherd checking up on his sheep, perhaps? Feeling more kindly disposed toward sheep lately, given all her recent . . . encounters, she started to refocus her telescope on the field, but realizing the time, Abigail hastily packed her telescope away in its case and made her way to the observatory. Lord Rochvale was already there, and she greeted him quietly before heading to her station in a very businesslike fashion, determined to concentrate on her work.

As she communicated with Lord Rochvale over the next few hours, a corner of her mind was occupied with the knotty problem of how to manage her attraction to him. The sooner they completed this blasted star chart, the better. Spending all this time with him was most trying as she was finding it harder and harder to hide her feelings for him and maintain sufficient focus.

Fortunately, they were making excellent progress as the weather had been most obliging. Indeed, it was the only obliging aspect of this whole sorry situation. She pressed her lips together in frustration. The problem with the Longmore household was that everyone seemed to be at cross purposes with one another. Abigail was on the verge of losing her heart to Lord Rochvale, while Henrietta could not be shaken from her mistaken belief that her cousin was in danger of falling in love with Mr. Burnby. Meanwhile, Sir Reginald appeared to harbor strong feelings for Lady Amelia while their new house guest had indicated an interest, albeit of as yet unknown quality, in Lord Rochvale.

Abigail sighed. Somehow, she seemed to have landed in the middle of a performance of *A Midsummer Night's Dream,* with all the attending confusion of romantic connections gone awry. Except this was real life, not a play, and she hated having to act a part—because that was what she was doomed to do while she waited for news of Lord Rochvale's engagement to Lady Amelia. If, indeed, they *were* secretly betrothed.

They did not appear particularly enamored of each other, but the affection of a long-standing friendship was most definitely evident between them. They had known each other since childhood, after all, and were clearly on excellent terms. A marriage of respect and liking might be what Lord Rochvale and Lady Amelia sought rather than the more passionate connection that seemed to exist between Lady Amelia and Sir Reginald.

One thing was clear, however. Everyone was keeping their own counsel. No formal announcement had been made as yet, which gave Abigail a dash of hope. But that was in some ways worse than having no hope at all, she thought gloomily.

She had a sudden desire to run away from it all, to turn back the clock to a time when she didn't feel so vulnerable and exposed, to when her hopes and desires weren't inextricably linked to the decisions and actions of another.

But she couldn't get away, which meant she needed to find some way to distract herself from her unsettled emotions.

Fortunately, the next day distraction arrived in the form of an invitation from Mr. Burnby to picnic at Burnby Place. The card was addressed to Lady Longmore and requested the pleasure of the company of the Longmores and their guests to dine *al fresco* on his estate the following afternoon.

Aunt Longmore peered at the invitation and wrinkled her nose. "I am certain Mr. Burnby would prefer a party of young people." She shook her head as she set the card aside. "I, for one, cannot abide picnics. Ants crawl all over everything, and bees are attracted to the cakes. It becomes an insect-repelling fest, and no matter how hard I try, I *cannot* sit quietly by as bees buzz around my head. I fear their sting and leap to my feet in a futile attempt to escape them. Most undignified at my age. And Longmore never can abide sitting about doing nothing. So you go, my dears."

Consequently, the next day, Abigail, Henrietta, and Lady Amelia piled into the coach for the short drive to the neighboring estate. A picnic had been set up under an old oak tree in a meadow, and Abigail gazed around with pleasure when she stepped out of the coach and made her way to the designated spot. How lovely it was to be outdoors. She had been cooped up inside far too much recently.

An array of food had been set out on a table under the tree's spreading branches, and Abigail's mouth watered when her gaze alighted on the plum cake and macaroons. She hadn't eaten much breakfast this morning, and her stomach grumbled in protest. If only she weren't perpetually hungry! And she didn't even have the excuse that she was still growing—Abigail had reached her full height years ago.

Turning to Henrietta, she saw the other girl looking around with an air of surprise. "Everything seems in excellent trim. Those fences were broken the last time I came here, and the meadows were terribly overgrown. I wonder . . ." She drew her brows together as Mr. Burnby and Lord Rochvale came into sight, emerging from a nearby woodland.

After greetings had been exchanged, they all settled down to enjoy the excellent repast Mr. Burnby had provided. Abigail repressed a smile when a bee began buzzing around the macaroon on her plate, imagining her aunt leaping to her feet and speeding away.

Henrietta and Lady Amelia were conversing with Lord Rochvale when Mr. Burnby moved to sit beside Abigail on one of the Witney point blankets spread out over the ground. "I haven't seen you in a while, Miss Grantham. I trust that you are well?"

"Oh, very well, thank you, sir. I have been occupied with astronomical matters of late."

Henrietta turned her head. "I see that you have made significant improvements to your estate, Mr. Burnby."

"Indeed, Miss Longmore. I am progressing steadily toward my goal." He rose to his feet and gave a small bow. "Would you ladies care to stroll about the gardens? They are only a step away, beyond that woodland."

"I should like that very much." Abigail rose to her feet.

"I am quite content to laze here," Lady Amelia said. "But you four go on. I need a nap after that large meal."

Henrietta and Lord Rochvale stood, and after advising a hovering footman to attend to Lady Amelia, Mr. Burnby led their small party through a narrow belt of trees that opened up unexpectedly into a most lovely garden.

"Oh, how pretty this is!" Abigail gazed around in delight. "That rose garden is exquisite." She hurried across the lawn to study the array of fragrant blooms on display while Henrietta and Lord Rochvale followed behind at a more leisurely pace. Mr. Burnby, who had stopped to have a word with a gardener, came up beside Abigail just as Lord Rochvale and Henrietta approached her from the other direction.

As she studied the distinctive Damask roses, Abigail's cheeks warmed as she realized that the posy and cap of flowers Mr. Burnby had presented to her at the masquerade ball must have come from this rose bed. She glanced at Henrietta, who was gazing at the roses, too, her face drawn. She said something to Lord Rochvale in a low voice, and he escorted her to a garden seat placed under a nearby tree.

With a murmured excuse, Abigail approached her cousin, who had withdrawn a delicate fan from her reticule. "Are you feeling unwell, Hetta? You've gone quite pale."

"I think it's just the heat, Abby. I felt overcome for a moment." She waved the fan in front of her face.

Lord Rochvale frowned. "May I escort you back to your coach? You must go home if you aren't feeling well."

Henrietta shook her head. "I don't wish to spoil the party." After a moment's hesitation, however, she allowed Lord Rochvale to assist her to her feet. Mr. Burnby came up to them at that moment, his brow creased in concern. "Are you unwell, Miss Longmore?"

"I need to lie down. The heat, you know." She studied the ground. "But don't let me interrupt your walk around the gardens."

"I am quite happy to return to Longmore," Abigail said. "It *is* an uncommonly warm day."

"Yes." Henrietta's voice was strained. "It is."

In silence, they walked back to the oak tree, where they discovered Lady Amelia fast asleep. Lord Rochvale studied her prone figure for a moment before looking back at Henrietta.

"When Lady Amelia wakes up, I will bring her back to Longmore in my curricle."

"Thank you, Rochvale," Henrietta murmured. "She looks so peaceful, I wouldn't like to disturb her."

Abigail turned to bid farewell to Mr. Burnby, who was studying Henrietta in some concern. "Would you not prefer to come up to the house to recover, Miss Longmore?"

"No, no, thank you. I'd like to go home."

"May I call on you tomorrow to see if you are feeling more the thing?"

"There's no need, Mr. Burnby. I believe it is merely a touch of the sun." Henrietta cleared her throat. "Your . . . your estate is looking quite splendid, sir. Indeed, I wish you every happiness here with your future wife."

And turning around, Henrietta hastened away to the carriage.

CHAPTER TWENTY-FIVE

ABIGAIL WAS READING a book in the library the next day when Aunt Longmore hastened into the room, her expression concerned. "Oh, there you are, my dear. I have just received a letter from your grandmother. She and Dorothea are in Bath, as your grandmother feels they have been trotting too hard in London these past few weeks." She looked down at the page in her hands. "Now that Dorothea is betrothed to Lord Castleroy, and she's had her coming-out ball, there is no need for them to stay in Town." She glanced up. "Your grandmama wants to know if we would like to join her in Bath for a short visit as Lord Castleroy currently has business in Macclesfield, and Dorothea is eager to spend time with you before her wedding."

Abigail set her book to one side. "I received a letter from Grandmama the other day saying she planned to travel to Longmore later in the summer. But I did not know they had decided to go to Bath first."

Aunt Longmore continued to peruse her letter. "Now that Dorothea is betrothed, your grandmother would like us to plan a mid-summer ball at Longmore to celebrate her engagement." She pressed her lips together. "This decision of your grandmother's to travel to Bath has come as something of a surprise to me as well. But it may serve me very well as she can bring Susannah to Longmore with her as she will be leaving her boarding school within the next few days." She pressed a hand to her forehead. "Unfortunately, I cannot leave Longmore while Lady Amelia is staying here. And I cannot send Henrietta to Bath with you as Lady Amelia will be left with no companions of her own age. So if you could accompany Aunt Mildred to Bath, that would be the perfect solution. I have asked Longmore if he can spare you for the next few weeks, and he says he can manage without you."

Abigail nibbled her bottom lip contemplatively. "We *have* made excellent progress with the star chart."

"That is what your uncle told me. So, would you like to travel to Bath, my dear?"

"Yes, indeed. I'd love to spend time with Thea before her wedding."

"That's settled then. I shall speak to your great-aunt, and hopefully, you can leave quite soon."

As her aunt bustled out of the room, Abigail stared blankly after her. Although she was delighted at the prospect of seeing Thea and her grandmother again, she had mixed emotions about leaving Longmore and Lord Rochvale. But perhaps it wasn't such a bad thing to gain some breathing room. At present, she was on tenterhooks as she waited for the announcement of his betrothal. The situation had put her all on edge, and getting away from Longmore Hall for a short spell might be the best thing for her state of mind.

Only a couple of days later, Abigail stepped out of the front door in the direction of the waiting coach. Great-aunt Mildred and Baker were already comfortably ensconced inside, but Abigail had forgotten a book she wanted to take to Bath and had slipped back to the library to retrieve it. She was studying the cover when she walked straight into a hard wall.

"What on . . . !" Looking up, Abigail realized that the hard wall was, in fact, Lord Rochvale's chest. As she met his amused gaze, betraying color rushed to her cheeks. "My lord!"

She took a hasty step back but somehow managed to stumble, and only Lord Rochvale's hands placed firmly on her shoulders prevented her from falling. "Reading while walking, Miss Grantham?" He raised his brows.

"I know. It's a dreadful habit. But I did *not* expect to encounter a boulder in the drive."

"A boulder?" His shoulders shook slightly. "You consider me blockish, my dear?"

"Not in the least. I realized a while ago that your placid demeanor disguises an unusually sharp mind."

His eyes were still alight with laughter. But, after studying her for a moment longer, he glanced at the footman who held the carriage door open for Abigail. "As much as I would like to continue this conversation, I mustn't keep you." He released her shoulders. "I trust you will enjoy your stay in Bath."

"Thank you, Lord Rochvale." Her cheeks still burned, and her breathing was rather shallow. His touch had the most disconcerting effect on her.

"I may see you in Bath in a couple of weeks as I wish to attend a lecture on ancient architectural remains at Westgate buildings." He offered her his arm. "And now, to prevent you from tripping over any more boulders, may I escort you the rest of the way?"

Abigail placed her gloved hand on his coat sleeve and walked silently beside him to the coach. He popped his head into the carriage and had a brief word with Great-aunt Mildred before stepping back. "Have a safe journey, my dear." He bowed. "I hope to see you soon."

Abigail's smile was rather tremulous as she dropped into a curtsy. *I hope to see you soon.* Never had words given her so much joy. She clutched them close to her breast as tendrils of hope unfurled in her chest. Maybe, just maybe, Lord Rochvale cared for her just a little.

They took the journey in easy stages, arriving in Bath at the end of the week. Thea and Grandmama were staying in one of the houses in the Royal Crescent, owned by Alexandra's husband, the Duke of Stanford. Abigail had stayed in the house the previous year when she had spent some time in Bath with Thea and their aunt Eliza, and her gaze rested fondly now on the curved façade of Bath stone, so bright in its whiteness it caused her to blink.

When the carriage came to a stop on the wide road, Abigail waited for Great-aunt Mildred to be helped down from the coach before climbing down herself and crossing to the pavement. As her aunt walked up to the front door, Abigail turned around and gazed at the beautiful lawn, surrounded with iron railings, and the broad gravel walk running beside it, where fashionable people promenaded most days of the week but especially on Sundays during the Season, when the Royal Crescent rivaled Rotten Row in its popularity.

The butler, Chadwick, opened the door and ushered them into the parlor, which contrived to be both cozy and grand at the same time, with its splendid marble fireplace, an inviting rosewood chaise longue, and blue paper hangings.

Abigail's grandmother, Lady Longmore, a handsome lady with elegant white hair, rose to their feet as Abigail and her great-aunt entered the room.

"You're looking very well, my dear! Astronomy appears to agree with you," she said as Abigail bent to kiss her. Patting Abigail's cheek fondly, she turned to her sister-in-law. "How lovely to see you, Mildred! I want to hear all your news."

Thea stepped forward then to greet her great-aunt and Abigail, and after the flurry of greetings, the two older ladies settled down for a comfortable coze near the fireplace while Abigail and Thea sat down on a sofa together.

"How are you, Abby dear?" Thea said.

Abigail shook her head. "Never mind about me, Thea. I want to hear all about your betrothal. Your letters scarcely told me a thing!"

"For good reason." Her sister's voice was somewhat sober. "I didn't want to cause you any anxiety, so I thought it would be best to tell you in person."

Abigail's eyes widened as she studied her sister's gentle face. "This sounds rather serious."

"It was. But fortunately, it all worked out in the end, so you can rest easy." Thea paused for a moment before proceeding to tell Abigail how the silken shawls she had created using chemical processes had been mistaken for imported silk from the Continent, which had resulted in her being targeted by unscrupulous smugglers in London, one of whom had resorted to kidnapping her, with the aim of marrying her to obtain her scientific secret.

"Fortunately, James came to my rescue. But it was a frightening few days on the road to Gretna Green with that villainous Sir Percival Ponsonby."

"Sir Percival actually planned to carry you across the border?" Abigail's mouth was agape.

"He wanted my dowry and planned to take me to France to set me to work there. A dreadful man."

"Oh, my dear. How awful. You must have been terrified."

"It was an awful ordeal, especially as I had no idea if Lord Castleroy would catch up to me in time. But he did, and Grandmama was with him."

"Grandmama braved such a long journey?"

"She said she couldn't bear to stay in London. I suppose after what happened to Alexandra during her Season, she couldn't face the uncertainty again."

Abigail shook her head, feeling quite chilled. During her eldest sister's first Season, Alexandra had become the target of Sir Percival Ponsonby's cousin, Edward Ponsonby, in a similar crime, which resulted in Mr. Ponsonby being forced to leave the country. So it seemed very much like a revenge attack on their family on Sir Percival's part.

Chadwick brought some tea into the room at that moment, which necessitated an end to their conversation, and while Grandmama poured out, Abigail caught up on the rest of the family news; thankfully, none of it as dramatic as Thea's recent experiences.

Abigail took a sip of her tea. "Aunt Longmore tells me she is planning a ball for you at Longmore Hall to celebrate your betrothal to Lord Castleroy."

Her sister smiled. "The whole family will be coming. Having all my nearest and dearest gathered together will be lovely." She hugged her middle, her eyes sparkling, and Abigail was amazed at the change that falling in love had wrought in her older sister. The perpetually guarded expression in her eyes had disappeared, and joy emanated from her now in an almost tangible way.

"You look so happy, Thea. I'm delighted for you."

"It's your turn next, dearest."

"Yes." Abigail's teacup rattled in its saucer. "I suppose it is." Except she had no desire to go to London to find a husband. She had already met the man she wanted to marry in an entirely different setting.

At that moment, the door opened, and her cousin, Susannah, tripped into the room. Small, dainty, and very pretty, Susannah seemed set to take the *ton* by storm as she was to be presented the following year. She embraced her great-aunt before hastening across to Abigail and clasping her hands. "Abby, dearest! I have been champing at the bit to return to Longmore, but Mama only relented recently. I believe she must have tired of all my plaintive letters."

Susannah sat on a chair close to Abigail and proceeded to pepper her with questions about her time at Longmore. "Has Papa been making you work exceedingly hard?"

"Yes. But I've enjoyed the work."

"Well, I'm glad he allowed you to visit Bath! I'm surprised he relented as once he begins a project, he rarely leaves it unfinished."

"Lord Rochvale is there to assist him, although Lord Rochvale did say he wishes to come to Bath next week to attend a lecture."

Susannah pressed her hands together. "Lord Rochvale will be in Bath? Oh, wonderful. He's my favorite person, you know. I always wanted him to marry Hetta, but it wasn't to be. Her heart belongs to another."

Her voice rose as she clasped a hand dramatically to her breast. When Abigail merely stared at her, Susannah continued, "Hasn't Hetta told you about Gerald Burnby?"

When Abigail shook her head, Susannah bit her lip. "Oh, dear. My tongue does tend to run away with me." She glanced at her great-aunt and then lowered her voice. "Mama mentioned in one of her letters that Gerald Burnby had returned to Burnby Place. Has Hetta seen him since his return?"

"Er . . . yes. He's been a regular visitor to Longmore Hall."

"He has? Oh, poor Hetta. Is she in a state?"

"I've noticed that she's a trifle perturbed by Mr. Burnby's presence. She doesn't refuse to see him, though."

"Mmm." Susannah stared off into the distance, her eyes pensive, before looking back at Abigail. "I think that's part of the problem. If she could just tell him off, it might clear the tumult in her breast. For years, she's been repining—ever since he disappeared to London and broke her heart." A scowl marred her smooth brow. "Scoundrel."

Great-aunt Mildred turned to ask Susannah what items she needed to buy to update her wardrobe before her return to Longmore Hall, which set the conversation in quite a different direction. But as the voices swirled around her, Abigail sat quietly, trying to assimilate the news about Mr. Burnby and Henrietta. Suddenly, it all made sense—her cousin's air of tension whenever Mr. Burnby came into their midst and her repeated warnings to Abigail that she needed to guard her heart. Poor Henrietta must have been deeply in love with Mr. Burnby for her hurt to run so deep. And how awful for Henrietta to witness Mr. Burnby's flirtatious behavior around Abigail!

Abigail gave a tiny shake of her head. What a dreadful muddle it all was. Fortunately, Abigail had not succumbed to Mr. Burnby's charm, but Henrietta did not know she was immune to him. No wonder her cousin had been so anxious when Mr.

Burnby spoke about his desire to set Burnby Place in order. If he could break one lady's heart, there was nothing to prevent him from breaking another's, especially as he had barely met Abigail when he had begun spouting about his desire to settle down.

Unless he'd had quite a different person in mind when he spoke about such things? Had he been flirting with Abigail to make Henrietta jealous? Casting her mind back over all their encounters, Abigail realized it was a likely possibility. Perhaps Mr. Burnby regretted leaving Henrietta and wished to win her back.

He had just chosen a truly idiotic way of going about it.

CHAPTER TWENTY-SIX

THE NEXT DAY Lady Longmore took her granddaughters to Milsom Street on a shopping expedition. Thea purchased various silk and lace items for her wedding trousseau while Abigail and Susannah were measured for pelisses by a dressmaker advertising fashions with a distinctly Parisian flair. Next, they stopped at a linen draper to find material for the new gowns Grandmama wished to order for Thea's betrothal ball.

"I'm so looking forward to it," Grandmama said as she examined the beautiful silks the shopkeeper brought for her inspection. "John and Emily have promised to attend, and Alexandra and Stanford have indicated they will be there as well, although they must leave the following day for Stanford Court. A family reunion will be wonderful as it has been an age since we all gathered together."

After Lady Longmore had chosen the fabrics she wanted, they left the linen draper and walked to Green Street, where Grandmama purchased straw hats for Abigail and Susannah before sending the footman who had accompanied them back to the Royal Crescent laden with packages and boxes. She smiled at her granddaughters. "Now let us go on to the Pump Room, my dears. I may even attempt to drink the waters as shopping is thirsty work indeed!"

As they walked along the street, Abigail listened with one ear to her grandmother's conversation while looking around at her surroundings. Bath was a lovely town, with its green spaces and elegant buildings, and its history filled her with delight. Founded sometime during the first century, the Romans had constructed a bathhouse around the famous hot springs, and it always fascinated Abigail to imagine the people who had once bathed in the natural spa and partaken of the healing waters all those centuries ago.

But, although she delighted in so many aspects of this city, she hadn't particularly enjoyed the time she'd spent at the select ladies' seminary she had been sent to here. Her aunt Eliza had grown increasingly concerned about Abigail and Thea's interest in scientific subjects and had suggested to Lady Longmore that a ladies' seminary would provide her nieces with the polish they needed before their presentation to Polite Society. And so Abigail and Thea had left Grantham Place for Miss Mason's establishment in Bath, where they had dutifully attained the various accomplishments required of young ladies who wished to be accepted by the Polite World.

But, although Abigail had submitted to the restraints on her behavior, she had secretly dreamed that one day she would be allowed to follow her passions rather than conform to the narrow expectations of Society. And her time at Longmore Hall had allowed her to do just that in ways she could scarcely have imagined. Her uncle had given her an amazing opportunity to work in the field she loved, while Lord Rochvale had shown her that not all gentlemen expected ladies to conform to the restrictive ideals upheld by the *ton*.

Abigail glanced across the street and stilled when she saw someone who looked very much like Mr. Burnby slipping into a building. She opened her mouth to say something but shut it again when her glance settled on her cousin. Susannah harbored real antipathy toward Mr. Burnby, and it might be awkward if Abigail drew her attention to him. As they drew nearer, she saw that the building Mr. Burnby had entered was the premises of an auctioneer and pawnbroker.

She remained silent, frowning a little as she walked beside her relations to the Pump Room, a spacious chamber constructed above the old Roman baths. However, when she entered the classical building, she set aside her contemplations and looked around with interest. All the world and his wife came here every morning to take the waters, and any student of human behavior would find it interesting to observe the comings and goings of the people assembled here.

Although Bath was a magnet for the old and infirm who sought cures for their various ailments, it also attracted a range of other people, including the more fashionable set, who attended the balls and concerts. However, Bath drew an extremely learned crowd as well who came to the spa town to hear lectures on topics ranging from experimental philosophy to ancient architecture—the exact reason Lord Rochvale was planning to travel to Bath next week.

Abigail hugged the thought of his upcoming visit to herself, amazed at the certainty of her positive regard for the viscount. Somehow in the past few weeks, she had fallen in love with him. She couldn't pinpoint the exact hour it had occurred. All she knew was that she was counting the days until she could see him again.

How had he grown so dear to her within such a short space of time? She shook her head a little, stunned at the all-consuming emotion. Lord Rochvale's kindness, his sense of humor, and his clever mind all contributed to the warm feeling she had for him. But something less tangible had caused her to lose her heart to him—the sense of being so at home in his company that nothing needed to be said; it simply was—like the most unassailable of facts.

She had not expected love to creep up on her in this fashion. Instead, she had envisaged it as some sort of arrow that would pierce her heart in a moment of instant recognition. But this slow knowing, this undeniable esteem . . . it warmed her from within, bound as it was with a frisson of attraction simmering just beneath the surface.

Bringing her mind back to more mundane matters, Abigail looked around the Pump Room, recognizing the faces of a few residents she had encountered in Bath last year when she had stayed here.

However, the rest of the people standing in small clusters or promenading about were unknown to her, and her gaze passed over them before she returned her attention to Susannah and Thea, who were discussing the best way to hem the edge of a shawl.

Grandmama disappeared in the direction of the pump, situated in an alcove at the back of the room, and Abigail was contemplating joining her there when a deep voice spoke in her ear. "Miss Grantham! Charmed to see you."

Abigail turned her head and encountered Mr. Burnby's green gaze. So she hadn't been mistaken earlier! She glanced across at Susannah, whose jaw set firmly in dislike before a mask of hauteur settled over her features.

Her younger cousin dipped into a stiff curtsy as Mr. Burnby murmured a how-do-you-do and bowed.

After introducing him to Thea, Abigail placed her head to one side. "Have you been in Bath for long, sir?"

"I arrived yesterday. A flying visit. Business, you know."

Abigail didn't know, but she forbore to press him further. A constrained silence settled on them until Mr. Burnby said, "I trust Miss Longmore is feeling more the thing, Miss Grantham? A pity she needed to leave the picnic early the other day."

"My cousin recovered quickly enough," Abigail said. "I believe it must have been the heat that made her feel so overcome."

"Indeed." He drew out his snuff box. "That fine weather we have been experiencing has resulted in my renovations at Burnby Place moving along at a faster pace than I anticipated."

"Renovations?" Susannah's eyes rounded. "I thought that London was your primary place of residence, Mr. Burnby."

"The country has been calling to me recently."

"Oh!" The surprise in her cousin's voice was patent.

As Mr. Burnby took a pinch of snuff, Abigail observed his box. A Roman coin of Julius Caesar's profile had been set on the hinged gold lid, and an intricate floral and foliage pattern decorated the border. "What a beautiful snuff box." Abigail studied it more closely. "That coin looks just like one I saw in the museum at Barcombe the other day."

"A pretty piece, is it not? I collect snuff boxes, and this one's a beauty." Mr. Burnby set the objet d'art back into his coat pocket just as Grandmama approached them, holding her glass of water. "Mr. Burnby." She nodded at him before taking a small sip of water.

Studying her grandmother's face, Abigail wasn't sure if her expression indicated distaste for the drink in her hand or for the man standing before her. "I heard from my daughter-in-law that you had returned to Burnby Place. Rusticating, young man?"

He bowed. "Indeed, your ladyship. And enjoying it immensely."

Grandmama narrowed her eyes before questioning him about the state of his grandfather's health. As Abigail contemplated Mr. Burnby's handsome profile, the idea that he had been using her to awaken jealous feelings in Henrietta's breast gathered momentum. One thing that had been puzzling Abigail was why Mr. Burnby had recited that romantic poem to her at the Flintons' masquerade. However, if he had mistaken Abigail for her cousin, it suddenly made a great deal more sense. Abigail's hair had been powered white at the ball, and she was very much the same size and build as Henrietta. It was entirely within the realm of possibility that Mr. Burnby had made a grave error.

For all Abigail knew, he might have inquired at Longmore Hall about what costume Henrietta had chosen to wear that evening. Winnicott was his old nursery maid, after all, and he could easily have obtained the information from her. But as Abigail and Henrietta had changed costumes on the day of the ball, Mr. Burnby may have presented the wrong lady with his floral and poetic tributes.

Abigail stilled. This theory seemed far more credible than the idea that Mr. Burnby had fallen in love with her at first sight. Not that she didn't believe it was possible to experience a *coup de foudre*—she had fallen in love with Lord Rochvale rather quickly herself. But, it *was* unusual to declare oneself so openly while still unsure of the other person's affection.

Mr. Burnby's voice had rung with sincerity when he had recited that poem to her. When he had realized his mistake, he must have gone to Henrietta to set matters to rights. But evidently, he hadn't succeeded.

That must have been why he left the ball early.

All the pieces of the puzzle suddenly fell into place. As Abigail regarded Mr. Burnby now, she hoped that his recent actions meant that he had reformed his way of life. But would he succeed in winning back his lady love? That remained to be seen. As Mr. Burnby bowed and took his leave of them, Abigail contemplated his recent actions in an entirely new light. She wouldn't be surprised if he managed the feat of winning back Henrietta's affections. It was clear that her cousin was not indifferent to him. When she had recognized those Damask roses in Mr. Burnby's garden the other day, she had become physically ill and asked to return home.

Her older cousin's feelings were most definitely engaged. The only unclear thing was whether she would trust Mr. Burnby enough to give him a second chance.

CHAPTER TWENTY-SEVEN

ABIGAIL WAS READING in the drawing room one morning the following week when Chadwick ushered Lord Rochvale inside. Taken by surprise, she set her book to one side and gazed up at him, unable to say a thing for a moment. She was alone as Susannah and Thea had just gone upstairs, and Grandmama and Aunt Eliza were out visiting an old friend who had recently arrived in Bath.

"My lord," Abigail said eventually, rising to her feet. She wanted to stretch out her hands to him in welcome but managed to restrain them at her sides as she sank into a curtsy. "Did you have a good journey to Bath?"

"It was uneventful, which is always a good thing."

He advanced inside, leaving Chadwick hovering uncertainly in the doorway. No doubt, the butler had not expected Abigail to be alone. As a compromise, he left the door open and stood in the hallway.

Abigail waved at a chair. "Pray be seated, my lord." Oh, dear. Why did she sound so formal?

"Thank you." He settled his large frame and looked across at her, a smile playing about his lips.

She cleared her throat. "Have the night skies been clear?"

"Clear enough. We've made good progress, although we miss our trusty assistant. Are you enjoying your stay in Bath?"

"Very much so. Seeing Susannah and spending time with my sister and grandmother has been lovely."

"And how is little Susie?"

"Quite grown up and therefore no longer addressed in the diminutive form," Susannah said as she tripped into the room, her face wreathed in smiles. "Although, on second thought, I'll accept such a form of address from you."

And, unlike Abigail, Susannah stretched out her hands to Lord Rochvale in warm greeting. After sitting across from him on the sofa, the younger girl chattered about her delight at having left school and her excitement at the prospect of Dorothea's upcoming ball. "I received a letter from Mama the other day, and she says I'll be allowed to attend. Isn't that beyond anything? I am so excited at the prospect. Will you be there?"

Lord Rochvale inclined his head. "I received my invitation for the ball before I left for Bath. I have already sent Lady Longmore my note of acceptance."

"Wonderful. Please will you save the first dance for me? I've had lessons with a dancing instructor, but I shan't be confident dancing for the first time in public with a stranger."

He smiled. "Very well."

And as he engaged her cousin in lighthearted conversation, Abigail saw him with fresh eyes. Lord Rochvale was handsome in an understated way, his well-cut clothes fitting his muscular frame perfectly. And although his attitude toward Susannah was somewhat avuncular, he exuded a virility that Abigail hadn't paid much attention to when she had ridiculously placed him in the category of men of her uncle's generation.

But now, as he spoke, his deep voice contrasting starkly with Susannah's light tones, his strength seemed indelibly stamped in his bearing, from the firmness of his jaw to the straight line of his shoulders to the quiet authority of his demeanor, hinting at reigned-in power. How attractive he was! And if Abigail had noticed it, surely other young ladies must be aware of it too? No doubt Lady Amelia, who was on very good terms with him, must appreciate his excellent qualities.

When Abigail had first arrived in Bath, she had lived in daily anticipation of receiving a communication from Longmore Hall announcing the marquess's daughter's betrothal to Lord Rochvale. However, as time had gone by with no word from her aunt or Henrietta, the tension in Abigail had eased as it seemed more and more likely that no such announcement would be made. Because surely, if they had entered into an engagement, it would have been declared to the world by now?

A lull in the conversation brought Lord Rochvale's attention back to Abigail. "Your uncle has entrusted me with discovering the exact date you will return to Longmore Hall. He won't ask your aunt to find out as she believes he has monopolized your attention enough and that you should be free to engage in the activities that other young ladies enjoy. But he begged me to make some inquiries while I am here."

Abigail opened her mouth and then shut it again, a mangled feeling of pain slicing through her at the realization that Lord Rochvale had called on her not for the pleasure of her company but at her uncle's behest. Perhaps something of her dismay showed in her face as a shadow of concern crossed Lord Rochvale's face as he considered her. However, Abigail pushed her turmoil aside and replied politely that her grandmother had not yet decided on the date she wished to leave Bath. "Although she seems set on remaining here for the next fortnight at least."

"Ah. Well, I trust she will decide to leave sooner rather than later." He paused. "You see, it isn't only your uncle who wishes for your return."

The look in his eyes was unmistakably warm, and a ray of sunshine seemed to emerge from behind a cloud. "I'm eager to return, my lord," she murmured. "I miss my work . . . and . . . and my fellow astronomers."

She flushed, looking down at her tightly entwined fingers. That was the best she could do. She couldn't tell Lord Rochvale directly that she had been pining for him. But lumping him together with her uncle in this way might give him some sort of idea about the nature of her regard for him.

Her grandmother and great-aunt entered the room then, and Thea came downstairs a short while later. The clamor of conversation that ensued was so voluble that Abigail wasn't surprised when Lord Rochvale rose from his chair a short time later and departed.

"How long will Lord Rochvale be in town?" Grandmama asked after he had left.

Abigail lifted her shoulders. "He didn't say. Although I imagine he won't wish to stay here too long as Uncle Longmore needs his help. We work in pairs on our star chart, you see, and with both of us gone, Uncle Longmore won't be able to get nearly as much work done."

Grandmama shook her head. "Once your uncle has fixed his mind on something, he is unflagging in his endeavors. Is there anyone else who understands astronomy who could assist him?"

"Sir Reginald Markham might have been able to help him, but he left for London before I came to Bath."

Her grandmother pressed her lips together. "Your aunt mentioned that to me in one of her letters. Odd that he's developed this bee in his bonnet about traveling to the polar region. It's quite bizarre the lengths some men will go to just to avoid matrimony! But they mostly settle down after a while, even if some only do so because Society and their families expect it of them."

"Perhaps Sir Reginald does wish to marry, but only once he has returned from his expedition," Abigail said.

"That would be more comprehensible if Lady Amelia were a young woman. But she is not. She is nearly thirty, and understandably, she wishes to marry now. Her mother, Lady Hythe, is most put out at Sir Reginald's recalcitrance. It is too bad of him, particularly as he raised Lady Amelia's expectations by paying her such marked attention." She released a sigh. "But that is the price of loving a sailor. They're restless by nature. It would serve him quite right if Lady Amelia sought consolation elsewhere."

"Well, maybe she will," Susannah said. "She has always been on the best of terms with Lord Rochvale."

"So Lady Hythe said. But no man likes the idea of being someone's second choice. But we shall see which way the wind is blowing soon enough, I suppose."

The conversation turned then to yet more discussion about Thea's betrothal ball. Abigail allowed the conversation to swirl around her head as her thoughts raced in one direction and then another. How disconcerting that so many people had expressed the possibility of Lord Rochvale marrying Lady Amelia. The complacency Abigail had begun to feel due to the lack of news emanating from Longmore Hall rapidly dissipated as a cold and lonely feeling settled in the region of her heart.

Looking back over her encounters with Lord Rochvale, he appeared to harbor a genuine fondness for Abigail. And, although his gentlemanly behavior could never be faulted, she had discerned an expression in his eyes on a few occasions that had stopped her breath. But could she be reading too much into those incidents? A momentary flare of attraction was not the same as love, and from her limited experience, most men exhibited some degree of warmth in the presence of young ladies. It appeared to be as natural to them as breathing.

Mr. Burnby was a case in point. Although Abigail was now convinced that he was in love with Henrietta, it hadn't stopped him from flirting with Abigail, even though he had no doubt done so to provoke a reaction from Henrietta. The games that potential lovers played in the complicated dance of courtship were often unconscious and quite primitive, and Abigail did not wish to ascribe more profound meaning to any of her interactions with Lord Rochvale when they might have been meant very little to him.

Yet somehow, she couldn't shake the idea that he might care for her—it was like a deep knowing engraved in the center of her heart, just waiting to be reached . . . if only she could traverse those *misleading, confusing, perplexing ways of true-false choices in a winding maze.*

CHAPTER TWENTY-EIGHT

A T THE PUMP Room the next day, Abigail encountered both Lord Rochvale and Mr. Burnby. Mr. Burnby caught her alone as Susannah and Thea had gone off to listen to the musicians playing in the gallery while Grandmama sought out her daily dose of water from the ever-dispensing pump.

Mr. Burnby offered to fetch Abigail a glass of the water for herself, and she was just informing him that she wasn't particularly fond of its metallic taste when Lord Rochvale approached, his brows slightly raised. "Good morning, Miss Grantham." He turned to his cousin. "What a surprise to see you here. Gerald. I thought you disliked Bath."

"I do, in general. But certain . . . business draws me here."

"Ah." Lord Rochvale's gaze was contemplative. "I see. How long do you plan to stay?"

"Not long. My business will be concluded soon enough. I've never been one to linger over things, as you know."

"You'll be returning to Burnby Place after this business is completed?"

"Yes, dear coz. My improvements to my home have made the place quite habitable. Indeed, it is quite a desirable residence these days. I must take you on a tour." He looked across at Abigail. "I must take you *both* on a tour."

When Lord Rochvale remained silent, Abigail said in a stilted voice, "That sounds delightful, Mr. Burnby."

He gave her his flashing smile. "If you'll bring Miss Longmore along, that should round off the party nicely."

Abigail smiled, relieved. "I shall suggest the plan to her when I return to Longmore."

"Do you know when that will be?" Mr. Burnby's bland expression did not mask the bright inquiry in his eyes.

"Not as yet. But we'll probably leave quite soon. Grandmama wishes to assist my aunt with planning my sister's betrothal ball in early July."

He bowed his head. "Ah, yes. I received my invitation a few days ago. I hope you will save a dance for me."

"If you stay long enough this time, of course, I will," she replied gently.

Although Mr. Burnby's smile did not shift, his gaze was alert. But before he could respond, Susannah and Thea returned, and after a few minutes of lively conversation, he took his leave.

Lord Rochvale studied Mr. Burnby's retreating back, his brow slightly furrowed. However, when Susannah asked him about his plans for the rest of the day, he collected himself and gave her his full attention. But, although he answered her politely enough, it seemed to Abigail that he was miles away.

He left a short while later, and Abigail sighed. She desperately wanted to speak frankly to him, but decorum dictated that a gentleman approach a lady with a declaration of love—not the other way around. She needed to wait for him to address her, even though it went very much against the grain with her to sit idly by in this passive way.

Her thoughts turned to Mr. Burnby. His inclusion of Henrietta in his invitation to tour Burnby Place helped confirm Abigail's suspicion that her cousin was indeed the object of his affections. How wonderful it would be if they could sort out their differences! Although Mr. Burnby might have had a wild past, he definitely seemed to have turned over a new leaf, as indeed he had once stated.

And although Mr. Burnby could be classified as a dangerous flirt, he had appeared most sincere when he had recited that poem at the masquerade ball, showing a heretofore unglimpsed part of his character.

Her belief that Mr. Burnby might be a good match for her cousin in spite of his past bad behavior was also based on something her grandmother had said last year when she was discussing Abigail and Thea's upcoming presentations with them. Grandmama had advised her granddaughters to beware of very young suitors, as youthful gentlemen often delayed marriage indefinitely. "Indeed, my dears, if they happen to meet their ideal woman while in an immature frame of mind, it is unlikely they will take the plunge into matrimony no matter how much they might care for her. Only once a man feels ready to offer his hand will he start to look about him more seriously for a wife. Men don't necessarily marry when they meet the right person. They marry when they determine the time is the right."

Her grandmother's pronouncement had seemed a little strange to Abigail at the time. Surely once a gentleman fell in love, he would wish to commit himself fully to his beloved. How could he not? But, when Abigail had put the question to her, the older lady had shaken her head. "Remember, Abigail, that while a woman tends to gain security when she marries, a man must consider whether he can provide for both her and any children they might have. Such responsibilities weigh heavily and can be burdensome for immature shoulders. That is why a young man may not offer for a lady he has paid court to even though he might be deeply in love with her. It is, therefore, wiser to consider the suit of a more mature gentleman who is ready to put down roots."

Sadly, that might also be why Sir Reginald had failed to offer for Lady Amelia. Although he appeared to be in love with her, the burden of marriage might be too heavy for him to bear while he still had a strong desire to explore the world. And while the baronet was of a reasonably mature age, he might still be at a stage in his life where he did not feel able to commit to the duties of a husband.

Thank goodness Lord Rochvale offered more stability! Abigail bit her lip when she remembered how indignant she had been when Aunt Longmore had informed her that Grandmama wished Abigail to marry a sensible man. How dreary it had sounded back then! But Abigail had since learned that being sensible did not necessarily equate with being dull. She would be delighted to throw her lot in with such a man now. If only he would ask her!

It dawned on her then that even if Lord Rochvale wanted her for his wife, he could not request her hand in marriage until he had received permission from John, her legal guardian. Of course, he could also speak to Grandmama, but her brother would be the correct person to approach should the viscount wish to offer for her.

Abigail straightened her shoulders, suddenly feeling better. John would be coming to Longmore Hall for Thea's engagement ball, which would provide the perfect opportunity for Lord Rochvale to speak to him. What Abigail needed to do in the interim was make it crystal clear to her beloved that she would be open to receiving his addresses. She wasn't quite sure how to go about it without appearing shockingly forward, but perhaps she could show him in a subtle way that she had fallen in love with him.

She pressed her lips together a little doubtfully. This sort of discreet behavior did not come naturally to her—not when she wanted to shout her love for Lord Rochvale from the rooftops. But she needed to take care. After all, she was in a somewhat precarious position as Lord Rochvale might still believe that his cousin was pursuing her. Henrietta had hinted as much in his presence, and Mr. Burnby's frequent visits to Longmore Hall could easily be misinterpreted.

Lord Rochvale probably did not know that Mr. Burnby's interest lay in quite a different direction. Therefore, it was up to

Abigail to make it clear to him that Mr. Burnby held no attraction for her while steering that gentleman firmly in Henrietta's direction.

Abigail set her jaw. She had some serious work to do when she returned to Longmore Hall. If only she could leave for Buckinghamshire when Lord Rochvale departed Bath! At this very moment, Lady Amelia could be weighing up the benefits of marrying her old friend after Sir Reginald's defection.

However, Abigail could only twirl her thumbs until her grandmother was ready to quit the spa city. And that might not be for a few weeks as Lady Longmore appeared to be having a wonderful time in Bath, visiting her old friends and drinking those dreadful waters every morning.

Grandmama didn't know that Abigail was eager to return to Longmore Hall for reasons of the heart. And she couldn't very well proclaim her wishes to her grandparent as they were based primarily on hope and not on any formal declaration on Lord Rochvale's part. Grandmama would not encourage Abigail to blatantly set her cap at the viscount, as to do so would be unladylike in the extreme.

So Abigail was stuck in Bath for the moment, unable to act. How frustrating it was to be a young woman in Society! If only she could hire a chaise-and-four and speed back to Longmore Hall to fight for her beloved. Instead, she needed to wait patiently, biding her time while hiding the fact that her heart was poised on the edge of a cliff, over which it could topple at any moment and shatter into a million pieces.

CHAPTER TWENTY-NINE

WHEN WILLIAM ENTERED the room where the lecture was to take place at Westgate Buildings, he surveyed the space with his quizzing glass before taking a chair in the first row so he would have ample room to stretch out his legs in front of him. Mr. Wood's talk was due to start at 7:30 pm, and according to the leaflet he had received at the door, he would be lecturing on "illustrations of History, exemplified by drawings of the remains of ancient architecture."

William glanced idly around the room to see if he knew anyone. He was nodding at a man he vaguely recognized seated in the back row when someone tapped his shoulder. "Fancy seeing you here, Rochvale."

He shifted in his seat. "Gerald! You're attending the lecture?"

His cousin took the chair beside him. "I'm not a complete ignoramus, you know."

"I never said you were."

"You didn't need to." His cousin studied the point of his highly polished shoe. "It's all in the lift of that cursed eyebrow of yours."

"Then it is most uncivil. My apologies," he said gravely.

"Ho!" Gerald half-smiled. "You always were bookish, William. I never could understand it growing up. But of late, I've developed an interest in ancient history. So here I am."

The room was filling up quickly now, and the lecturer, who had been conversing with Lord Blenton in the corner, walked to the front and stood behind a table, greeting everyone formally.

As a hush settled over the room, Mr. Wood gave a brief history of the Roman foundations of Bath, showing a series of illustrations of how the city appeared all those centuries ago, before concluding: "As you can see, the Roman influence on Bath has lent it a distinct air of grace. And even now, so many years later, that influence lingers. As the town developed and the foundations for new buildings were dug, numerous ruins were unearthed as well as evidence of great art and culture."

He surveyed the room. "Even today we occasionally find coins engraved with the heads of such lofty personages as Nero, Antoninus, Adrian, Trajan, and other great figures from ancient history. And magnificent pieces of sculpture such as the well-preserved bronze head of a statue of either Apollo or Minerva—we're still uncertain which one—have also been uncovered. Other artifacts draw interest from both casual observers and historians alike, particularly several crudely carved coffins constructed of stone and a sepulchral altar in near-perfect condition unearthed in Sidney Place in 1793." He paused. "Naturally, in order to preserve such treasures for posterity, the Corporation houses them in a secure building. This museum is in Bath Street, and I encourage you to visit it."

He bowed in response to a round of applause and walked off, a sheaf of papers held under his arm.

Gerald rose to his feet. "Well, William, I must be off. I just want a word first with Mr. Wood. A very interesting lecture, wasn't it? It's quite piqued my interest in the subject. When do you return to Barcombe?"

"Within the next few days."

"Hmm." His cousin regarded him with a speculative gleam in his eye. "Rumor has it that a betrothal is on the cards for you and Lady Amelia. But I've my doubts. I suspect your interest lies in an entirely different direction."

William raised his cursed brow. "Indeed?"

Gerald shook his head. "Miss Grantham is just as clever as you. She'll suit you admirably."

William remained silent for a moment and then broke into a smile. "So you're no longer pursuing her?"

"I never was."

"What about all this talk of yours about settling down?"

"I am planning on settling down. Just not with Miss Grantham."

"It's Henrietta?"

Gerald heaved a sigh. "It's always been Henrietta. But I wasn't in a position to marry her before."

William drew his brows together. "I suppose your luck's turned at the tables?"

His cousin bent his head. "Let's just say that my luck has turned."

William was about to question Gerald further when Lord Blenton approached, requesting him to value an item he had recently purchased from an antiquities dealer in London. William offered to stop at the older man's house in the Crescent the following day to look at it. With a word of thanks, he walked off, but Gerald had moved away by then.

Before making for the door, William had a final look around the room and spotted his cousin conversing with Mr. Wood. He frowned as he turned away. Gerald had effected considerable changes in his life—furthering his classical education and now contemplating marriage. But he had his work cut out for him if he wished to win back Henrietta. Although his sister's friend had never mentioned her failed love affair, William had witnessed her starry-eyed fervor for Gerald and the slow dousing of that light when his cousin had left for London all those years ago.

As he stepped outside, a weight fell off his shoulders at the realization that the field was now clear for him to pay his addresses to Abigail. Although he had long since concluded that Abigail had no real interest in his cousin, Gerald's mischievous presence had been a complication he could well do without.

The only dark spot on the horizon was how his cousin had contrived to make enough blunt to set Burnby Place in order. It was entirely possible he might call on William to bail him out of financial difficulties in the near future. At the gambling tables, vast fortunes could exchange hands with the mere throw of the dice. And that was no doubt how Gerald had come into his fortune.

William tightened his jaw. Hopefully, he wouldn't lose it again just as quickly.

CHAPTER THIRTY

ABIGAIL RELEASED A happy sigh as the carriage turned onto the road that led to Longmore Hall. Finally, they were here, and she was counting the hours until she could see Lord Rochvale again. A reminiscent smile settled on Abigail's lips as she remembered the night she had met him on this very road when she had noticed the zodiacal light—that false dusk had ultimately led to the truest of loves.

How long ago that now seemed, but it was, in fact, only a few short months ago. Amazing how life could carry on in the same staid manner for years and years, and then one day, something might happen, and it would never be the same again. That something for her had been twofold—meeting Lord Rochvale and being allowed to pursue her passion for astronomy at Longmore Hall.

Abigail had missed her work so much since she had been in Bath. A sense of guilt assailed her as the coach drew up in front of the house. What she had thought would be a brief trip to Bath had turned into a month-long expedition. At times, Abigail had felt as if she had traveled to the polar region herself, so far had she felt from Longmore Hall during her sojourn in the spa city. But now she was back, and soon she would resume her observations.

And she would see Lord Rochvale again. Somehow, somehow, she would ensure that she managed to show him what was in her heart.

A footman let down the step, and Grandmama climbed down from the carriage, followed by Susannah and Abigail. Great-aunt Mildred and Thea were following in another carriage and should be arriving soon.

Instead of hastening after her relations to the front door, Abigail paused and looked up at the sky, allowing the sun to settle on her skin, warming her with the lightest of kisses. She closed her eyes, imagining her reunion with Lord Rochvale and how she could show him without words that she loved him.

She released her breath in another joyous sigh and smiled at Davison as he wished her good afternoon. After handing him her outdoor things, she made her way to the drawing room, where she could hear a clamor of voices.

When she stepped inside, Henrietta hastened across to her side. "Abby, dear, how lovely to see you! We have missed you so." She pressed her lips together. "Although, on balance, I suspect Papa will insist that he's missed you the most. He has complained nearly every day since your departure, saying it has made his job much harder."

Abigail pressed her cousin's hands. "But Lord Rochvale has been helping him, has he not?"

"Lord Rochvale's had other pressing concerns. Quite a lot has happened since your departure. I . . ."

Henrietta broke off as their grandmother's voice drifted across to them. "Betrothed, Margaret? When did this happen? Lady Hythe will be delighted. I must write to her at once."

Abigail raised her brows. "Who is betrothed?"

Henrietta shook her head. "Such news cannot be kept a secret for long. I am sure it will be around London within the week. Lady Amelia announced her betrothal a few days ago and returned to Hythe Place this morning to plan her wedding."

Abigail stared at her cousin. "Lady Amelia's betrothed?"

"Yes. It's the most wondrous thing. I've never seen her so happy."

Uncle Longmore strode into the room at that moment. "Thank heavens you're back, Abigail. With Rochvale so caught up in his own affairs these days, I'm making slow progress on our star chart."

A feeling of dread settled in the pit of Abigail's stomach. "Good morning, Uncle. Lord Rochvale cannot assist you anymore?"

"Not at present. But I suppose it's understandable considering the circumstances."

Abigail opened her mouth and then shut it. "If you would excuse me, sir, I need to retire to my bedchamber."

"Yes, of course, niece. You've just arrived, have you not?"

She nodded as she turned away. Hastening toward the door, she slipped through the breakfast room next door and out into the hall. She had just set foot on the first step of the staircase when the front door opened behind her. Spinning around, she froze as she met Lord Rochvale's gaze.

"My lord!"

"Good morning, Miss Grantham. I thought you might be back when I saw the coach outside. I trust you had a good journey?"

"I did, thank you."

Abigail stared at him for a moment, quite at a loss for words. Eventually, she placed her hands behind her back, all the better to wring them out of sight. "I've just heard your news, my lord. I . . . I wish you very happy."

A look of faint surprise crossed his face. "Er . . . thank you."

"I gather you'll be too busy now to continue work on the star chart."

"I hope to return to the project at a later date, of course, but I am not in a position to practice astronomy right now."

"Yes." Her voice rose slightly. "Seeing as how your time is otherwise engaged." She winced at her unintentional pun. "Or rather—*engaged*." Oh, dear. Even worse.

"Yes, indeed. Although I'm still assessing some items for your aunt, hence my presence here today." He studied her for a moment, a faint line between his brows. "Are you quite well, my dear? You seem rather feverish."

"I'm . . . I need to retire to my bedchamber."

A look of understanding crossed his face. "Ah, yes, of course. Let me not keep you."

Abigail hurried up the stairs, her heart pounding in time with every step she took. When she reached her room, she closed the door behind her, pressing her hands against the wooden panel for one agonized moment before kneeling in front of the bed and resting her elbows on the mattress.

Her worst nightmare had come true, and she could do nothing about it. Once a betrothal was announced, it was considered almost as binding as a marriage.

Lord Rochvale was lost to her forever.

Tears streamed down her face as she bowed her head, allowing them to fall unchecked onto the counterpane. She had spent so many hours in this pose, mourning first her mother and then her father. And now, the familiarity of sorrow stole over her again. Except it wasn't a physical death she lamented this time. Rather, it was the demise of her hopes and dreams, which in some ways, was even worse, as the bleakness of a life without Lord Rochvale in it stretched endlessly before her, depressing as a dirge.

She was like that carving of the girl in St Mary's Church, bent over in perpetual grief, joy seeping out of her like lifeblood from a wound, destined always to lose those she loved. She raised her head. How unfair it was! Lord Rochvale wasn't even Lady Amelia's first choice. She had merely chosen him as a husband because her true love had gone away.

If only Abigail had discovered in time that she loved him. But she hadn't. And she suspected, on some level, that she hadn't wanted to. She had enjoyed skimming along the surface, removing the cream from the top while avoiding deep feeling.

And no matter how much she tried to convince herself that

the timing of her realization had merely been off, the truth was that she had been willfully ignorant, frightened of the power of her emotions. She had deliberately avoided examining them, hoping to circumvent anything that could recreate the depth of grief she had experienced upon her parents' deaths.

And so, she had put her head down, grazing in green pastures where starlight always shone, casting its glow upon everything in its path, and no harsh reality ever needed to be confronted.

But she needed to face it now. And the stark outline of this landscape, a landscape without Lord Rochvale in it, was utterly cold and colorless.

Yet somehow, she needed to survive in it. Abigail held her head in her hands and exhaled slowly.

She had risen from the ashes twice before. Could she do it again?

CHAPTER THIRTY-ONE

WHEN ABIGAIL WENT downstairs a few hours later, Lord Rochvale had left, and only Aunt Longmore and Henrietta were in the drawing room. Abigail sat on the sofa beside her cousin and folded her hands neatly on her lap. Somehow she had to endure hearing about Lady Amelia and Lord Rochvale's betrothal. Probably best to face it sooner rather than later. But it was still a horrible ordeal.

Henrietta smiled at her. "Did you enjoy your time in Bath, Abby? You disappeared so quickly earlier that I didn't have the chance to find out."

"I did, thank you. Grandmama ordered me loads of new gowns in preparation for my Season next year. I didn't fully grasp until recently what a vast wardrobe a London Season requires."

"Indeed. It's fatiguing just thinking about it."

"I believe you saw Gerald Burnby when you were in Bath?" her aunt said. "He called on us when he returned, but we've seen neither hide nor hair of him since. Rumor has it that he's gone up to London again."

"I saw both Mr. Burnby and Lord Rochvale when I was in Bath."

Her aunt's eyes narrowed. "I shall be surprised if you arrive in London heart-whole, my dear, what with all the gentlemen falling at your feet as they have. It was as I predicted. Since the

Flintons' ball, you are the belle of the district. We received a number of invitations requesting your presence at various events when you were away."

Henrietta gazed at her intently. "So are you still heart-whole, Abby?"

Her cousin's color was a little high, and Abigail suspected she might still believe Mr. Burnby was pursuing her. How to set her mind at rest? "I am certainly not contemplating matrimony with anyone," she said carefully.

"You aren't?"

Abigail shook her head. "I doubt I shall ever marry."

"Don't be ridiculous, Abigail." Her aunt's tone was a little sharp. "Of course you will marry. You just haven't met the right gentleman yet. I confess I had high hopes in one direction, but there . . ." She sighed. "One cannot love to order."

The door opened then, and Davison ushered Mr. Burnby into the room. He sat in an armchair beside Aunt Longmore and spoke about his recent trip to London before turning to Abigail. "Will you walk a little way with me in the gardens, Miss Grantham? I have recently become interested in classical civilizations, and I'd like to ask you something."

She blinked. "I'm no expert on the subject, sir. Lord Rochvale would be a better person to ask."

"But I would prefer to ask you." His smile was cajoling.

Abigail looked at her aunt. "I'm not sure . . ."

"You may go, Abigail. I always encourage the expansion of knowledge in young minds. Especially in minds which have not previously been inclined in that direction." Aunt Longmore gave Mr. Burnby an old-fashioned look, which he blithely ignored as he rose to his feet.

Abigail compressed her lips, dismayed at Mr. Burnby's timing. Now Henrietta would be even more convinced that he was in pursuit of her. But she couldn't easily say no, so she stood, accepted his proffered arm, and allowed him to lead her outside.

They traversed the lawns in silence for a while before Mr.

Burnby stopped and turned. "Miss Grantham, I'm afraid I'm in a spot of trouble, and I was hoping you could assist me."

"So you don't wish to speak to me about classical civilizations?"

"This spot of trouble relates to one *particular* classical civilization, so I did not draw you away mendaciously."

"I'm all at sea, sir."

"I shall explain. But first, I would like your promise that you will keep my confidence."

Seeing the earnest expression on his face, Abigail suspected he might wish to confide in her about his feelings for Henrietta, so with a smiling nod, she acquiesced.

"Thank you." He remained silent for a moment before saying, "A few months ago, I came across some Roman artifacts at Burnby Place. I believed they were valuable, but as I didn't wish to leave Bucks at the time, I entrusted the items to my old nursery maid."

"Annie Winnicott? But what does she know about ancient artifacts?"

"Very little. But her brother, Tom, works for an antiquities dealer in London. She told me about Tom's occupation a few years ago as she is very proud that her brother has done so well for himself. I obtained the name of the dealer from Annie, and after I confirmed his credentials with Rochvale, I wrote to him. He suggested I hand over the artifacts to Tom, who was planning a trip home to see his ailing mother who lives retired on the Barcombe estate. Tom planned to take the artifacts to Town with him. But, his journey was postponed, so Annie stored the artifacts, which included two Roman urns, in the attic opposite her bedchamber. However, Lady Longmore came across one of the urns one day . . . and you know what transpired next."

Abigail gazed at him. "*Winnicott* took it from the butler's pantry?"

He nodded. "I overheard your aunt asking Rochvale to examine some family heirlooms, including a marble urn she'd found in the attic. I was concerned it might be one of my urns, so I asked Annie to see if it had been placed in the butler's pantry and to take it along with my other Roman artifacts to the Barcombe Maze and set them in the hedge embrasures, where her brother could then collect them without drawing too much attention."

When Abigail said nothing, he went on, "However, when I made my request to Annie, I did not know that Rochvale had already examined the urn and informed Lady Longmore that it was of great value." He walked on with his hands behind his back, staring straight ahead.

"Because of what Rochvale said, a huge furor was created that neither Annie nor I expected. She had only managed to get the urn and its twin as far as the Italian garden—they are a bit heavy—but the hope was that they would blend in with the other garden ornaments until such a time as Tom could collect them there or I could take them on to the maze. But then the Bow Street Runner arrived, and Annie took fright and returned the urn to the butler's pantry. After he left, she took the second urn back to the attic and told me she had washed her hands of the whole affair."

"With good reason, Mr. Burnby. I have never heard such a crazy tale! But why all the secrecy?"

He shot her a quick glance. "When I inherited Burnby Place, it was in a poor financial state. I did not wish to be bothered with responsibilities at that age, so I made no effort to maintain it, preferring to live in London." He cleared his throat. "I had fallen in love with Henrietta, but I had no desire to settle down. And so I left." He paused. "However, I couldn't put her from my mind. And when I returned to visit my grandfather recently, I realized I never would." He fell silent once again. "When I . . . stumbled across the Roman artifacts, I devised a plan to sell them so that I would be able to set my estate in order and offer for Henrietta. But things have gone slightly awry." His mouth twisted ruefully.

"Why didn't you tell Lord Rochvale and your grandfather about the artifacts? Surely it would have been better to approach them?"

"They would have wanted to place them in that dashed museum of theirs instead of selling them. So, I thought it would be best to go my own way. It's easy enough to be high-minded about preserving history when you've a lot of blunt at your disposal. Not so much when the readies have run out."

"I see." Abigail furrowed her brow. "Though I don't understand how I can be of any help to you, sir."

"I have lost both my Roman urns and cannot claim them without involving Annie. She'd lose her job and reputation, and I cannot allow that. But there is one more artifact that Annie stored for me in the attic which I hope you'll retrieve for me—a bronze statue of Venus. I consulted with a dealer in Bath about it the other day, and he says it should fetch a fair price."

"So that's why you went into that antiquities shop in Green Street!"

Mr. Burnby stiffened. "You saw me?"

"I was walking to the Pump Room when I noticed you across the street."

"You never mentioned it."

"I was with Susannah."

"Ah." He remained silent for a while. "Well, that dealer offered to buy it from me. It's locked away in an old chest under a mattress in the corner of the attic, so thankfully, it was missed during that initial search." He took a key out of his pocket. "Would you be so kind as to retrieve it for me?"

Abigail widened her eyes. "You're very confident that I will keep your secret, Mr. Burnby."

The corners of his mouth turned up. "Some people radiate trustworthiness, Miss Grantham. You are one of them. And you have sympathetic eyes."

"You didn't think to approach Henrietta?"

He stretched out his hands. "Every attempt I've made to speak to her thus far has ended in disaster. I tried to declare myself to her at the Flintons' ball but only succeeded in driving her further away."

"You mistook me for her."

His brows flew up. "You guessed?"

"It's the only explanation that makes any sense."

He tapped the key against his palm. "Yes. Well, Annie told me what Henrietta planned to wear that night, but you swapped costumes. I made a dashed fool of myself in the end." His tone was slightly accusatory.

Abigail smiled weakly. "I suppose the course of true love never did run smooth."

"Ho! Never a truer word was said."

They walked on in silence for a few minutes before Abigail stopped. "Very well, sir. I will help you. Where must I put the statue?"

"You're an angel, Miss Grantham. If you would place it in the Italian garden, I'll look for it there."

She accepted the key from him before saying briskly, "We had better head back if you don't want Henrietta to imagine that you are proposing marriage to me. You haven't done your case any good, Mr. Burnby, by flirting with me in front of her. She is convinced that you are pursuing me."

"I hoped to make her jealous."

"A very foolish strategy, if I may say so."

"Yes." He frowned at the ground. "I realized that too late."

When they returned to the house, Abigail bid Mr. Burnby goodbye before walking to the staircase. Now was as good a time as any to search for that statue. When she reached the corridor that led to the attics, she looked around. The coast was blessedly clear. Stealing down the passage, she opened the attic door before closing it swiftly behind her. Then, walking to the corner, she leaned over and shifted the mattress off the chest. Removing the key from her reticule, Abigail was about to set it in the lock when the door creaked open. Dropping the key, she spun around.

"Miss Grantham?" Lord Rochvale came closer. "I was in the Gallery when I saw you slip past."

"Oh!" What poor luck. Abigail lowered her gaze and spotted the key lying on the floor. Taking a tiny step forward, she covered it with her slippered foot. That should keep it out of sight. "Lord Rochvale! How do you do?" How ridiculously formal she sounded.

His grey eyes surveyed her, and her cheeks warmed. No doubt guilt was stamped all over her face. As a child, whenever their governess had confronted the Grantham children about any misdemeanor, Abigail was always singled out as the guilty party. She just had one of those faces. And even when she was perfectly innocent, she had somehow always *felt* as if she were the one who had sinned. And now that she truly *was* guilty, she could only imagine her expression of shame.

Lord Rochvale shut the door and came over to her. "Is anything the matter?"

Abigail shook her head. "Nothing!" Her voice came out as a squeak. "I was just . . . checking on something."

He set his hands on her shoulders, searching her face. "You seem perturbed."

"In-indeed?" She stared fiercely at his chest, suddenly perturbed in quite a different manner. And then, raising her head, she melted into his gaze.

CHAPTER THIRTY-TWO

WILLIAM STUDIED ABIGAIL'S flushed face. He shouldn't, he really shouldn't . . . but he couldn't resist. Not anymore. Her hair was coming loose, a few curls brushing her cheeks. He tucked them behind her ears as he lowered his head, his lips mere inches from hers. The faint scent of roses drifted up to him as her eyes met his for an endless moment. And then he kissed her.

Her lips were soft and yielding, and his hands tangled in her hair, drawing her ever closer. A current sparked between them, electrifying in intensity, and he deepened the kiss, unwilling to draw back, tasting the sweetness of her mouth.

He must stop. He needed to stop.

But it was Abigail who pulled away first, her eyes huge in her white face. "We mustn't, my lord. We cannot. Lady Amelia!"

"Lady Amelia?" He frowned as he looked over his shoulder to see if she were there. But the door remained closed. He returned his gaze to Abigail. "What of her, sweetheart?"

"What of her?" She stepped back. "You dare to ask that, my lord?" And with a heaving breath, she placed a hand over her mouth and fled, wrenching the door open.

William stretched out a hand and then hastened after her. "Abby!"

But she didn't stop, and he stared at her retreating form disappearing through the attic door, his brows drawn together. Why had she mentioned Amelia? It made no sense unless the rumors circulating in the village about a possible engagement between them had come to her ears. But Amelia's recent betrothal to Sir Reginald, when he returned to Bucks a few days ago, should have put an end to all those murmurings.

Unless Abigail had yet to hear the news? She had just arrived at Longmore Hall, after all. He walked over to an attic window and stared outside. When he had seen Abigail earlier, she had wished him very happy. Which meant . . . she must believe that *he* was to marry Lady Amelia.

What a damnable muddle! And now she was upset because she thought he had kissed her while engaged to another woman. He sighed. Abigail would discover her mistake soon enough, but it was a complication he could well do without. Especially at this stage of his courtship.

He turned around, and his gaze fell on a key on the floor near a mattress on the far side of the attic. Bending down, he picked it up and looked around the small space, noticing the chest beside the mattress had a lock on it. Had Abigail been trying to open it? With a slight shrug, he shoved the key inside, turning it easily.

Lifting up the lid, he frowned a little as he pulled out a small bronze statue. He examined it carefully before placing it back in the chest and locking it again. If he weren't mistaken, the statue was yet another Roman artifact. How odd that three such items had been discovered up here in such a short space of time. And it looked as though Abigail had been searching for it. She'd appeared dismayed and almost guilty when he'd walked inside, although he didn't quite understand what she had to be guilty about.

He pocketed the key and left the room. Abigail had most likely dropped it, and returning it to her would provide him with an excellent excuse to seek her out again. And he wanted to find her as soon as he could to advise her about Lady Amelia's betrothal to the baronet.

However, when he went downstairs to the drawing room,

the ladies had gone. "Have you seen Miss Grantham?" William asked Davison when he went back to the hall.

"Miss Grantham and Mr. Burnby met in the hall a few minutes ago, my lord, and went outside.

"Ah, excellent. Thank you, Davison. Did you see in which direction they went?"

"I believe they walked toward the Italian garden, my lord."

William nodded and set out after them, heading to the enclosure, which had an orangery serving as one of its walls. As he stepped into the peaceful retreat, he saw Gerald and Abigail on the far side, at the foot of a stairway, with statues on each step, leading up to a fountain supported by the arms of four stone Cupids.

Gerald was pointing at one of the statues when William came up to them. And for the second time that day, Abigail looked like a ghost when she turned to face him.

"My lord!"

"Rochvale!"

Gerald and Abigail spoke simultaneously, similar notes of unease in their voices. He studied them both before taking the key from his pocket. "I believe you dropped this, Miss Grantham?"

"Oh! Oh, yes, indeed. Thank you, my lord."

When she reached out to take the key, her fingers brushed his, and she blushed rosily, which only heightened her beauty. If only he could speak to her in private! "I fear I have interrupted you."

"Oh, no, indeed, sir. Mr. Burnby was just pointing out these statues to me. I believe they are Italian?"

"I wouldn't know," he said gravely.

She shook her head. "But you know all about antiques, Lord Rochvale!"

"These statues aren't antiques. They have decorative elements from the Classical Revival, but they aren't from the Roman era."

Her eyes rounded. "You can determine that from just a glance?"

"I can determine many things from just a glance."

If anything, she blushed even rosier.

Gerald cleared his throat. "I was just . . . er . . . pointing out the more interesting features of this garden to Miss Grantham."

"Ah." William studied his cousin lazily. "Is this due to your recent interest in Roman history?"

"Yes. Yes, indeed, coz. Have a particular interest in statues these days."

Abigail stepped closer to Gerald, and when he looked at her, she gave an almost imperceptible shake of her head. William frowned. Just what was his disreputable cousin dragging Abigail into now? He knew that expression on Gerald's face of old. When they were children, he had frequently attempted to involve William in his mischievous escapades with varying degrees of success. William knew very well how to handle him. Abigail did not.

He bowed. "I hoped for a word with you, Miss Grantham. May I escort you back to the house?"

"I'm . . . I'm rather enjoying my stroll in the garden." The look she sent him was quite panic-stricken, and William suppressed a sigh. Attempting to deepen his courtship was becoming more complicated by the hour. Some other factors seemed to be at play. How helpful it would be if he knew what they were.

He looked from Gerald to Abigail and then at the statues lined up neatly in an ascending row. Statues. They were appearing with some regularity in conversation these days. When Abigail had paid that visit to Barcombe, she'd mentioned a Roman figurine in the maze, similar to the one he'd shown her in the museum. William had wanted to search for it after her visit because, as far as he knew, no such statue had ever been placed in the hedge embrasures. But, unfortunately, he had not found the time. And now, another bronze sculpture was in the chest upstairs. Merely a coincidence?

However, an ever more significant question was why Gerald

had suddenly evinced a desire to learn more about artifacts from the Roman period. When William had bumped into Mr. Wood the day after he had given his lecture in Bath, the man had mentioned in passing that Burnby had asked him numerous questions about classical antiquities. As Gerald had never displayed an interest in scholarly pursuits before, William found his behavior highly suspicious. Still, he had dismissed it, having far too many other matters on his mind.

But, although William had been willing to give Gerald the benefit of the doubt, now he wondered if his cousin's transformation could be due to something else entirely.

Further investigation was warranted before he could act. So, with a civil bow, he murmured, "I hope to see you tomorrow, Miss Grantham."

Half an hour later, he returned home and went straight to the maze. He hadn't walked along these complicated passages for years but remembered the entire plan like a map imprinted on the inside of his head. It made the simple pleasure of exploration quite useless to him, which was why he never bothered to venture within—there was no challenge in traversing such familiar paths.

However, he had forgotten how peaceful it was to walk along in complete privacy without people demanding things from him every second of the day, which, as the heir to a very ill relative on death's door these past few weeks, had been his lot in life of late.

William walked up and down, searching all the niches in the hedge walls until he found what he sought—a carved bronze figure of the goddess Venus. He gave a quiet whistle as he removed the statue from its vegetative shelf. As he examined it carefully, his jaw tightened—it was an exact replica of the statue in the chest at Longmore Hall.

Odder and odder. A pair of matching Roman urns had been found quite by chance at Longmore Hall the other day. And now, this set of identical statues from the same period had come to light.

Just what was going on?

CHAPTER THIRTY-THREE

ABIGAIL RETIRED TO bed early, hoping to have a few hours of sleep before working with her uncle on the star chart. However, she stared dry-eyed up at the dark canopy, a million thoughts buzzing through her head as a mélange of images, some good, most not, swirled in her mind's eye.

Purposely avoiding thinking of Lord Rochvale and that shattering kiss, she turned her thoughts to his cousin instead. Her efforts to help Mr. Burnby had truly set the cat amongst the pigeons, embroiling her in a dreadful tangle. What had seemed like a simple enough task had now turned into a monumental deceit, which made her feel terrible. She hated sneaking around but felt unable to tell the truth due to her promise to keep Mr. Burnby's confidence.

She should never have agreed to assist him, especially as she was becoming more and more suspicious about the provenance of Mr. Burnby's Roman artifacts. What were the chances that he had merely stumbled across those antiquities at Burnby Place? Could he have possibly excavated them in the grounds of his property? Although the idea seemed fanciful, Abigail cast her thoughts back to her visit to the village of Stone when Lord Rochvale had speculated that a Roman barrow might lie beneath the foundations of the church.

She had asked her uncle about the area's history upon her

return from the church, and he had informed her that the valley had once been under Roman rule, which meant there was a high likelihood that there might be as yet undiscovered archaeological remains in the local countryside. Had Mr. Burnby perhaps found a barrow of some sort? And, if he had, was he secretly digging it up?

She rose from her bed, trying to shake off the unsettled feeling that she had somehow landed in the middle of a labyrinth with no knowledge of the correct path. She grasped the candle on the table beside her bed, and the soft glow of the light enabled her to find her telescope. Somehow she needed to take her mind off these circular, unhelpful thoughts.

Setting the instrument upon its tripod stand, she aimed her lens at the vault of the sky as she began sweeping the heavens in a familiar motion. And calm slowly seeped into her as she recognized, as always, how insignificant the ways of men were in comparison to the vastness of the firmament, where stars sang together in such joyful chorus.

After half an hour or so, Abigail was directing her telescope downward in preparation for ending the session when she noticed the flickering light she had seen once before near the river.

She narrowed her eyes as she observed the flashing motion. The light was moving up and down evenly, like someone holding a lantern patrolling along a boundary. Who could it be? Had Uncle Longmore employed a watchman to guard his property at night as a deterrent to poachers? Alternatively, it might be a shepherd protecting his flock from would-be sheep thieves. She observed the blinking light for a few more minutes before packing away her telescope and hurrying downstairs to the observatory where Uncle Longmore awaited her.

"Glad to see you, niece. We should start making excellent progress now that you are back."

She stepped up to the telescope she always used. "When does Lord Rochvale plan on joining us again?"

"Who knows? He feels the need to be attendant at night,

which is sensible, I suppose."

"Yes, indeed." Lady Amelia no doubt expected Lord Rochvale to dance attendance on her every evening now that they were betrothed. "Do you know when the ceremony will be?"

He cast her a look of vague irritation. "It's not quite time to administer his last rites yet, niece."

Abigail swallowed her own annoyance. Why did men always talk about weddings in such a negative fashion? Last rites, indeed! As if Lord Rochvale was heading to his death by committing himself to marriage. Even more annoying was the habit some gentlemen had of referring to matrimony as "parson's mouse-trap" as if they were victims of some kind of fatal conspiracy set up by females to rob them of their liberty.

Best not to show her irritation to her uncle, however. So in a brisk voice, she asked him what he required from her that evening and, upon receiving his instructions, set to work.

After finishing their measurements for the night, Abigail turned to ask Uncle Longmore the question that had been playing on her mind. "Do you have a gamekeeper patrolling the boundary of your property, sir? I saw a light moving up and down earlier."

"Not I." Her uncle studied the star chart, his hands behind his back. "Burnby's had more of that sort of problem since he has been absent from home for such long periods. But now he's back, I'm sure matters will improve." He glanced across at her. "Where did you see this light?"

"Near the river," Abigail said. "It seemed as though someone was patrolling."

"More than likely, Burnby's sheep are being stolen, and he's set a shepherd to watch his flocks by night."

She nodded as she stepped away. "Well, I bid you goodnight, Uncle."

"Until tomorrow, then, niece. Delighted to have you home."

The smile he gave her was unusually sweet, and as she walked away, Abigail was warmed by the thought that he considered Longmore Hall her home.

After Winnicott helped her to undress and left her to herself, Abigail took her telescope out again and trained it on the same spot she had been studying earlier. But this time, she saw two lights in the vicinity—one on the boundary and another a fair distance away. However, this second light came and went, almost as though someone were moving in and out of a building.

Abigail watched for a few more minutes before putting her telescope away, reluctant to climb into bed where there were no distractions and she would be forced to reflect on the devastating news she had learned this morning—although it seemed an entire lifetime ago since she had heard that Lord Rochvale was betrothed to Lady Amelia.

If only she could leave Longmore Hall and return to Grantham Place! But, with her entire family heading here for Thea's betrothal ball early next month, there was no use making up an excuse to escape, as she would be forced to come back anyway.

How would she manage to see Lord Rochvale and Lady Amelia together, knowing full well that they did not love each other—that they had settled for a marriage of convenience?

Her anger flared as she considered the utter waste of lives lived without love. William and Amelia would grow old together in comfortable companionship, settling for peace rather than passion, as Abigail had once been tempted to do. But at least she had recognized the cowardice of her behavior and tried to change—unlike Lord Rochvale, who, without a vestige of spirit, had submitted to dull domesticity.

And, indeed, it was against Lord Rochvale that her anger burned most fiercely. She could understand Lady Amelia's wish to marry for safety, as women did not have many choices in their society. But Lord Rochvale had the whole world at his disposal and had chosen the most lackluster of paths—rather like coming to a dead end in a maze and accepting its finality without looking for another way out.

She turned around, hugging her middle. That was what rankled most of all—the thought that she had ascribed heroic characteristics to Lord Rochvale when he hadn't deserved them at all. The man she believed she had fallen in love with had a light in his eyes that his current course of action denied.

She sighed as she climbed into bed and pulled the covers over her head. How could she have misjudged his nature so completely? Abigail had hoped that anyone who gazed at stars every night would have more imagination than to aspire to a dull, lonely life with no joy or desire in it. But perhaps Lord Rochvale did not wish to reach for the stars. After all, he had told her most concisely that her wish to see a comet must be tempered by the knowledge that such occurrences were rare.

And perhaps that was how he liked to live his life—weighing up the odds while never believing that maybe, just maybe, he would be blessed with a one-in-a-thousand chance of discovering something rare, beautiful, and unique.

How devastating that she had harbored the barely-recognized hope that Lord Rochvale might have wished upon the very same star as hers. But falling in love and living happily with her beloved had eluded her in much the same way as a falling star vanishing into space.

And nothing would ever be the same again.

CHAPTER THIRTY-FOUR

AFTER BREAKFAST THE next morning, Abigail went upstairs to retrieve Mr. Burnby's bronze statue. He had taken her to the Italian garden the day before to show her where he wanted her to leave it. And, although she had agreed to place the figurine there for him, her promise had been given before she began to suspect that Mr. Burnby might not be giving the proper care and attention to the antiquities he'd suddenly found himself in possession of.

He had insisted that he did not wish his cousin to learn of his discoveries. And although the viscount was the ideal person to consult regarding Roman ruins, he was also the man who had left Abigail's dreams in ruins and, therefore, the last person she wanted to speak to, even though she desperately wished she could confide in someone knowledgeable about her concerns.

Perhaps the best thing to do was simply place the statue in the garden and wash her hands of the entire matter. She had enough problems of her own without adding more to their number—namely, the fact that she had no idea how she was going to face Lord Rochvale today without giving away the depth of her feelings.

If only she could disappear for a day or two to gather her composure! But she couldn't. So the next best course of action open to her was to avoid Lord Rochvale until she could better control her emotions.

How could she do that, though, when he might arrive at Longmore Hall at any moment and request to see her? Her grandmother and Thea planned to go out in the coach today to pay a couple of morning calls, and Abigail was sorely tempted to accompany them. But she had assured Mr. Burnby that she would deliver the statue to the Italian garden. And she did not like to renege on her commitments even though nagging doubts were plaguing her about his honesty.

Hastening up the stairs to the attic, she unlocked the chest and peered inside. The statue was still there, thank goodness. When she picked up the bronze carving, she saw that it looked just like the figure she had seen in the Barcombe maze the other day. It must be part of a matching set. After wrapping the figure in a shawl, she left the room.

Crossing the lawn a few minutes later, she kept a sharp lookout for Lord Rochvale. But she did not encounter him or anyone else as she traversed the gravel path leading to the enclosure. Although Abigail had made sure she had concealed the statue properly within the folds of fabric, anyone who cared to look at the bundled shawl would be able to tell that she was hiding something.

Abigail sent up a prayer of thanks as she slipped into the Italian garden. Unwrapping the statue, she placed it on the stairway Mr. Burnby had shown her the day before. The anxiety she had been feeling drained away, and she sagged for a moment against a stone pillar before rising to her full height once again and walking to the entrance.

Peeking around the tall hedge, she drew back at once when she spotted Lord Rochvale on the far side of the lawn in conversation with the head gardener. Now what was she to do? She could remain hidden in the Italian garden in the hope that his lordship would not find her, or she could go back to the house via the stables and sneak upstairs to her bedchamber. Really, it was no choice at all.

With her present luck, if she stayed here, Lord Rochvale would discover her, and considering what had transpired the last time she had encountered him in an isolated spot, she did not wish to take the chance.

It still hadn't completely sunk in that the viscount had kissed her while already committed to another woman. Perhaps in a marriage of convenience, a lady did not expect fidelity from her husband. But Abigail was straight-laced enough to abhor the idea, and the more she considered Lord Rochvale's behavior, the more inexcusable it seemed. Of course, she hadn't covered herself in honor by responding to him with such abandon. But still, she accepted her guilt . . . she did not know if Lord Rochvale accepted his.

At all costs, she needed to avoid him today.

Darting out from behind the hedge, she sped across the grounds toward the stables at the back of the house. Glancing over her shoulder, she failed to see the viscount anywhere, and heaving a sigh of relief, she slowed her pace. But her momentary calm vanished at the realization that this was merely a postponement of an inevitable appointment.

An impending sense of doom pervaded her at the coming confrontation. Lord Rochvale was no fool; if he'd looked in that chest yesterday before returning the key to her, he would want to speak to her about its contents. And what, in all honesty, could she say? She wasn't in a position to tell him anything about the bronze figure as the story involved other people—one who could lose her job, and the other the hand of the lady his cousin hoped to win. So Abigail was committed to silence, a silence that stretched her nerves.

She nodded at a groom, who was polishing a saddle in a somewhat desultory fashion, before continuing along a rough track that led back to the house from the other direction. A footman opened the front door for her, and Abigail took a tentative step inside, afraid of coming face to face with the man she was so studiously avoiding. Instead, she came face to face with the bronze statue, now on the hall table. She blinked twice as she stared at it, horrified. How in heaven had it got back here? Someone must have found it and brought it inside. But who? Lord Rochvale, no doubt, while searching for Abigail in the gardens.

Which meant that he was still here. She glanced at the footman, who had taken her hat and cloak from her, before handing them to the porter, who had already walked off. "Please see if my aunt is in the drawing room, Peter."

"Very well, miss."

As the manservant walked away, Abigail hastened to the bronze statue. Making sure the porter was out of sight, she stuffed it in her shawl before leaving the house again. A pity she no longer had her outdoor things, but she didn't have time to reclaim them. Not when Lord Rochvale might appear at any minute. She would take that dratted statue across to Burnby Place and leave it in a safe spot in the grounds there. Evidently, it wasn't wise to leave any precious items at Longmore Hall—too many people were crawling about to hide anything successfully here for long.

Abigail returned to the stables, where she found the groom. "Please leave that and accompany me on a walk."

The groom set the saddle to one side and rose hastily to his feet. She recognized him as the young boy who had accompanied her on a ride around the grounds the other day. "Yes, miss. Just a moment, miss."

He picked up the saddle and took it inside, leaving Abigail to look around anxiously. Time was ticking by. Fortunately, he didn't take too long, and within a few minutes, he reappeared. Abigail cleared her throat. "You may walk twenty paces or so behind me, Timmy. I like solitary walks." She half-smiled as she turned away, hoping the explanation would suffice as to why she would be hastening ahead of him. She did not intend for him to see where she hid the statue, as that could cause the kind of talk she was desperately trying to avoid.

Abigail walked ahead of the boy, looking over her shoulder several times to see if he was following at an appropriate distance. Fortunately, he was, and Abigail sighed with relief that her hastily conceived plan might work.

When she reached the stone bridge separating Longmore Hall from Burnby Place, she hurried across it. Now was the perfect time to find a spot to hide the statue. A hedgerow marched along on her right side, and she stopped to examine if there were any niches within the vegetative border where she could place her burden. Then she would measure the number of steps back to the bridge and inform Mr. Burnby of its exact location.

Pushing aside some interlinked branches which crackled under pressure, she peered through the gap in the hedge. It enclosed a pasture with a shepherd's domicile on one end. But it wasn't a typical field. The grass had been dug up all around the hut, which was built on a mound similar to the rise the church in Stone had been constructed upon.

Abigail bit down hard on her bottom lip. So, her suspicions might be true. Mr. Burnby could be excavating Roman ruins here. But it was difficult to see things clearly from this side of the hedge. Lowering her head, she saw an Abigail-shaped hole at the bottom of the border, just large enough for her to creep through and have a better look. But she would have to be quick as Timmy would be coming along at any moment now.

Getting onto her hands and knees, she crawled through the gap and was still in this unseemly position when a voice boomed in her ear. "Now, what have we here?"

She nearly fainted in fright as she looked up at a man's red face. The guard. How idiotic of her to have assumed that he would only patrol the property at night. She should never have allowed her curiosity to get the better of her in this way.

Abigail rose quickly to her feet. If he realized she was a lady, he would apologize and let her go. But what a pity she had donned her plainest cambric gown this morning as she did not appear particularly grand, especially as she'd torn her dress while climbing through that hole.

Trying to imitate her grandmother's most imperious accents, she said, "I am a lady out for a walk, my good man, and I resent your familiar tones."

He lifted his bushy grey eyebrows. "Oh?" He folded his arms. "On your own?" He studied her hatless head, and Abigail flushed in mortification at how shabby she must look. No proper young lady would ever go out without some sort of covering on her head, let alone on her own. She had no idea where Timmy was—he'd been quite far behind the last time she looked back. She needed to brazen this out. So with a regal nod, she said in a clear voice, "If you would excuse me."

As she turned back to the gap in the hedge, her mind raced as to how she could contrive to get back on the other side without crawling out on all fours again. Setting her parcel on the ground, she froze in horror when the fabric fell partly away, and the edge of the statue showed.

The guard must have noticed it, too, because he said in a rough voice, "Just a moment, girl." He removed the shawl from around the bronze figurine and scrutinized it for an endless moment. Eventually, his mouth tightened. "This here statue looks like one I've seen afore." He studied her with suspicious eyes. "You're going nowhere until the master's spoken to you."

And taking her elbow in a firm grip, he marched her across to the hut.

CHAPTER THIRTY-FIVE

WILLIAM WAS SEATED in an armchair in Longmore's study reading an article when Davison scratched on the door and entered. "Forgive me, my lord. I was looking for Lord Longmore."

"He just stepped out." Noticing the perturbed expression on the butler's face, he set the journal to one side. "Is anything the matter?"

"I do not wish to bother you, my lord, if you are busy. I shall wait for his lordship."

"Lord Longmore said he would be gone for an hour or so."

"Oh! In that case, I should be grateful for your assistance. It regards Miss Grantham."

"Miss Grantham?" William rose to his feet. "What's happened?"

"It is just that she went out for a walk earlier. She asked Timmy, the groom, to accompany her but informed him that she preferred to walk ahead of him, which she did. But then she simply vanished out of sight. He looked everywhere for her but couldn't find her."

William frowned. "Where did he lose her?"

"On the boundary of the estate. He saw her cross the bridge that leads to Burnby Place, but when he followed her there, he couldn't find her.

"How old is Timmy?"

"Fourteen or so. Just a lad, really."

"Please bring him to me. I'd like to question him."

"Very well, my lord."

The butler stepped out the door and reappeared with the young groom in tow.

"Now tell me in detail what happened," William said.

However, the groom recounted the same tale that Davison had told him, adding nothing new. William tapped his fingers on the edge of the table before standing up. "Let me go and look for Miss Grantham. Perhaps she took another path, and Timmy missed it."

Davison was handing William his hat when Henrietta walked into the hall. "You're leaving now, Rochvale?"

He accepted his cane from the butler. "I'm off to look for Miss Grantham. She went out earlier with a groom, but he somehow contrived to lose her."

"Where did the groom last see her?"

"At the bridge that leads to Burnby Place."

"Let me come with you, Rochvale. I can help you look for her."

William nodded. "Be quick, though. She's been gone for quite some time."

Henrietta hastened up the stairs and, five minutes later, came back into the hall. They left the house together, taking the shortest way across the estate to the bridge where Timmy had last seen Abigail.

"I hope Abby hasn't fallen and twisted her ankle," Henrietta said. "But I'm afraid that's the most likely explanation."

"Yes. I thought the same thing. That boy should have kept pace."

"Abby's a fast walker, and Timmy has the lethargy of many people his age. I've never understood why youth is so frequently equated with boundless energy. Many people below the age of twenty are the most exhausted beings imaginable."

"True." He smiled faintly but failed to look at her as he came to a halt on the other side of the bridge, surveying his surroundings. "There's only the single path."

"Yes."

"Let us walk on." Unease settled on him as he wondered where Abigail could be. He was scrutinizing the ground when he noticed a scrap of material in the hedge on his right. Bending down, he set his cane on the ground and removed the small piece of fabric. "Could this be from Miss Grantham's gown?" he asked, showing it to Henrietta.

She glanced at it. "Yes. She was wearing a white cambric gown at breakfast this morning."

William studied the hole at the bottom of the hedge. "Perhaps she went through that gap. But why?" Picking up his cane, William engaged a mechanism at the top and pulled up a cleverly concealed telescope. Then, holding the stick upright, he directed the telescope through a slightly higher gap in the hedge before setting his eye on the monocle.

Abigail was visible in the distance through the open door of a shepherd's hut, seated on a chair, with a man wielding a truncheon standing above her.

"Well, I'll be . . ." He swiftly turned to Henrietta. Not wishing to alarm her, he spoke in a neutral voice, "Some rather unusual activity appears to be taking place in this field. My cousin appears to be excavating it. Let us walk around to the gate and enter that way."

Henrietta peered through a hole in the hedge. "This isn't some sort of new agricultural method?"

"No." His voice was grim.

When they came to the gate, which led into the meadow, a lock was clamped on it. William climbed over the barrier before offering Henrietta his hand. "Let me help you." She managed to clamber halfway up, and then William grasped her under her arms and swung her over. "I'll go on ahead, Hetta. Meet me there."

He set off at a run along the path that marched beside the meadow. When he came to the hut, he slowed. William had returned the small telescope to its resting place, and he now held the cane in one hand, ready to brandish it as a weapon.

Abigail was seated on a stool near the door, her ankles tied, looking belligerently up at the burly man standing guard above her.

"Why won't you listen to me? How many times must I tell you that I'm a friend of Mr. Burnby's? When he arrives, he will be most displeased to find me tied up in this way."

"He'll be here soon enough, girlie, and you can explain yourself to 'im."

William's shadow fell across the doorway. Abigail glanced up, an expression of relief crossing her face as her eyes met his. She turned back to the guard. "Do you need Mr. Burnby to release me? Or will his cousin's word suffice?"

The words fell from Abigail's lips just as William came up behind the guard and wrenched the truncheon from his hand. The guard made a grunting sound and swiveled, drawing his fist back. But before the man could plant him a facer, William drew his cork and sent him sprawling to the ground.

Leaving the man groaning on the floor, William hastened to Abigail's side, taking her hands in his. "Did he hurt you, sweetheart?"

She shook her head.

"But he frightened you?"

"A little. But I suspect his bark is worse than his bite."

He dropped a kiss on her lips just as a commotion arose outside. Rising swiftly to his feet, William stretched out his walking stick like a sword as Burnby and Henrietta burst into the room.

Gerald's gaze swept from Abigail to his henchman, who was rising to his feet, a bloody handkerchief held against his nose. "What have you done, man?" he said urgently.

"Just following yer orders, sir." The guard's voice held a note of injury.

"Untie this young lady at once! Good heavens, are you all right, Miss Grantham?" Gerald hastened across to Abigail, his face as white as a sheet. "How did you get here?"

"I was bringing this across to Burnby Place for you." She pointed at the statue beside her chair. "I planned to hide it in your hedge."

"In my *hedge*? But . . . why? We agreed . . ." He cleared his throat as his gaze fell upon his cousin and Henrietta. "Perhaps we should discuss this another time."

William folded his arms. "This is as good a time as any."

Gerald hesitated a moment, but when he met William's eyes, an expression of resignation settled upon his features. "Very well. The game's up anyway, I suppose." He pointed at the door. "Out, Jacob. I'll talk to you later."

As the guard trundled toward the door, William crouched to untie the rope from around Abigail's ankles. Turning back to Gerald, he indicated the bronze figure on the floor. "I presume your field is the archaeological site this statue originates from?"

"It is." His cousin's voice was wary.

William frowned. "It's a matching set?"

Gerald shook his head. "By Jove, William! How did you know? Sometimes you're too canny by half."

"I found a statue just like this in the maze at Barcombe." He nodded at Abigail, who had risen to her feet. "And, yesterday, I saw its match in the chest at Longmore. I'm not sure which one this is." He raised his brows as he directed the question to Abigail.

She hesitated a moment. "I took the figurine from the chest to the Italian garden this morning, my lord. But when I came back to the house, I saw it in the hall." An expression of dawning understanding crossed her face. "Did you leave the statue from the maze in the hall this morning, by any chance, my lord?"

"I did. I brought it across from Barcombe."

"Oh, dear." Abigail sat down squarely on her chair again and stared at the ground. "If only I'd known."

William turned back to his cousin. "Did those Roman urns

that were discovered at Longmore also come from this site?"

"Yes. I arranged for them to be stored there briefly, but unfortunately, they were . . . er . . . discovered." When William continued to stare at him, Gerald cleared his throat. "I'll explain it all to you once we're on our own, coz." He wriggled his shoulder in Henrietta's direction and said in a mumble. "Ladies present, you know."

William sighed. "I'd like to clear this matter up now, Gerald. And I'm sure the ladies do not wish to be kept in the dark any more than I do." He turned back to Abigail. "Why did you bring that statue here? Did you know about this site?"

"No. But when I saw the statue in the hall, I decided to take it to Mr. Burnby's estate as I couldn't believe it had already been found in the Italian garden right after I had left it there. I was searching for a suitable place to hide it in the hedge when I looked through the gap and realized that this field might be an archaeological dig."

"So you crawled through that gap?"

She pressed her lips together. "Yes. Perhaps not the wisest thing to do. But I was so curious! I already suspected Mr. Burnby might be digging at Burnby Place."

Henrietta, who had remained silent the entire time, now marched into the center of the room, stepping around a giant hole on one side, surrounded by wooden planks, which served as a protective barrier. She folded her arms. "I demand an explanation at once! You could be talking Greek for all the sense you're all making."

William nodded at his cousin. "I believe it must fall on Gerald to enlighten you."

"Well, Mr. Burnby?" Henrietta began tapping her foot. "I'm waiting."

Gerald raised his hands as though he were surrendering to a foreign army. "It's a long story, Hetta, but it mostly involves you."

"Me? How on earth could it involve me?" She glared at the

pile of dirt lying beside the giant hole. "And I did not intend that pun."

Gerald's expression was imploring. "You're the reason I've done all this." He pointed at the hollow in the ground. "That's a shaft-pit, m'dear. The shepherd who used to live here found some Roman pottery in his garden earlier this year. He informed me of the discovery, and I found a stonemason who agreed to do some exploratory foraging." He darted a look at William. "We unearthed quite a few treasures, I'm pleased to say. Sold some to raise funds to set my estate in order." He paused before looking back at Henrietta. "I want to marry you, Hetta. But in order to do so, I needed to restore my fortunes, which I'm pleased to say I have."

Henrietta stared at him. "But . . . but I don't understand. You want to marry *me*? I thought you were pursuing Abigail. You've been flirting with her ever since she came here, and you gave her those Damask roses at . . . at . . . the Flintons' ball." She glanced at her cousin before looking down at her feet.

Gerald took a step forward. "They were meant for you, my love. I found out from Annie what you were planning to wear that night and gathered my courage to recite that dashed poem to you. But then you changed costumes with Miss Grantham at the last minute, and I declared my love to the wrong lady."

Henrietta stared at him. Then she began to laugh. She pressed a hand to her lips. "Oh dear, oh dear. And all this time, I believed that you must be violently in love with Abby to go to such romantic lengths—dressing as a shepherd to recite Christopher Marlowe to her."

"Miss Grantham told you that?"

"No, no. Great-aunt Mildred overheard you quoting the verses to Abby, and *she* told me about it. And then you came over and tried to do the same with me, and I . . ."

He stepped even closer. "You sent me away with a flea in my ear."

She nodded as Gerald grasped her hands. "Darling Hetta, will you listen to me?"

William looked across at Abigail, who stood motionless beside the stool. When he indicated with a discreet movement that they should leave, she inclined her head and followed him out of the door.

Abigail looked around at the architectural site as they stepped outside. "Can you believe people once walked around here, going about their daily lives so many centuries ago?" Her voice was carefully polite. "The idea never fails to fascinate me."

William studied her averted face. Evidently, her confidences were at an end. But now was not the time to press her to speak. When they returned to Longmore Hall, he would request a private audience with her. Bending down, he examined a nearby trench. "Thankfully, whoever Gerald hired to dig these fields seems to have done a careful job." He rose to his full height again. "When did you suspect my cousin might have an archaeological site on his property?"

"When I returned from Bath, Mr. Burnby told me that those Roman urns belonged to him—that he had stumbled across them at Burnby Place. But I wondered if he might not have dug them up when I saw a guard patrolling this field on a couple of occasions at night."

"You *saw* that? Oh, of course, your telescope." He smiled. "I should have known."

Her aloof expression lightened somewhat. But then Jacob came into view, and she turned around again, her back stiff. William's hand tightened on his cane. The patience he'd always prided himself on was wearing very thin.

CHAPTER THIRTY-SIX

A BIGAIL STAYED AS far away from Lord Rochvale as possible on their walk back to Longmore Hall, strolling beside Henrietta, who kept up a stream of conversation with Mr. Burnby, effectively deflecting attention away from the silence of the other two members of the party. Before parting ways in the hall, they all agreed that no mention should be made of the urns or the statues to keep Annie Winnicott out of trouble.

Uttering a word of farewell, Abigail set off in the direction of the staircase, her blessed means of escape from what was becoming an impossible situation. However, Lord Rochvale detained her by the simple expedient of placing his hand on her arm. She stared at it for a long moment before looking up at him.

"I believe you are under a severe misapprehension, Miss Grantham," he said quietly. "May I speak to you privately?"

Abigail peered around his shoulder for Henrietta, but she was still with Mr. Burnby on the other side of the hall. "Sir!" Abigail removed his hand from her arm as though it were a particularly venomous snake. "Your behavior is not that of a gentleman. You have kissed me—twice now!—all the while betrothed to another woman. It is beyond the pale."

"That would indeed be true if I were betrothed to someone else. But I am not."

She gazed at him, her lips slightly parted. "But Henrietta told me that Lady Amelia recently announced her betrothal."

"She did. But she is to marry Sir Reginald, not me."

"But . . . but, I don't understand." Abigail took a step back. "Everyone has been saying that you've been unusually occupied. I assumed it was because you were engaged to be married."

"My grandfather is gravely ill at present. That must have been what they meant."

"Oh! Oh, yes, of course. I am very sorry to hear that Lord Barcombe is ill."

He removed his watch from his pocket and frowned. "I'm afraid I cannot stay. But I hope to speak to you soon. When does the rest of your family arrive at Longmore Hall?"

"Next week."

"Excellent. I am looking forward, in particular, to making your brother's acquaintance." He took her hand in his and kissed it. "Your servant, ma'am."

On those words, he turned to take his hasty leave of Mr. Burnby and Henrietta before striding toward the door. Abigail stared at his retreating form as she tried to change her view of him from an unscrupulous rogue, devoid of all honor and principles, to a gentleman of integrity who wished to marry her. For he would never have mentioned his wish to meet her brother if he did not intend to make her an offer, would he?

Abigail trudged up the stairs, feeling like she had as a little girl when she had spun around in circles and fallen on her back, staring up at the revolving sky. Except that the scenery shifting now was within her mind, though it was taking just as long to adjust to the new picture.

Abigail opened her bedchamber door before sinking into the armchair in the corner of the room. Sometimes she dreamed of people she knew and liked. But in her dreams, they treated her badly, and she woke up with an altered view of them, even though they had done nothing wrong. And later, should she happen to see them during the day, she would look at them strangely, still holding onto a grudge, angry with them for their imagined actions, even though it wasn't logical or fair.

That was how she felt about Lord Rochvale now. Although he had not wronged her in any way, the adverse feelings she had been nursing against him just would not fade away. Especially because, in some ways, she had been deliberately fanning those flames, relieved that he wasn't the man she'd believed him to be.

Abigail had been so quick to accept that Lord Rochvale was engaged to Lady Amelia, ignoring all evidence to the contrary that he'd shown signs of harboring tender feelings for her. Had she done this perhaps because somewhere deep inside, something was very wrong?

She leaned back in her chair, pressing her hands hard onto the wooden arms. To find out how she had set herself on such a disastrous course, she needed to find out what that something was. Because although she had been desperately unhappy at the news of Lord Rochvale's betrothal, she had also been conscious of a sense of release. For at the back of her mind, the excruciating fear existed that she would lose him one day anyway, so it might as well be now.

A tear squeezed out of her eye. What if he, too, died young as her parents had? Or perhaps it would be Abigail's life that was snuffed out first, and William and any children they had would be the ones left alone, devastated, and stripped of light.

The thought lacerated her, and another tear rolled down her cheek. Would she ever recover from the loss of confidence her parents' early deaths had wrought in her? She was always looking ahead, surveying the horizon for any hint of change because she knew, of old, that some changes came in with devastating effect, changing the shape of one's landscape forever.

She sat in the chair for hours, staring straight ahead, trying to come to terms with what she had been avoiding for years—that living involved irrevocable loss, and nothing could change that. She might try any manner of things to protect herself from it, but once she made herself vulnerable to another human being, she lost all control over when that blinding strike of grief would pierce her once again.

For it would.

How tempting it was to live a detached life, exempt from the griefs of other people. But in order to do that, one needed to avoid deep involvement and, consequently, deep love. And did she want to live her life like that? Like a stone thrown across the water's surface, rippling but never sinking to profound depths?

No. She didn't. She released a slow breath. But that meant that she needed to take a chance on love . . . to take a chance on William. However, she would be doing so knowing full well that it was ephemeral, like a comet shooting across the sky, here one moment, gone the next, in a moment of utter brilliance . . . but so worthwhile and unforgettable. A light that showed that hope could exist in darkness, shining brightly with the resilience that made you think all was well with the world.

Indeed, love was like a star shining in the universe, always visible but not always attainable. But if you reached for it with hope and determination, a showering of light might rain down on you like a celestial mystery, awesome in its wonder, with the promise that more was to come . . . the promise of a life well lived.

And that was always worth reaching for.

CHAPTER THIRTY-SEVEN

ABIGAIL DID NOT see Lord Rochvale for the next week. Her uncle informed her that he was dealing with all the estate matters his grandfather had once directed from his sick room. She kept an eager eye out for him, but he did not appear, and she chastised herself for her selfishness in wishing for his attention when it was necessarily focused on a very ill relative.

As the days went by, her knowledge of her love for him grew deeper and deeper as she held on to his last words to her—that he looked forward to meeting her brother. Her lips curved into a soft smile. How like William it was to go about the business of matrimony in the correct manner! He would not circumvent the appropriate way of doing things. Rather he would approach situations with a proper plan of action, being the last person to propose marriage before establishing first that her guardian would permit it.

And how she loved him for it! After years of feeling as though her feet were treading on shaking ground, William represented the stability she had been lacking. When her mother died, her father had fallen apart, and Abigail had needed to rely heavily on her brother and sisters for emotional support in a very uncertain time. And although they had provided comfort, she had always felt as though her world was not as warm as it should be, as they were all dealing with grief in their own ways and unable to do more than provide a shoulder for each other to cry on when things were hard.

But now she felt the joy of having someone who was fully supportive of her. She did not have to fight for his attention as she had needed to jostle for support in her family. Instead, he appeared to like her despite her flaws, not finding them annoying as close family members tended to do. It felt like a brand new start, with uncharted territory stretching ahead of her. And how lovely it was that she would be the one responsible for marking those important measurements!

So she waited, biding her time, looking forward to the day when she could announce her love to the world. She had not told anyone about her feelings for Lord Rochvale, although she suspected Henrietta knew. However, her cousin was so caught up with her love for Mr. Burnby that she barely seemed to be walking on this earth, so airborne were her steps.

She and Mr. Burnby had announced their betrothal, and the engagement ball meant to celebrate Thea's engagement had now extended to Henrietta, not to mention Lady Amelia's upcoming nuptials, which were due to take place as soon as the banns had been read.

Indeed, there was a distinct air of festivity in the air at Longmore Hall, which made William's grandfather's deteriorating health all the harder to bear. How sad that life, in its inevitable cycles of mourning and dancing, weeping and laughing, had coincided simultaneously at a point of joy and sorrow for William. And although Abigail would eagerly open her arms now to embrace, she understood that, for him, it must necessarily be a time to refrain.

It was, therefore, with great joy—and a dollop of relief—that the news came to her ears at the end of that week that Lord Barcombe had turned the corner and appeared to be on the mend. When her uncle told her the glad tidings one evening just before they started their work in the observatory, she clasped her hands together. "Do you think Lord Barcombe will make a full recovery, Uncle?"

"So his physician says. Although you never know with these quacks. Can't abide having medical men about me, you know. Always give me the fidgets with their predilection for blood-letting. Never could abide the sight of blood. Or leeches, for that matter," he added thoughtfully.

Abigail gave a delicate shiver. "I hope that I never have to submit to such a thing."

"It befalls us all in the end, I'm afraid. As mere mortals, we so often end our lives at the mercy of doctors, prodding and poking us, and none of our former position or power means anything at all. Life's a great leveler, niece. Never forget that."

"Yes, Uncle."

"Speaking of leveling, when do you plan to marry Rochvale? He fell head over ears for you the moment he met you. Been waiting for the announcement for ages, but you young people take your time these days."

Abigail blinked. "How . . . how did you know? That is . . . his lordship hasn't offered for me yet."

"He will."

Abigail's eyes opened wide at the realization that her uncle, who never appeared to notice anything of a personal nature, must have observed Lord Rochvale's feelings for her even before she became aware of them. How surprising people were! But then Uncle Longmore knew Lord Rochvale very well, so he would likely be attuned to his state of mind. But she never would have thought that the older man, so caught up in his particular field of scientific study, would be aware of such things, let alone recognize Lord Rochvale's intentions before Abigail did. She smiled at him. "I truly hope he does."

"Never known two people better suited to each other. If you happen to be blessed with a good mind, it's important to marry someone who can meet it. It's the best recipe for a good marriage, I'd say."

"Not everyone values intellectual pursuits, however."

"No. But if you *do* happen to value them, you'd be a fool if you ignore that aspect of marital companionship. Too many do."

Abigail nodded, wondering about his marriage to her aunt. Although they did not share a love for astronomical activities, Aunt Longmore, in her rather long-suffering way, appeared to understand her husband's passion for this branch of natural philosophy and did not place too many obstacles in his path to pursuing it. And that, for a busy man of science, must be a boon indeed.

Sometimes simply not standing in someone's way could be as liberating as a more obvious show of support. Indeed, there were many ways to love someone. And what appeared to be most important was that you cared for your beloved in the way that they needed, no matter how idiosyncratic or different it might be.

Hopefully, Abigail would learn to love Lord Rochvale in just such a way.

All he needed to do was ask.

CHAPTER THIRTY-EIGHT

THE REST OF Abigail's family arrived the following week. The house filled with bustle and activity as the servants prepared for the ball and various family members caught up on each other's news. Abigail was particularly pleased to see her older sister, Alexandra. She ensconced herself in the drawing room with Alexandra, Thea, and their sister-in-law Emily to hear all about the recent London Season as well as the various gardening projects Alexandra had taken on in her role as the Duchess of Stanford.

Their Aunt Eliza gravitated to the older members of the household, spending a deal of time with Great-aunt Mildred, Aunt Longmore, and Grandmama, which suited Abigail very well as her aunt was a fussy chaperone, and Abigail did not relish having her behavior censored all the time.

John headed straight to the library, spending hours reading the astronomical texts on the bookshelves, while the Duke of Stanford spent time with Uncle Longmore in his study, discussing the latest article he had written for the Royal Society.

Abigail kept an eye out for William, but he did not come to Longmore Hall on the day of John's arrival. Perhaps he planned to give the family some time to settle in before seeking her brother out, but Abigail found herself wishing that the patience that typified her sweetheart would be less in evidence on this occasion.

However, on the second day, William arrived and requested a meeting with John in the library. Abigail happened to be with her brother at the time, showing him the work she had been doing on the star chart. But, when William entered the room, she jumped up from the table and, with a stammered excuse, walked to the door.

William smiled at her as she approached, but his eyes were slightly questioning as she stopped beside him. However, her beaming expression must have reassured him because the stiffness in his posture disappeared, and the bow he gave her was gallant indeed.

As she disappeared out of the door, she heard John ask William a question about his observational methods, leaving Abigail wishing for the first time in her life that astronomical matters would fail to dominate the conversation.

Deciding it would be best to get some fresh air rather than wait around anxiously for William to reappear, Abigail hastened upstairs to fetch her bonnet and shawl before walking outside just as a carriage rolled up the drive. Lady Amelia and Sir Reginald descended from the coach, and Abigail hastened toward them, smiling in greeting.

She hadn't seen the couple since their betrothal and now spent some five minutes conversing with them before stepping away and saying, "Let me not keep you. I was just stepping out for a stroll in the garden."

Lady Amelia looked around. "I'm tempted to join you, Miss Grantham. The grounds are looking quite splendid, I must say." She returned her gaze to Abigail. "I hope to see you later, but if I don't, we shall see you at the ball."

Abigail glanced from Sir Reginald to Lady Amelia. Witnessing the happiness radiating from them both, she gave a contented sigh. How wonderful that they had sorted out their differences. And although Sir Reginald would no longer be going on that expedition, he had chosen another journey that promised to be just as rewarding.

Abigail dropped into a quick curtsy and, with a word of farewell, turned away, her steps leading her inexorably to the Italian garden, where she sat on the carved stone bench, enjoying the sound of cascading water from the Cupids' fountain.

She had just fallen into a daydream about William when her imaginings seemed to conjure him up, and he stepped into the enclosure. Her eyelids fluttered as she rose to her feet and took a step in his direction.

He swiftly covered the distance between them. "I thought I would find you here after Amelia said you were in the garden."

She contemplated him lovingly and then collected herself. "I was so pleased to learn of her betrothal to Sir Reginald. Such excellent news."

"Indeed, although I'm not nearly as interested in her betrothal as I am in my own." He took one more stride and swept her into his arms, gazing down at her. "*Trip no further, pretty sweeting. Journeys end in lovers' meeting.* Those words have been a refrain in my mind ever since I met you, darling Abby. Will you marry me, sweetheart?"

She lifted her face to his. "It is my heart's truest desire."

He kissed her gently at first and then with more urgency, drawing her into a world of sensation she'd only begun to discover in the attic the other day. Somehow the strings of her bonnet became entangled in her hair, and William eventually plucked the offending covering from her head and tossed it away, loosening her curls as he ran his fingers through them. Finally, he drew back, cupping her face. "Happy, my love?"

She gave a tiny nod. "Almost too happy. It doesn't feel quite real."

"It is clearly my duty to reinforce it then," he said gravely, lowering his head once more. And, for the next while, there was nothing except William. Darling, wonderful William.

Eventually, he took her arm and led her to the bench. As he drew her down beside him, Abigail spotted her bonnet perched atop a stone statue of Cupid. She giggled. "Look where my hat ended up."

He followed her pointing finger. "I clearly have impeccable aim." He smiled as he looked back at her, his gaze lingering on her face. "And impeccable taste."

"For a man of few words, my lord, you are using them most charmingly today."

"Even the most tongue-tied fellow must think of how to portray what is in his heart on a day like this."

"With a little help from Shakespeare?" She twinkled at him.

"Indeed." He settled back more comfortably against the bench, stretching his legs out. "You can be thankful it wasn't Christopher Marlowe."

"Oh, yes. Poor Mr. Burnby."

"Hmm. I need to have a few words with that cousin of mine—selling priceless artifacts to pawnbrokers. If my grandfather knew . . ."

She twisted to face him. "I heard from my uncle that Lord Barcombe is no longer so gravely ill?"

"Thankfully, he turned the corner a few days ago. It's been a difficult few weeks."

The words came out sparely, but Abigail sensed a depth of emotion beneath them. With William's parents dying so young, Lord Barcombe must have stood more in the role of father to him than grandfather while he was growing up. William certainly seemed to hold him in high esteem. Abigail only hoped she would be able to meet the earl when he was a little better and, hopefully, once she was married to William, relieve him of some of the burdens he'd carried alone for so many years.

Married . . . She released a slow breath. She couldn't quite believe she would be William's wife soon. How had the course of her life altered so entirely within such a short space of time? A few months ago, she had been looking forward to furthering her astronomical studies and then going to the Capital for her first Season. And now, without even setting foot in a London ballroom, she was betrothed to the man she loved, her future stretching happily before her.

William brushed her cheek with his knuckles. "You seem pensive, my love. Anything the matter?"

She took his hand in hers and cradled it before pressing a kiss on the back. "No, no. It's just that in a blink of an eye, my life has changed completely. In the past, my experience of change has always been related to negative things. But now the change is for the good, and it feels . . . strange for it to be the other way around." She drew in a deep breath. "I'm afraid it's hard to recognize it as real."

He pressed the lightest of kisses onto her palm. "I love you, Abigail, and that is the most real statement I've ever made—if that is even grammatical English."

She sighed. "Oh, William. I love you so very, very much!"

And then she was back into his arms, and all thought was swept away as William reassured her in a way that words simply couldn't.

And it felt most real.

When Abigail returned to the house, she sought out Henrietta, who Winnicott informed her, was in her bedchamber. Eager to share her news, Abigail pushed the door open, which was slightly ajar, and called out, "Are you busy, Hetta?"

Her cousin was seated at a table, writing some letters. She set down her pen. "I would welcome a respite. I'm writing to inform various friends of my betrothal." She studied Abigail's face, her head tilted to one side. "Am I correct in assuming that you are the bearer of some happy news too?"

"Is it so obvious?" Abigail sank onto the bed, hugging her arms. "Lord Rochvale has just offered for me, and I accepted."

"Oh, splendid, Abby! I am so pleased for you both!" She rose and kissed Abigail on both cheeks before returning to her chair. "You know, I suspected the first day you met that Rochvale had fallen in love with you."

"Really?" Abigail's eyes widened. "How did you guess? I

confess I had no idea."

Henrietta leaned back in her chair, a slight crease between her brows. "It had something to do with a particular light in his eyes. I'd never seen it before. I hadn't believed in love at first sight until I saw Rochvale fall at your feet like that. I felt dreadfully sorry for him, you know, being forced to work with you. And then Burnby came on the scene, complicating matters even further."

"I took Mr. Burnby to task for trying to gain your attention by flirting with me as he did. He told me he hoped to make you jealous."

"Well, he succeeded! I was in agonies for months. And even though I told myself I was a fool for loving him, I couldn't stop." She shook her head. "You know, sometimes I could shake that man. But I love him madly."

"Have you set a wedding date?"

"Not yet. We've been uncertain about Lord Barcombe's health. But he seems to be recovering." She hesitated. "I want to tell you something, Abby, but please keep it to yourself. It's such a fantastical thing that when Burnby told me, I thought I had stepped into the pages of a romantic novel."

"Oh? It sounds intriguing."

Henrietta shook her head. "When Burnby discovered those Roman urns in that shaft-pit in the shepherd's hut, they were filled to the brim with gold coins. Can you imagine? There were ever so many, and he sold them for a fortune which is why he has been able to put his estate in order. Do you know much about Roman coins, Abby?"

"Very little. Lord Rochvale would be the right person to ask."

"Oh, no—he's barely recovered from learning Burnby's plans to dispose of the urns and those statues. He's actually offered to buy the statues so that he can place them in his museum. I don't know what he'd think of his cousin selling those coins."

"Has Mr. Burnby kept any?" Abigail sat up straighter. "In Bath, I saw that he had a snuff box with a Roman coin embedded on the lid."

"He kept a few of each type but sold the rest. That must have been one of them. He was quite indignant when I told him that he should have more respect for historical artifacts." Her lips curved into a smile. "He said that without them, he would never have been in a position to offer for me, quite disregarding the fact that he had stumbled upon an important archaeological discovery."

"I suppose not everyone ascribes value to such things. But however regrettable it may be that he sold them so quickly, it shows the depth of his devotion to you that he put love above all else."

"Yes." She shook her head. "He may have his faults, but his heart is in the right place. And he assures me his wild days are behind him."

"I'm so happy for you, Hetta."

"I had all but given up on love, you know. But now, my whole world has opened up. And I'm so grateful."

Joy shone from Henrietta's face, and Abigail sighed. What a transforming effect love had had on her, like a flower in the sunshine, unfurling in its warmth. And this effect was not just visible in her cousin's countenance, but also in Lady Amelia's and Thea's, and according to Henrietta, in Abigail's.

A certain light in the eye, a curve to the lips, the blush of excitement on the cheek—it was as though love was a blossoming ray of loveliness, bringing light and brightness to the world.

And how eager they all were to be captivated by it.

CHAPTER THIRTY-NINE

THE DAY OF the ball dawned bright and clear, and from the early hours, the house was a hive of activity. Winnicott and Baker made several last-minute alterations to the ladies' ballgowns while Davison bustled about ensuring that the large ballroom, which had been opened a few days ago, was spotlessly clean and aired.

A number of people from the neighborhood had already left London and returned to Bucks, and most of them had accepted the engraved invitations Aunt Longmore had sent out. On the day of the ball, Abigail spent most of the morning with her sisters, chattering nineteen to the dozen about the upcoming festivities.

"As you are to be married before your first Season, Abby, I'm delighted we can celebrate your betrothal today as well as Henrietta's." Thea's brow creased. "What is the collective noun for a group of betrothals?"

Abigail wrinkled her nose. "A rash of betrothals?"

Alexandra, seated in the window seat of the drawing room, burst out laughing. "Oh, no, Abby! How unromantic. I don't think such a word exists, but I'm sure we can contrive one ourselves. Any ideas?"

Abigail smiled. "A galaxy of betrothals?"

"Much better!" Alexandra hugged a cushion to her stomach, her expression dreamy. "Especially as falling love can be compared to being touched by starlight."

Their grandmother and Aunt Eliza joined them then, and the conversation turned to the special dinner that the Longmores were hosting at the Hall before the ball.

"I believe Sir Reginald and Lady Amelia will be there," Grandmama said. "I must say that I'm glad he chose to marry rather than haring off to the other side of the world on that sea adventure."

"Do you think that in years to come, Sir Reginald will regret not taking the opportunity when it arose?" Abigail said thoughtfully.

"Perhaps," Grandmama said. "For some gentlemen, adventure is more important than anything. But it is a question of priorities, and Sir Reginald no doubt realized that he would lose the lady he loved if he went ahead with his plans. Sometimes difficult choices need to be made, and a measure of loss will be involved, no matter what you decide."

Abigail nodded. Even falling in love and marrying involved some sort of loss—the forfeiture of one's freedom and liberty of action. And, although Abigail had hoped to marry one day she would not have been required to do so as she would inherit a sizeable independence on her twenty-first birthday. Her brother had also always made it quite plain that she would always have a home at Grantham Place, which meant that, unlike many young ladies, Abigail could have had a fulfilling life if she'd chosen not to marry.

But she did choose to marry. She chose it with her whole heart. And she couldn't wait to dance the night away in the arms of her beloved.

Later that afternoon, Abigail twirled in front of the mirror, turning first this way and then that as she viewed her ivory gauze gown with its short, puffed sleeves and high bodice. The frock, brocaded with blue silk flowers, was worn over a delicate satin slip—grand enough for a ball gown without being too elaborate for someone her age.

Abigail's headdress was on loan from her aunt, an exquisite pearl hairpiece set on the crown of her head. Winnicott had pulled Abigail's copper curls back into a chignon, allowing a few loose ringlets to frame her face in a pleasingly elegant fashion.

After fastening her pearl necklace, Abigail pulled on her gloves and slid her feet into her slippers. Winnicott had left a short while ago to put the finishing touches on Henrietta's ensemble, and Abigail savored this rare moment alone to catch her breath before the busy evening ahead.

She tweaked a slightly wayward curl back into place and straightened her petticoats before leaving her bedchamber and going downstairs. Gazing in wonder at the beautiful flower arrangements Alexandra had placed on every available surface, she walked to the very end of the hall, unable to resist sneaking a look at the ballroom before everyone arrived.

She passed into an antechamber where two footmen stood to attention in front of the ballroom doors and slipped inside, gazing around the splendid space, designed in the lavish style of Louis XV, with numerous portraits of various Longmore ancestors hanging on the walls. The rather supercilious-looking ladies and gentlemen stared down their noses at the place of revelry beneath them as musicians tuned their instruments in a minstrels' gallery at the far end.

Since the ballroom was built onto the side of the house, it had been possible for the architect to set a massive skylight in the center of the ceiling to serve as a natural source of light. However, Aunt Longmore had not neglected to light hundreds and hundreds of candles in the wall sconces between the paintings. All in all, the effect was one of dazzling splendor, and Abigail couldn't help thinking that such brilliance augured wonderful things for the evening ahead.

She couldn't wait to dance around this room in William's arms because, now that Abigail was a betrothed lady, her aunt had informed her that she would be allowed to dance the waltz with her betrothed even though she wasn't officially out.

She turned away and stepped out the door, making her way to the drawing room, where all the guests for dinner were due to assemble. Lady Amelia and Sir Reginald were already there, conversing in a group near the window with Stanford, Alexandra, Henrietta, and Mr. Burnby. John and Emily stood near the fire talking to Thea and Lord Castleroy, who had arrived earlier that day. The baron was smiling at her sister when Abigail entered the room as he murmured something in her ear which made her laugh, and Abigail thought again how happy Thea looked.

Abigail turned when she felt a tap on her shoulder and looked up at William, a smile trembling on her lips. He said nothing for a moment as he gazed into her eyes. Then he shook his head. "I need to borrow from Shakespeare again, Abby, as words fail me." He took her hand and raised it to his lips. "Your loveliness surpasses that of a summer's day."

The light in his eyes made her breath quicken, and everyone else faded into nothingness until the older members of the party arrived. Abigail came out from under the spell that seemed to have been cast on her and progressed to the dining room with everyone else. She sat beside William at the long dining room table, but for once, she wasn't looking forward to the special banquet the Longmores' French chef had prepared for them.

She did not plan to eat all that much, as the last thing she wanted was to dance around the ballroom on an overly full stomach. She pressed her lips together to prevent herself from giggling. Hopefully, William would not think she was sickening for something when she turned down most of the dishes offered to her this evening. She would eat something more substantial at supper later in the evening.

Lord Castleroy was seated to her left, and Abigail was delighted to have the opportunity to catch up with him as she hadn't seen him since she left London. After asking him about his sister, Anne, who was about to be married, she learned about his plan to take Thea to Italy on their wedding trip as they wished to visit Como, the home of silk, which they were both passionate about.

Silk had brought her sister and Lord Castleroy together in the same way that Abigail's passion for stars had thrown her into William's path. Interesting how one sort of passion often begot another. She blushed at the direction her thoughts were taking and turned back to William, smiling, just as Uncle Longmore rose to his feet to propose a wonderful toast to first Thea and then to Lord Castleroy, the guests of honor at the ball.

He then went on to toast the Duke of Stanford and Alexandra on their recent marriage, Lady Amelia and Sir Reginald on their engagement, and speak some especially kind words about Henrietta and Mr. Burnby. Eventually, he turned to William and Abigail. "And, finally, I am delighted Lord Rochvale will soon be joining our family. I have worked closely with him for many years and can attest to his integrity, honor, and eye for beauty, which is partly, I suppose, why he was drawn to my niece but, I know, not the only reason."

After raising his glass in a toast to William, Uncle Longmore sipped his wine as he studied Abigail thoughtfully. "My dear niece came here some months ago to assist me with a star chart project I'd agreed to undertake. And although the work required of her was of the most tedious kind imaginable for a budding astronomer, Abigail participated in the project with great diligence, never complaining that she couldn't do what I know she truly wanted to do—sweep the sky for comets." His eyes twinkled a little as he smiled at her.

"Abigail's faithfulness in addressing this task is a testament to her excellent character and bodes well for her marriage, as she has shown a maturity beyond her years in understanding that drudgery makes up a great deal of human existence." He surveyed the sea of faces before him. "A singularly unromantic statement to make, no doubt, with so many recently-betrothed couples here tonight. But it has been my observation in my middle years that mountain-top moments do not come to us frequently in this life but only upon occasion to sustain us as we trudge in the valley below.

"Although it is tempting to believe these moments should make up the bulk of our lives, they cannot. But we often expect them to, railing at our misfortunes when they fail to appear. But only giants have large enough strides to leap from hilltop to hilltop, and we are mere men and women taking much smaller steps." He looked back at Abigail. "But it is the constant walking that builds the necessary endurance to climb those upper slopes that lead to those flashes of pure inspiration so integral to a life well lived." He raised his glass to her. "So, my dear, as you embark on this new journey with those beautiful stars in your eyes, I wish you every happiness and joy."

Abigail blinked away tears as she smiled at her uncle, amazed at his insight into her struggle with the more mundane aspects of astronomy and thankful for his encouragement to keep striving. Everyone raised their glasses, a few gentlemen saying, "Hear, hear," as they drank her health. And as Abigail gazed around at her close friends and family, she was grateful beyond measure for the love and blessings in her life.

Later, at the ball, William led Abigail into the first country dance. Although he had promised the first dance to Susannah in Bath, Lady Longmore had informed her daughter it behooved Lord Rochvale to partner Abigail for the first dance as they were now betrothed.

However, William danced the second dance with Susannah, and Abigail did not dance with him for a couple of sets after that, because although she was engaged to William, it would not be at all the thing if she only danced with him tonight. And so she chattered to and smiled at the gentlemen who asked her to dance, all the while wishing to throw etiquette to the winds and step into William's arms.

When the time for the first waltz arrived, Lady Longmore went up to the minstrels' gallery. A hush settled on the crowd as she raised her voice: "As you know, this ball was initially planned to celebrate the betrothal of my lovely niece, Dorothea Grantham, to Lord Castleroy. However, since the announcement of their engagement, three more couples in our midst have become betrothed. And so I propose now that Lady Amelia and Sir Reginald, Henrietta and Mr. Burnby, and Abigail and Lord Rochvale join Dorothea and Lord Castleroy for a waltz to celebrate their engagements."

Within a few moments, William was at Abigail's side, and when the musicians played the first strains of the waltz, he swept her onto the floor, twirling her round in breathless motion as he gazed down at her as though they were the only two people in the room. And, indeed, it felt as though everyone else had faded away as he held her close, so very close that she did not know where she ended and he began within the intimate circle of his arms.

She wanted the waltz to go on forever, but of course, it had to end, and Abigail felt a keen sense of loss at the removal of the protective barrier of William's arms. Bereft, she blinked and came back to earth as he stepped away to speak to an acquaintance.

A strange sense of confusion suddenly settled on her that she could be so deliriously happy without the presence tonight of the people she had once loved more than anyone in the world. How could she feel such heights of joy with her parents gone? It felt . . . unseemly somehow, and wiping away her tears, Abigail hastened to the ballroom doors. She needed a few moments on her own to collect herself.

Her feet led her almost of their own volition to the observatory, where the telescope had been set up, no doubt by Uncle Longmore, who would want to escape from the festivities sooner rather than later as it was a startlingly clear night.

As Abigail put her eye to the eye-piece and began sweeping, the mangled feeling within her began to fade away. She drew in a deep breath, allowing the night sky, her companion of old that had seen her through some of the darkest hours of her life, to calm her as it always did.

And then she saw it—the brightest of bright lights in the

position where the sun had gone down a few hours earlier, its tail stretching out by a few degrees as it headed straight up into the night sky. She held her breath, unable to believe the evidence of her eyes. But, it was incontrovertible. She wasn't mistaken.

A pair of hands settled on her shoulders, and Abigail stepped slowly away from the telescope, leaning back against William as she gazed into the distance, where the comet was visible even to the naked eye. Without a word, she stretched out her hand. "Look, William. Just look!"

His hands tightened on her shoulders. "Unbelievable. It can't be."

"It is, my love. It truly is."

Abigail stepped to one side so that William could look through the telescope. And for the next while, they took turns observing the amazing phenomenon, caught up in absolute wonder.

Eventually, William stepped back. "I wanted to give you the stars and the moon, my love, but I never dared hope that you would receive your comet." His voice was slightly teasing as he smiled at her.

"I never stopped hoping to see one even though I knew it wasn't likely. But sometimes extraordinary things happen if you keep looking up."

"Yes. You had more faith than I did, sweetheart, that you would eventually receive your heart's desire."

She tilted her head. "Did I?"

The smile faded from his lips as he drew her into his arms, gazing down at her. His thumbs gently stroked her cheeks. "Perhaps not, seeing as how my heart's desire is standing right before me."

He lowered his head then, and his lips touched hers in a searing kiss that burned across her senses like the comet trailing across the sky behind them. Eventually, he drew back, placing his hands on her shoulders as he carefully searched her face, an expression in his eyes she'd never seen before. "I'll always remember how you look tonight. Abigail in the moonlight. Dreaming and teaching others to dream. Do you know what a rare gift that is? To have such hope and light shining from your eyes that you cause others to believe in miracles . . . to believe in the impossible. To believe in love."

"Oh, William." She touched his cheek, deeply moved. "My dearest love."

He swept her back into his embrace, and she became lost to everything then except the magic of his arms around her and the warmth of his lips as starlight shone above them, casting a glow upon an enchanted world where only the two of them existed.

The End

Author's Note

The Great Comet of 1819

The Great Comet of 1819, also referred to as Comet Tralles, was discovered by Johann George Tralles in Berlin, Germany on July 1, 1819. François Arago, a French mathematician used polarimetry to analyze it, and it was the first comet to be measured in this way.

Its brightness and visibility were extraordinary, and many people other than astronomers saw it, including the English poet John Keats and his wife Fanny.

Friedrich Bessel's Star Chart Project

Friedrich Wilhelm Bessel (22 July 1784–17 March 1846) was a German astronomer who initiated a star chart project in 1822, which led to a remarkable advance in understanding of the night sky and the methods for observing and recording it. His aim was to create a more accurate and complete star chart, as those of his day were invariably riddled with mistakes and inconsistencies. Bessel practiced obtaining three key measurements within the space of a minute with his assistant F. W. A. Argelander, to make sure it could be done, and then invited other observatories to participate in his mammoth star chart project. It was this project that ultimately led to the discovery of Neptune in 1846.

Though I could find no direct evidence of it, I thought it likely that Friedrich Bessel could have asked some of his astronomer friends to evaluate the potential of his project, which is why, in our story in 1819, Lord Longmore agrees to participate in a trial.

Acknowledgements

Many thanks to my amazing editor, Courtney Brown.

References

British Sculpture and Church Monuments. "Buckinghamshire Church Monuments." http://www.speel.me.uk/bucks/cheshamch.htm.

Egan, Pierce. *Walks Through Bath: Describing Everything Worthy of Interest Connected With the Public Buildings, the Rooms, Crescents, Theatre, Concerts, Baths, Its Literature &c., Including Walcot And Widcombe, and the Surrounding Vicinity*. Bath: Printed for Meyler and Son, 1819.

Herschel, Mrs. John. *Memoir and Correspondence of Caroline Herschel*. London: John Murray, 1879.

Jason Clark Antiques. "Regency Period Cased Telescope on Stand by Joseph Smith of Royal Exchange London." https://jasonclarkeantiques.co.uk/products/regency-period-cased-telescope-on-stand-by-joseph-smith-of-royal-exchange-london.

Kronk, Gary W. *Cometography: A Catalog of Comets*. Vol. 2, *1800-1899*. Cambridge: Cambridge University Press, 2003.

Parry, William Edward. *Nautical Astronomy By Night*. 1813.

Smyth, W. H. *Ædes Hartwellianae: Or Notices of the Manor and Mansion of Hartwell*. London: Printed by John Bowyer Nichols and Son, 1851.

Stauberman, Klaus. "Exercising Patience: On the Reconstruction of F.W. Bessel's Early Star Chart Observations" *Journal for the History of Astronomy* 34, no. 1 (2006): 19-36.

About the Author

Alissa Baxter wrote her first Regency romance during her long university holidays. After travelling the world, she settled down to write her second Regency novel, which was inspired by her time living on a country estate in England. Alissa then published two chick lit novels, The *Truth About Clicking Send and Receive* (previously published as *Send and Receive*) and *The Truth About Cats and Bees* (previously published as *The Blog Affair*).

Many years later, Alissa returned to her favorite era. She writes Regency romances that feature women in trend-setting roles who fall in love with men who embrace their trailblazing ways… at least eventually. Alissa currently lives in Johannesburg with her husband and two sons.

These are my social media details:
Alissa's Instagram page: alissa.baxter.author
Alissa's Facebook group: Alissa's Regency Companions
Alissa's Twitter page: @alissa_baxter
Alissa's Facebook page: facebook.com/alissa.baxter.writer
Alissa's website: alissabaxter.com
Alissa's blog: alissabaxter.blogspot.com